Maggie's Pleasure Palace

Palace

The murder of Thelma Goodrich

By Bill Shuey

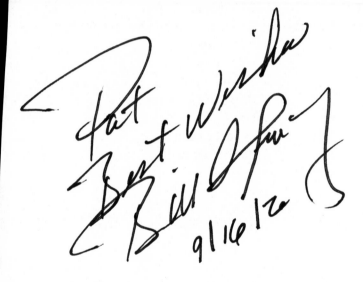

Pat
Best Wishes
Bill Shuey
9|16|12

1

Other books by Bill Shuey

A Search for Israel
A Search for Bible Truth
Unholy Dilemma – A Search for Logic in the Old Testament
Unholy Dilemma 2 – A Search for Logic in the New Testament
Unholy Dilemma 3 – A Search for Logic in the Qur'an
Have a good week – Ten years of ObverseView musings
East of Edin
Retribution
A Killing in Dogwood
The Cattlemen
The Texican
The Horsemen

Maggie's Pleasure Palace

The murder of Thelma Goodrich

ISBN 13: 978-1688420045
ISBN 10:

Printed in the United States of America

Dedication

My wife of forty years, Gloria, has implored me to write a second mystery novel. With some degree of reluctance, I agreed to honor her request.

No one could ask for a more loyal and loving companion with which to journey through life. I dedicate this novel to her; in the hope this effort is worthy of her trust in my writing skill and meets her expectations.

Acknowledgements

As with my earlier literary efforts, the team is what makes the endeavor come together, not just the author.

My sister-in-law Bern proofread the book and was instrumental in correcting the prose for grammar and punctuation.

My brother Ken helped design the cover art and did his normal fine job.

Marisa Mott, a friend from my Florida days, created the cover and wrap.
www.cowboykimono.com

Betty Henderson and Stormie Saucerman put the finishing touches on the book.

And last but never least, my wife Gloria who is always supportive of my literary efforts and this was no exception.

Chapter 1

Maggie's Pleasure Palace was a brothel on the outskirts of Dallas, Texas. The establishment was operated by Maggie Ellen Branceer. The facility was staffed by twelve to fifteen girls of varying ages, sizes, and shapes. Technically, prostitution was illegal, but the luminaries around Dallas would occasionally enter Maggie's Pleasure Palace for an evening's entertainment. Maggie didn't entertain the clientele. She just made sure the paying customers were well taken care of and left happy. The bawdy house wasn't elegant. In fact, it was weather beaten on the outside. But on the inside, it was comfortable and masculine. The furnishings had men in mind and were made of earth tone fabrics and rich leather. The bar had drawings of ladies in immodest attire and paintings of western landscapes. The dining room featured a stuffed longhorn head with a seven-foot tip to tip horn span, a large fireplace, tables to accommodate thirty diners, and T-Bone steaks as the specialty. A Chinese cook named Ling prepared food for the guests and was a world-class chef.

The employees' rooms were clean and always well maintained. The girls' rooms were on the second floor. The kitchen, dining room, and bar were on the ground floor. Someone built the building in a T shape. The one-story part contained Maggie's office, her private living quarters, and a comfortable room for Ling. There was also a well-appointed room for a guest who might drop in to see Maggie. Maggie relegated the rest to storage. There was one room on the second floor which was nicer than the others and was always locked. The bar was well stocked with bonded whiskey that was shipped in from the east. Rot-gut booze wasn't allowed in the building. Maggie hired two piano players who alternated playing from 6 PM to midnight every night of the week. Occasionally, a cello player from Boston, Massachusetts, who had moved to Dallas would come in at night and play tunes with the throaty deep sounds only the large string instrument could provide. Once a month, weather permitting, Maggie would host a bare-knuckle fight in a ring which they would erect for the event. It always drew a big crowd. Men came for the fights, the excellent steaks, the good whiskey, and, the girls. Sometimes, the men just wanted female companionship and, at other times, more. Maggie gave attention to detail. She even had several loads of small rock hauled in and placed in front of the building so that men wouldn't track mud onto the carpet in the foyer.

The girls who worked in Maggie's were happy. The clients were happy, and Maggie was happy. The money rolled in. The men who frequented Maggie's were of means, and she tolerated no nonsense. Maggie's was a gentlemen's establishment.

Maggie knew a gonorrhea infected employee would hurt her business. Thus, she had the girls regularly checked, and if an infection was detected or even suspected, the doctor would treat the woman with one of the medications available. The girl would be out of business until the doctor gave her a clean bill of health.

****

Gonorrhea, colloquially referred to as the "clap," is a sexually transmitted infection caused by the bacterium Neisseria gonorrhoeae. Infection may involve the genitals, mouth, or rectum. Infected men may experience pain or burning during urination, discharge from the penis, or testicular pain. Infected women may experience burning during urination, vaginal discharge, vaginal bleeding, and/or pelvic pain. Unfortunately, many women who are infected display no symptoms at all.

During the middle 19th century, the treatments of choice were cubebs, an Indonesian variety of pepper which used the dried powdered unripe fruit, and balsam of copaiba, which was extracted from a South American tree. Silver nitrate was also used and proved to be more effective than the organic plant extracts.

****

It was June 1874. Business was good, and the customers were leaving well satisfied with the food, liquor, and female companionship. Not every male customer who entered Maggie's tasted of the girls' wares. Some just wanted a good steak and a few drinks. That was fine with Maggie. All the income went to the bottom line. Maggie was generous to a fault with her girls. She allowed them to keep 30% of their take and didn't charge them a dime for room and board. Most women in their profession fared far worse. Some were basically held in slavery. The women who worked at Maggie's were there because they wanted the income. Most stayed a couple years, saved a few hundred dollars, and then went west to San Francisco or east to New York City in search of a husband or to go into business for themselves. They didn't necessarily stay in the oldest profession in the world. With seed money, they entered whatever vocation interested them. Maggie heard from some of the girls that left her employment occasionally and was pleased they were doing well.

Every Sunday morning, Maggie and all the girls had breakfast together at 8 AM sharp. At the breakfast, Maggie heard complaints, if there were any, and then she sponsored a Bible study. Maggie felt the girls needed a spiritual element in their lives. Certainly, they were engaged in the world's oldest profession, but that didn't necessarily make them bad people. In the 19th century, love often wasn't a consideration in marriages. A woman wanted security, and a man wanted sex and someone to cook and clean. Maggie kind of figured she was supplying a service the same as a wife would provide. She got reimbursed for her services with money. Married women got reimbursed in kind: a home, security, and whatever finery the husband could afford.

Once the Bible study was concluded, the girls had the rest of the day to themselves to do whatever they desired. Most went for a walk, sewed, or just laid around and relaxed.

On June 21, 1874, thirteen girls showed up for breakfast at 8 AM. Thelma Goodrich wasn't at the table by 8:10 AM, and Maggie sent Beverley Scott to go to Thelma's room to make sure she was awake and to get her down to the breakfast gathering. In a couple minutes, Beverley was back, looked at Maggie, and said, "Thelma's gone. Her clothes and personal effects are all gone. She must have left sometime during the night. I saw her around 10 PM, so she was still here then. Peaches was the only living, breathing thing in the room." Peaches was the pale orange-tan colored cat which was kind of community property amongst the girls at Maggie's. The visitors to the establishment thought it interesting that a cat wandered the halls and rooms of the sporting club.

Maggie asked the girls if they knew where Thelma had gone and why. No one knew for sure. Joyce Baker said that Thelma was sweet on someone, but she never would say who it was. Joyce supposed Thelma left early Sunday morning and met whoever she was planning to run away with. None of this made any sense to Maggie. Her girls could leave any time they wanted and, normally, on good terms. There was no reason to sneak off in the middle of the night. Nope. Sneaking off to meet a boyfriend didn't wash. Something else was going on here.

11

Maggie's opinion was to prove prophetic. There was a whole lot else going on!

****

James Boutwell was a deputy U.S. marshal stationed in Austin, Texas. On June 20, 1874, Marshal Boutwell left Austin with Freddie McElpine to deliver him to Dallas to stand trial for his part in a bank robbery. James wasn't in any hurry and stopped every evening and made camp while on the trail. Dallas was around 200 miles from Austin, and James would be happy if he got the prisoner to Dallas by the 24th of June.

James didn't get paid a salary. He got paid for each warrant he served, or prisoner delivered. In between missions, his time was his own. He had learned that hurrying really didn't make much sense. There were plenty of warrants, robbers, killers, and bandits. There was seemingly always a ready supply of men who wanted to break the law.

Chapter 2

James Boutwell looked more like an actor in a theatre troupe than a deputy U. S. marshal. He was just over six feet tall, with ash colored hair he wore collar length, dark blue eyes, and sporting a Van Dyke moustache and chin whiskers. He wore a striped pair of broadcloth pants, a leather vest, a slouch hat, expensive brown boots, and seemed to always wear a clean shirt. James was clean and well-groomed any time he could find a bathtub and barber shop. Some of his friends accused him of being a clotheshorse, but it was good-natured ribbing. James' mother had told him early on that clothes made the man. Any time he appeared for a meal with dirty clothes his mother would tan his hide. The early message his mother instilled was to stay with him his entire life. His mother would be proud.

James was born in Neosho, Missouri, on May 21, 1844. He left his father and mother's large farm at the start of the Civil War. The Boutwells didn't own slaves and didn't believe it was right to own another human being. James didn't want to be in a position where he might have to kill a neighbor who had joined the Confederate Army, so he shunned the Union army. And he didn't want to fight on the side of the Confederacy to help continue the practice of slavery. Left with no real choice, on June 1, 1861, James packed up his possibles, saddled his horse, and rode off towards Texas. He had a Sharps carbine in a scabbard and carried a Colt Dragoon revolver in a cross-draw holster. James was seventeen when he left home, but full grown and capable. He had worked on adjacent farms since he was twelve and saved every dime. The money allowed him to purchase the horse, saddle, and the weaponry. When he left home, his Dad gave him a few dollars to help with the cost of his travels. When James arrived in Texas, he had $73.57 in his pocket, a good horse, and no marketable skills or prospects. Well, that wasn't entirely true. He could pitch hay, cut sprouts, and milk a cow. None of these skills would serve him well in Texas. James stopped along the trail and worked odd jobs, slept in barns, and ate a few free meals after splitting some wood or mending something broken. He stopped in the little town of Paris, Texas, on July 6, 1861, to rest up a mite, eat a decent meal, and look for work before traveling on.

****

The town of Paris, Texas, was founded by merchant George W. Wright, who donated fifty acres of land in February 1844, when the community was designated as the county seat by voters. Paris was incorporated on February 3, 1845. The settlement was named for Paris, France, by one of Wright's employees, Thomas Poteet. Paris was on the Central National Road. The road began at John Neely Bryan's crossing on the Trinity River and ran to the south bank of the Red River in the northwest corner of Red River County. At the start of the Civil War,

14

Paris had about 700 residents and was becoming a center for cattle ranching and farming.

****

James stopped in front of the Paris Café, tied his horse to the hitching rail, removed his rifle from its scabbard, and walked into the eatery. He sat down and ordered biscuits with blackstrap molasses and coffee. The coffee came first. As he was sipping on the scalding hot brew, a large man wearing a frock coat and black narrow brim hat walked over to his table and said, "You look able bodied. Why aren't you off with the Confederate Army?"

James looked at the man, thought him mighty bold, but replied, "Sir, I just rode into this town. The only thing I'm interested in joining this fine morning is some biscuits and molasses. I left Missouri a few weeks ago because I didn't want to join the Confederacy or the Union and fight against my neighbors. We didn't own slaves and don't hold with slavery, but I will not fight and kill southerners." After finishing his discourse, James ignored the man and continued sipping on his coffee. The man just stood there. In a minute James looked back up at the man and said, "Sir, is there something else I can help you with?"

The man rubbed his chin and finally said, "I'm Jefferson McMasters, and yes, maybe there is. I own the Red River Ranch north of here. It's the Red River Brand. Some of my drovers left the ranch and

15

went off to fight in the war, leaving me short-handed. Would you have any interest in working on my ranch? I'll pay you a dollar a day plus found. You'll get to work in all kinds of weather, fight Indians and cattle rustlers, and deal with rattlesnakes, scorpions, and Gila monsters. Does that sound like a fun way to make a living?"

James looked at McMasters and said, "No, it doesn't sound like fun, but I like a challenge. When would you like for me to start?"

McMasters said, "Well, no reason to put off hard work, be at the ranch in the morning in time for breakfast. That would be 6 AM sharp!"

James started working on the Red River Ranch on July 7, 1861. He worked for McMasters during the war years. McMasters was one of the more visionary cattlemen in Texas. He knew he couldn't sell beef to anyone but the Confederates and, although it infuriated their paymasters, he demanded gold for the cattle they purchased. McMasters continued to breed cattle, round up feral cows, and build up his herd. He knew, once the war was over, he could sell his beef to the markets in the northern states. He wanted to be ready.

McMasters took a liking to James and taught him all aspects of the cattle business. James was a quick study and learned from McMasters early on. After working for a few months and seeing how McMasters got paid for his cattle, he approached the ranch owner. After chatting for a few minutes James said, "Sir, I would rather you just hold my pay or pay me in gold and/or silver. I don't think Confederate money will have much value after the war. I just don't see any way the South can win the war. I'm not much on drinking and ain't gonna pay a woman for sex, so I have little need for my pay."

McMasters laughed and said, "You don't miss much, James. I'll keep your wages recorded in a ledger. If you need money, just let me know and I'll deduct it from what I owe you." In June 1863, McMasters gave James the job as the foreman, and a $.25 a day raise in pay. At nineteen years of age, James was the ramrod of one of the largest cattle ranches in northeast Texas. Only one of the cowpunchers had a problem taking orders from James. One broken nose and two loose teeth later, he decided James was the boss.

In March 1864 a man named Marcus Nedfelt robbed the mercantile store in Paris, killed the owner and his wife, and shot another man as he was making his getaway. Rufus Smallwood, the county sheriff wanted to form a posse to go after the killer, but all that was left in Red River County was old men and young boys for the most part. Smallwood and McMasters were longtime friends. Smallwood rode to the Red River Ranch and asked McMasters if he could borrow a couple of his drovers for a few days. James was standing near McMasters and said, "I don't mean to butt in, Sir, but almost all the drovers are out rounding up and branding cattle. If this will only take a couple days, why don't I go along with the sheriff and let the men keep at their work."

McMasters laughed and replied, "Well, I guess I could do your job for a couple days. Go ahead." James got some of his possibles together and rode off with the sheriff. Sheriff Smallwood swore James in as a deputy sheriff and handed him a badge. On April 1, 1864, James was a lawman. When they got to Paris, the sheriff got a pack horse out of the livery and placed panniers on the animal. After getting provisions for a few days, Sheriff Smallwood and James headed towards the little settlement of Lenoir, Texas. The sheriff informed James that Nedfelt had two brothers in Lenoir who owned a small cattle spread. No one seemed to know where they got their cattle to start the operation or how their herd kept increasing.

Smallwood was kinda long in the tooth, perhaps in his late fifties, but he seemed in good health, sturdy, and determined. As they rode along, Sheriff Smallwood told James about some of his experiences as a lawman. It seemed he had been a peace officer in both Kansas and Oklahoma Territory before moving to Texas and taking the job as sheriff of Red River County. While wearing a badge, men he tried to arrest had shot Smallwood three times, but only one was a serious wound. He reckoned he had arrested more than 2,000 men and a few women for various crimes or lesser offenses like public drunkenness or unlawful discharge of a firearm.

The time went by fast and they arrived in the small settlement of Lenoir (it was later named Powderly) after about an hour in the saddle. The tiny town had a marshal, so Smallwood and James stopped by to see him and get directions to the Nedfelt spread. They found the marshal sitting in his small office drinking a cup of coffee. Marshal Zeb Franks stood and said, "Hello, Rufus. It's good to see you."

Smallwood returned the greeting and got right to the point. They were there to find and arrest Marcus Nedfelt. They needed to know the location of the Nedfelt spread. Sheriff Smallwood knew that the ranch was in the far northern edge of Lamar County near what would become Chicota. But he had never had occasion to be at the ranch, or as strange as it seemed, in that part of the county.

Marshal Franks was noticeably nervous and replied, "I don't think Marcus is at the ranch. He would know you would be after him and would have gone somewhere else."

Smallwood merely said, "Humor me, Zeb. Give me the directions."

Marshal Franks told Smallwood how to find the small ranch. After which he opined, "I would be careful out there. There are rumors of the Nedfelts being free and easy with the cattle they brand. There isn't much need for law out there in that part of the county. My jurisdiction stops at the town limits. I think you are riding into a hornets' nest."

Smallwood thanked Marshal Franks and walked out of his office. James followed along. They walked down the street a few yards, stopped at a hole-in-the-wall eatery, got plates of beans seasoned with chilies, and a cup of coffee. Smallwood said he always tried to eat before going to arrest someone. His worse fear was being killed when he was hungry. If Smallwood was going to leave the earth, he wanted to do it on a full stomach.

After they had eaten, Smallwood took the packhorse to the livery. He explained to James that he hadn't known what their needs might be and now didn't think he would need the extra provisions. He had learned from experience that it didn't cost much extra to always be prepared. If Nedfelt wasn't at the ranch or ran when they arrived, they would need the pack horse and provisions if they had to spend some time tracking the man. Smallwood said he had learned his lesson on being prepared the hard way. It would be a short ride to go back and get the pack horse.

The Nedfelt ranch house was around eight miles northeast of Lenoir. They crossed Sanders Creek, which was a tributary of the Red River. When they got to within a couple hundred yards of the ranch house, they saw they had a problem. There was nothing but sage and random patches of grass between them and the ranch house. There was no way to get close to the dwelling without being detected.

They were sitting on their horses with Smallwood trying to decide how to proceed. James was just there to do what he was told. As Smallwood was pondering, dirt kicked up a few feet in front of the horses, followed by the report of a rifle.

Smallwood turned to James and said, "Guess we'd better back the horses up a mite. That shooter might do better the next time." They moved their horses back.

They had absolutely no idea how many people were in the ranch house. Smallwood presumed Marcus Nedfelt was there; otherwise, why would they shoot? After they had retreated around twenty yards, they dismounted and loosened the cinches on the horses. Smallwood turned to James and said, "Let me think on this a spell. Had I known we were going to sit on the plains and look at a cabin, I would have brought the packhorse."

James couldn't help but chuckle and replied, "Pays to be prepared."

Chapter 3

Smallwood didn't seem to find James' comment humorous but didn't rebuff him with a reply. Right now, food stuff wasn't a consideration. They had to find some way to root the men out of the cabin. Obviously, they couldn't advance through an open expanse without getting lead in their hides. The thick walls of the structure sheltered the men in the cabin. If Smallwood and James advanced towards the cabin, all the occupants would have to do is just keep shooting until the two of them were on the ground with bullets in their bodies. Obviously, just walking or riding down to the cabin and hoping for the best wasn't a viable plan.

After a few minutes, Smallwood looked at James and said, "Aren't you glad you came along. The only option I see is for us to wait til dark. We can try to sneak up close to the cabin and find protection behind the tack shed, privy, or have partial cover behind the corral. I grant you, it's not a great plan, but I've got no other ideas." James didn't know what to say, so he said nothing. He wanted to say that he should have stayed on the McMasters' ranch, but he kept his thoughts to himself.

James had his Sharps carbine and Smallwood had one of the new Henry repeating rifles. Both men carried Colt Dragoon pistols. Their four weapons probably wouldn't match up well against an unknown number of people. On the other hand, if the men in the cabin came out to make a fight of it, they would have to come out the door one by one. James liked their chances if they could get the men to leave the cabin. James looked at Smallwood's Henry rifle and kinda wished he had one. It was an interesting weapon for the time.

****

The original Henry rifle was a sixteen shot .44 caliber rimfire breech-loading lever-action rifle, patented by Benjamin Tyler Henry in 1860. The Henry was an improved version of the earlier Volition, and later Volcanic models of repeating rifles. The Henry used copper (later brass) rimfire cartridges with a 216-grain bullet charged with 25 grains of black powder. Production of the new rifle was low (150 to 200 a month) until the middle of 1864.

The manufacturer never issued the Henry on a large scale, but it showed the advantage of rapid fire several times during the Civil War and later during engagements between the Army and Plains Indians. Perhaps one of the best examples of the superiority of rapid fire was the Cheyenne and other tribes' destruction of the 7th Cavalry. The Army elected to arm the soldiers with single-shot rifles at the Battle of Little Big Horn, and many of the Indians had repeaters. Besides having them greatly outnumbered, the hostiles had the cavalry outgunned.

The New Haven Arms Company manufactured the Henry rifle. The Henry evolved into the famous Winchester Model 1866 (Yellow Boy) lever-action rifle in 1866. Shortly thereafter, the New Haven Arms Company was renamed the Winchester Repeating Arms Company. Smallwood had somehow gotten his hands on one of the new Henry repeaters.

****

The night of Saturday, the 16th of April 1864, displayed a waxing Gibbous moon. In layman's terms, it was almost a full moon. The problem with being able to see at night is that people can see you. It would be relatively easy for a lookout in the cabin to see Smallwood and James as they approached the cabin. On the other hand, it would be difficult for a shooter to get a sight alignment to shoot at them accurately in the low light conditions. Or at least Smallwood hoped the lookout wouldn't be able to get a good bead on them.

They started towards the cabin at 2 AM. Smallwood made it to the outhouse and James got behind the tack shed with no shots being fired from the cabin. The question was, now what? They were close to the house, but it would be daylight in a few hours. What then? Smallwood and James would be cornered and wouldn't be able to get back to their horses before nightfall. Unless someone from the Nedfelt group came out to use the privy, or for some other purpose, they were in no better position than they were when they were more than 200 yards away. James and Smallwood had brought their canteens, so water wouldn't be a problem. But since it was mighty chilly at night and cool during the day, they wouldn't need much water, anyway.

Smallwood saw no reason to continue waiting for something to happen and around 4 AM hollered "This is Sheriff Rufus Smallwood. I'm here to arrest Marcus Nedfelt for robbery and murder." There was no response from the cabin for a couple minutes.

The door to the cabin opened slightly and someone hollered "Law dog, Marcus ain't here. We ain't heard nothing about him robbing or killing anyone. You need to get off my property."

Smallwood replied, "Each of you need to come out of the cabin with your hands in the air. I'll then search the house. If I don't find Marcus, I'll be on my way."

The same man hollered, "Like hell, we will. You ain't searching anything, Law dog." Before closing the door, the man took a shot at the outhouse knocking a shard of wood off the structure. James fired his Spencer at the door and splinters and shards of wood flew. James and Smallwood could hear the man holler, followed by loud cursing. Apparently, a piece of wood had found a place on his body to pierce.

Smallwood had yet to fire. The cabin was roughhewn, with logs as the side walls, and what appeared to be a solid door. There was no way a .44 slug would penetrate the logs and probably not the door. There didn't appear to be any other openings in the cabin other than the front door. Smallwood chuckled and said to himself, "Looks like we're involved in a Mexican standoff."

The sun peeked over the eastern horizon slightly after 6 AM. Nothing had been resolved, and other than a man having some wood splinters in his hide, both sides of the standoff were unscathed. Nothing happened until around noon. A man came slowly out the cabin door holding his gun belt in one hand and a rifle in the other as high as he could reach them. He hollered, "Don't shoot. I have no part in any of this. I just work on the ranch."

Smallwood didn't know any of the Nedfelts by sight and wasn't going to take any chances on the man being one of them. He hollered, "Walk straight towards the outhouse. I'll tell you when to stop." The man took three or four steps and the door opened. A man stepped out and shot the man who was attempting to surrender in the back. James had taken aim at the cabin door when the man walked out. Immediately after the man in the doorway had back-shot the other man, James fired. The back shooter spun around and fell against the door frame. The report of the Sharps reverberated in the midday air. The man struggled to remain upright. Someone grabbed him and half dragged, and half supported him back inside the cabin.

James didn't know exactly where he had hit the man, but it really didn't make a great deal of difference. A .52 caliber Sharps carbine used a 475-grain bullet. With the big hunk of lead being pushed by 50 grains of black powder, it made a mighty big hole in a human's flesh. This was the first time James had ever shot a human being, and he didn't enjoy the experience. But a man who would shoot another man in the back as he walked away trying to surrender wasn't worth losing sleep over.

The man who had attempted to surrender was trying to crawl to Smallwood, but he wasn't making a great deal of progress. Smallwood couldn't come to the man's aid without exposing himself to the guns in the cabin. He hated having to watch the man struggle, but there was nothing he could do. After a few minutes, the man stopped moving and lay still.

Around 3 PM the door opened slightly, and a voice hollered, "Leonard is hurting bad. That bullet one of you fired dun tore half his shoulder off. What are the terms if we surrender?"

Smallwood thought for at least a full minute and hollered back "Since I can't identify Marcus, I would have to arrest everyone in the cabin and take all of you back to Paris and let the people there sort out who's who. All I can promise is that I'll deliver all of you alive."

After Smallwood finished, there was silence for a few minutes and then the same voice hollered "We're coming out. One of you law dogs hurt

Leonard bad and we'll have to support him for him to walk."

Smallwood responded, "Just make sure I can see your hands, and everything will be fine." In a couple minutes, two men supporting another man between them came out the door of the cabin. They started walking towards the outhouse. James left the cover of the tack shed and walked to the corner of the cabin to be closer and have a clear view of what was going on. When the men supporting the wounded man took a few steps, they were blocking Smallwood's view of the cabin door. Suddenly two men burst out the cabin door and started shooting. One of the men supporting the wounded man got hit from behind and went down. James was about twenty feet from the two men and shot the shooter with his Sharps. The impact of the bullet knocked the man off his feet. Smallwood shifted his position to get a clear shot and put a bullet in the second shooter.

The man who remained standing supporting Leonard Nedfelt hollered "Don't shoot. I just work here. I didn't want the Nedfelts to kill me, so I went along to stay alive."

Sheriff Smallwood walked to the three men. He bent over and checked the man on the ground. He was dead. The wounded man, who the outlaws had referred to as Leonard Nedfelt, was in bad shape. James' Sharps bullet had hit the man in the front of his right shoulder, shattered the joint, and blew bone and tissue out the exit site. His associates had wrapped the entire shoulder area with what appeared to be an old blanket they had cut up for that purpose. If he lived, he would be a one-arm man.

James checked the uninjured man for weapons, found none, and put manacles on him. James had him and Leonard sit down on the ground. Leonard fell over and passed out. The second man who had been supporting Leonard Nedfelt died a few minutes later. James walked to the last man he had shot with the Sharps. His bullet had hit the man in his side. The bullet entered his chest, penetrated a lung, and burst his heart. He was graveyard dead. Sheriff Smallwood walked to the man he had shot and leaned over to check for a pulse. Suddenly the man lunged up and buried a knife in Smallwood's chest immediately below the rib cage and above the stomach. James had seen what had happened but couldn't react quickly enough to stop the knifing. He drew his revolver and fired as fast as he could get it into service. The bullet hit the man who had stabbed Smallwood right between the eyes.

James rushed to Smallwood's side. The knife had entered Smallwood's spleen and left him with just minutes to live before he bled out. Smallwood looked at James and weakly said, "You did good, Son. I couldn't have asked for better help. Getting careless can get you killed. I got careless. You're well suited to the law. I wish you would consider being a lawman." Smallwood's eyes fluttered a few times, and he gasped loudly and took his last breath.

Deputy Sheriff James Boutwell had a colossal mess on his hands. He had five dead men:

one who had been back shot by Leonard, one James had shot with his Sharps, one man who was supporting Leonard when the two men burst out of the cabin and began firing, one James shot after he had knifed Sheriff Smallwood, and of course Sheriff Smallwood. And he had one badly wounded outlaw who probably couldn't ride, and one man who could be an outlaw or civilian. James took the manacles off the uninjured man and had him go to the corral where they both began saddling horses. Once they got all the horses saddled, they began loading bodies. After getting all five corpses on their horses and secured so they wouldn't fall, James used a belt from one of the dead men and bound Leonard's fragmented arm to his side. He and the uninjured man got Leonard laid across his saddle on his horse. James tied Leonard's good arm to his boots so he wouldn't fall. Unfortunately, there just wasn't any other way to transport the injured man.

James tail tied all the horses. He took the lead reins of a group of three and the uninjured man took the other three mounts. The column started out to Paris, Texas. Since it was on the way, James stopped in Lenoir and asked the marshal if he knew any of the dead men other than Sheriff Smallwood. The marshal looked at each of the bodies and said that two were the Nedfelt brothers, Marcus and Chad. He didn't know the other two dead men or the man on the horse. The injured man was Leonard Nedfelt. Now that the marshal had identified everyone, James thanked the uninjured man for helping him and told him he was free to go. James left with the five dead men and Leonard Nedfelt. The six horses carrying the bodies and Leonard were tail tied behind James. It was a strange-looking caravan! Sheriff Smallwood had no known kin, so James took his Colt Dragoon revolver and Henry rifle and scabbard. He placed the Dragoon in his saddlebags and secured the Henry and scabbard to his horse.

When James arrived in Paris, a crowd quickly formed. Everyone was sorry to see Sheriff Smallwood was dead. He had been well liked. A young woman, probably in her late twenties or early thirties walked up to James and asked, "How did you manage to bring all three of the Nedfelt brothers to justice? They have been running rough shod over people around the northern part of Lamar County for years. Sheriff Smallwood was a good man but was all on his own for the most part and it's a big county. I'm going to send a wire to my father and tell him about you. Where can you be contacted?" James told the lady he worked on the Jefferson McMasters' ranch outside Paris, Texas. James thought the lady's comments were just so much nonsense and put them out of his mind.

After eating supper, James went to the livery, stabled his horse, and rolled up in his ground cover and blanket to get a well-deserved night's sleep. The following morning, he was up early and rode to the McMasters' ranch, ate breakfast, and went back to work. It had been an experience he would never forget.

James was in Paris, Texas, a couple weeks later getting supplies for Mr. McMasters and was told that Leonard Nedfelt had died from an infection due to the shoulder wound.

Chapter 4

On May 13, 1864, James Boutwell was riding the eastern edge of the McMasters ranch looking for stray cows when Jeff McMasters and a telegraph operator, who was in a tizzy, rode up. Obviously, McMasters had seen the wire because he was grinning from ear to ear.

James opened the wire and read it silently. The short of it was that James Speed, Attorney General of the United States, was offering a commission as a Deputy U.S. Marshal to James Boutwell. If James wanted the position, he was to report to his new office in Austin, Texas, forthwith and in no event to arrive later than May 25, 1864, to assume his duties as district marshal. His badge and other credentials would be waiting for him at the courthouse in Austin when he arrived. James thought back to the young woman he had met. Sometimes you just never know. He figured the woman's father was probably some low-level bureaucrat in the Lincoln Administration. She fooled him! James told the telegraph operator to send a reply. "*Honorable James Speed. Stop. I accept the appointment. Stop. James Boutwell.*" James paid the telegraph operator to send the wire and then turned to McMasters and said, "I guess I'd better get my possibles together, he didn't give me a great deal of time to get to Austin."

Jeff McMasters congratulated James and said he would get his money in order so he could have it when he left to ride to Austin. James got his possessions packed, said his goodbyes to the drovers on the ranch, and rode out on May 16, 1864, to start a new life as a peace officer. James rode with some urgency but didn't wear down his horse or himself and arrived on May 23rd. The greeting James received at the Austin courthouse made him wonder if he smelled bad. After talking to the judge and assuring him that he had no interest in getting involved in the war's politics, the judge seemed to settle down some. After swearing James in, the judge said that he had several warrants that had been gathering dust for some time and would appreciate James serving them as soon as possible.

The judge assigned James an office in the courthouse annex equipped with a cot, desk, and room to store his meager belongings. James worked amicably with the Texas authorities during the Civil War and never once got involved with trying to identify or arrest Confederate spies. In fact, Texas was a Confederate state, so he had to walk a delicate balance to keep his authority, capture killers and outlaws, and still stay well clear of the war disputes.

After the horrible Civil War ended, Marshal Boutwell had other problems. Texas became inundated with scalawags, profiteers, cutthroats, and every other example of human life at its worst. Money was scarce, and often those who didn't have greenbacks wanted to steal it from those who did.

On May 3, 1872, bandits held up the Harris stagecoach in the hills between Austin and Round Rock. They took the strong box which contained a small payroll. The bandits ordered the passengers out of the coach and relieved them of their possessions. One passenger, who had more courage than sense, drew his revolver and was killed for his trouble. A firearms dealer, Jackson Barnhardt, recognized one robber as Emanuel Clements. It seemed he had been involved in a card game with Clements in the Indian (Oklahoma) Territory a few months prior. Barnhardt was 100% sure that one robber was Emanuel Clements.

James talked to Barnhardt, the driver, and other passengers. They couldn't identify the other two men that robbed the stagecoach. Marshal Boutwell went to his office and looked through his stack of wanted posters and found one on an Emanuel Clements, Sr., aka Emanuel Mannen. It seemed Clements had killed two men in July 1871 in the Indian Territory. The information James had on Clements indicated he was an associate of John Wesley Hardin. That wasn't good news at all!

James would have to find three bandits and arrest them all by himself. He had tried a time or two to form a posse from the residents of Austin and each time the effort had proved futile. The general opinion was Marshal Boutwell was getting paid to chase down killers and bandits. That was only true in a general sense. James got paid for each warrant he served. He didn't get paid anything unless he was successful. James got his horse from the livery, saddled the mount, put his Sharps carbine and his relatively new Winchester 66 Yellow Boy in their scabbards, mounted the horse, and headed for Round Rock.

Shortly before arriving in Round Rock, James' horse threw a shoe. He walked the horse into the settlement, stopped at the blacksmith shop, and left the horse to have the shoe replaced and the others checked. He walked catty-corner across the street to Thomas Oatts' store, which also served as the post office and saloon. When James entered the store side of the building, a man was at the counter buying some supplies. It was a temperate day and Marshal Boutwell had foregone his coat. When the customer saw the marshal badge, he turned and ran out of the store.

James knew a lawman's badge intimidated some folks, but he had never seen anyone run away after having seen one. He walked out the door just as the man was about to mount his horse. The man drew his revolver and James drew his new Navy Colt. The man's pistol misfired, and James shot him in the chest. The man fell to the ground and blood started coming out of the man's mouth. Within a couple minutes he was dead.

Boutwell felt lucky. He had also experienced a misfire incident with his Colt Dragoon, which almost cost him his life. After that incident, he bought a Navy Colt revolver that had been converted to the .38 caliber metallic cartridge. He had liked the balance and the .44 caliber of the Dragoon better, but the Navy Colt pistol was less likely to misfire. It really didn't matter the size of the slug, if it didn't come out of the barrel.

Once the smoke settled, a small crowd of people gathered to gawk at the dead man. James said to no one in particular, "Does anyone recognize this man?"

Everyone just shook their heads. In a minute an older man walked up, looked at the dead man, and said, "I saw him this morning down by Brushy Creek camped with two other men. If the other two haven't gone on, you'll find them there."

James mounted his horse and started towards Brushy Creek. When he got a mile outside of Round Rock, he saw the stream. He followed the flow upstream for about a mile. When he rounded an oxbow, he spied two men camped about 250 yards away. He got off his horse, pulled out the Sharps, and started walking towards the men. When he got to within 100 yards, he laid the Sharps across the saddle and hollered, "I'm Marshall Boutwell, both of you are under arrest. Both men grabbed their rifles and ran towards a small copse of trees. The man nearest James didn't quite make it. James fired and a 475-grain slug hit the man in his side. He went down like a fallen tree and didn't move. The other man took cover.

Brushy Creek was aptly named. Small trees and brush covered both sides of the creek. James put the Sharps in its scabbard, pulled out his Winchester, rode his horse into the stream, and started towards the man while using the foliage for cover. When he got to within about seventy-five feet of the trees, he saw the man aiming a rifle at him. James shot and hit the man. The man also shot and hit James. The slug hit James just below his left shoulder, tore through his flesh under his armpit, busted a rib, and tore a reasonably large hole in the side of his back when it exited.

James levered another shell into the Winchester and shot again. The man turned and leaned against a tree. James started the horse up the creek bank but fell off the horse. The shock of the bullet and the blood loss had taken the starch out of him. The cold water kinda revived him and after a couple minutes, he mounted his horse and rode up the bank. The man he had shot was nowhere to be seen.

James rode his mount to the tree where the man had been standing. There were several splotches of blood on the ground and a blood trail leading away. James was getting dizzy and knew he was in no condition to track the man. With great effort he stayed in the saddle and made it back to Round Rock. There was no doctor in the town, but someone found a mid-wife. The woman cleaned the entrance and exit sites of his wound, bound his chest to support the broken rib, and suggested he get in bed and stay there a couple days.

James got a room behind Oatts' store. A man who saw him ride up to Oatts' store was nice enough to take the saddle off his horse and place it in the tiny room. Another man led the horse to the livery. James put his head on the saddle and was asleep in minutes and never moved the entire night. The next morning, Mrs. Oatts brought him a chamber pot and said she would take it away and empty it when she brought him some breakfast. He lay around most of the day. Midafternoon James got up, walked to the livery, got his horse, and walked back to Oatts' store. A drover was kind enough to saddle James' horse. He mounted the animal with some difficulty and rode off slowly towards Austin.

When he got to Austin, he left his horse in the livery and asked the hostler to take the saddle off the animal and give him a scoop of oats. James slowly walked to his office and lay down on the cot. The ride had exhausted him, and he immediately fell asleep. He wasn't up to speed yet.

As he rested on the cot, his thoughts turned to the man who had shot him. James had killed two of the men who were traveling with Clements, so the man toting the two pieces of .44 lead was probably the leader of the group. From the looks of the blood trail, the man could bleed to death, but there was no way of knowing. James had left the dead man where he had fallen, and the two horses picketed beside the camp. Clements could have returned, mounted one of the horses, and rode somewhere to get medical attention or hole up while his wounds healed. It all depended on exactly where the bullets had hit the outlaw. James had heard of men being shot four or five times and still surviving.

As it turned out Clements did get back to his horse and made it to a farmhouse further up the creek. They didn't know he was a killer and took care of him for a few days until he recovered sufficiently that he could ride. Clements wasn't in the greatest of health, but he rode off from the farm and headed north. Since Marshal Boutwell was in somewhat the same condition, he couldn't follow the outlaw.

****

Emanuel "Mannen" Clements ran for sheriff in the newly formed Runnels County, south of Abilene, Texas, in 1877. He lost in a hotly contested election. By 1880, Clements had amassed numerous horse and cattle herds on his McCulloch County ranch, which lay east of San Angelo, Texas. He was suspected of rustling, but lawmen could never prove it.

On March 29, 1887, Mannen Clements got embroiled in an argument in the Senate Saloon in Ballinger, Texas. The argument escalated and someone went for the law. City Marshal, Joseph Townsend, arrived and attempted to arrest Clements, but he was having none of it. Clements resisted arrest and was shot and killed in the ensuing gunfight. Another killer and outlaw died the way he had lived!

Chapter 5

James recovered from the gunshot wound he had received trying to capture Emanuel Clements and suffered no long-term effects of the injury. Marshal Boutwell's life got back to normal, whatever that was, and he began serving warrants, transporting prisoners to other locations, or returning them to Austin. He also made his presence known in and around Austin. He figured by being visible to the town's people; it helped with upholding law and order in the town.

On June 20, 1874, James got a transport order on Freddie McElpine to take him to Dallas, Texas, to stand trial. Dallas was about 200 miles from Austin. Marshal Boutwell got Freddie on the stagecoach when it left Austin on Sunday, June 21. James tied his mount and a spare to the rear of the stagecoach and swung his saddle and an old one for the spare horse onto the roof. He had McElpine get into the coach and he then climbed inside and sat across from the outlaw. Two dusty days and three stops to use the privy, change horses, and get a bite to eat and they were in Waco.

On the 24th the stagecoach stopped at a waystation near modern day Carl's Corner, Texas. They were now about fifty miles from Dallas, give or take. James was tired of being jostled around and eating dust. He told Freddie to use the privy and get a bite to eat. They would ride their horses the rest of the way to Dallas. The prisoner started complaining and James asked him if he would like to make the trip tied over his saddle? Freddie allowed he would shut up and ride the horse. Dallas was too far for a comfortable one-day ride, so James stopped and spent the night about fifty yards off the trail they were using. James got a skillet and a couple of coffee cups out of his saddlebags. After getting a small fire started, he placed some smoked bacon in the skillet, added some coffee to the cups, and pushed them close enough to the fire for the water to boil.

After eating and drinking their coffee, James had Freddie carry his saddle to a pine tree about six inches round, put down his ground cover and lay down with his blanket. James took one manacle loose, had the outlaw reach around the tree, and attached the other end to his wrist. Now that Freddie was secured for the night, James could rest without worrying about the outlaw getting any bright ideas. The next morning James heated two cups of coffee, saddled the horses, drank a cup, gave one to Freddie, and got started to Dallas.

Marshal Boutwell had been to Dallas several times through the years. He had delivered a few prisoners and once had helped put down a riot in the town. He found the town dirty and filled with undesirables. As they rode along, two men approached them from the north. When James got close to the men, he instinctively placed his hand on the butt of his revolver. Something just didn't seem right here.

When the men got to within about thirty feet of James and his prisoner they stopped. James looked at them and said, "Something I can do for you, fellas?"

The men looked at James, one sneered and the other looked frightened. The man on the right said, "I'm Jonas McElpine. When you didn't show up on the stagecoach, I figured you decided to ride into Dallas. You can turn Freddie loose and we'll all go our separate ways." The second man seemed nervous, fidgeted, but said nothing. James analyzed the situation. The talker no doubt knew how to use a gun. On the other hand, the fidgeter probably wasn't much of a gunman and might even wet his pants if gunplay started. James kept his focus on Jonas and just used his peripheral vision to watch the nervous Nellie.

After a few moments of silence James said, "Now you two have a decision to make. The only way you get Freddie is to kill me and I doubt you can do that. Either pull your pistol and get a free trip to boot hill or drop your weapons on the ground and ride ahead of us to Dallas. Your choice!"

The talker went for his pistol and James put a chunk of lead from his .38 in the man's brisket. Jonas looked surprised, sat motionless for a couple seconds, dropped the pistol, and fell to the ground. Nervous Nellie threw his hands up and said, "Don't shoot. Please don't shoot. Jonas and Freddie are my cousins. Nothing would do but I come along. I'm no help with a gun."

43

James eased his horse over to the man, relieved him of his pistol and rifle, and put the pistol in his saddlebags. Boutwell shucked all the cartridges out of the rifle and handed it back to the nervous Nellie and said, "If you even look like you want to take that rifle out of its scabbard I'll put a bullet right between your beady eyes." The man looked like he was about to pee in his pants and assured James he wouldn't touch the weapon.

James looked from one man to the other and said, "The dead man's your kin, load him on his horse and tie his wrists to his boots." They both complied and got the man on his horse and secured. They were still around ten miles from Dallas. James told the two men to ride in front of him, the nervous Nellie was to hold the dead man's horse's lead, and just walk their horses. After walking the horses for about five miles, James saw a group of buzzards circling in the sky a couple hundred feet away in the sage.

Marshal Boutwell turned to the nervous fellow and asked, "Did you see the buzzards when you came down the trail?"

The man replied, "Yes. But Jonas thought it was just a dead animal, so we didn't investigate."

James turned his horse towards the buzzards and said, "He was probably right, but let's take a look." When they got to the buzzards, one of the scavenger birds was on a reasonably small female body. James shot his pistol, and the buzzards scurried off and some flew away. He told both men to get off their horses. He told the nervous fellow to look at the woman and see if he knew her. When nervous Nellie saw the woman's face, he vomited and turned chalky white.

He looked at James and said, "Yes I know her, or at least I know who she was. Her name is Thelma Goodrich or Goodson, or something like that. She worked at a brothel called Maggie's Pleasure Palace right outside Dallas."

James said, "You look a little green around the gills, sit down beside Freddie, and don't move around." He walked over to the dead body and looked for evidence of foul play. He saw no obvious knife or bullet wounds and no tears on the woman's clothes. There was a scarf around her neck. The woman's legs were splayed, but when James lifted her dress, her bloomers were in place. That would indicate that she hadn't been violated. It was unlikely anyone would violate her and then go to the trouble of replacing her unmentionables.

James took the ground cover off his horse, spread it out next to the body, rolled the corpse onto the ground cover and wrapped it around the body. He picked the body up, placed it on the horse Freddie had been riding, and secured it with a length of rope.

Freddie looked at the marshal and said, "How am I gonna get to Dallas?"

James looked at the outlaw and said, "You're gonna ride double with your cousin, or I can bust your head open, tie you to the saddle, and let your cousin walk. Your choice, I like her better dead than

I do either of you alive." Freddie grumbled but got on the horse with his cousin.

As they were about to ride off James looked at the nervous fellow and said, "By the way, what's your name?" The man replied his name was Jonathan T. Scruthers. James was to later discover that Scruthers was an attorney and the mayor of Dallas.

When James arrived in Dallas, he turned the dead body of Jonas McElpine over to city marshal John Earl Framington. Since Scruthers had done nothing beyond accompany McElpine, he couldn't be charged with anything. James told Scruthers to go on home and turned Freddie McElpine over to the marshal to be locked in a jail cell. James turned his horse and started off with the dead woman's body. The marshal wanted to know where he was going with the body. James told him he understood the dead woman worked at Maggie's Pleasure Palace. He would take the body there for a positive identification.

Marshal Framington said, "This is a local matter. I'll take care of it. Just leave the body on the horse."

Marshal Boutwell looked at the city marshal and replied, "I reckon not. I'll turn the body over to the undertaker once the owner of the brothel makes a positive identification. That is unless you are a customer of the place, have used her services, and want to make the identification." Framington huffed but said nothing else.

Marshal Boutwell followed Marshal Framington's directions, rode to the brothel, hitched his horse to the rail in the front of the building, and walked inside. A very attractive raven-haired woman who appeared to be in her twenties met him at the door. The woman's enthusiasm waned when she saw James' badge. She cautiously asked, "Are you here for business or pleasure."

Marshal Boutwell replied, "I need to see the owner of this establishment."

The young woman scurried off and in a couple minutes a buxom, well-dressed woman of a certain age came walking up and said, "I'm Maggie Branceer, what can I do for you today, Marshal?" James explained that he had a female body outside on a horse and had been told that she worked at Maggie's Pleasure Palace.

James said, "Miss Branceer, I would appreciate it if you would walk out to the horse with me and make a positive identification of the woman."

Maggie Branceer looked at Marshal Boutwell and said, "Its Mrs. Branceer. Let's go. I hope it's not who I fear it may be." When they got to the horse, James raised the ground cover. Maggie gasped, blanched, and stepped back. She said, "My God. What happened to her face?"

James softly said, "Ma'am, animals found her I'm afraid. Do you know her?"

Mrs. Branceer teared up and said, "Yes. She worked here and when we met for breakfast this past

Sunday morning, we discovered her missing. Her name is Thelma Goodrich."

Marshal Boutwell gently asked, "Then it's Goodrich, not Goodson?"

Mrs. Branceer replied, "Certainly it's Goodrich, or at least that is the name she used while she was working here. Where did you get the idea, it was Goodson?"

James looked at Mrs. Branceer and said, "Is there someplace I can put these horses and perhaps ask you a few questions?" Mrs. Branceer walked with James around the building and showed him a stable large enough to house a dozen horses. Right now, there were only two in the stable. James led the horses in and loosened their cinches and gave them a scoop of oats from a barrel.

After getting the horses squared away, James walked to the back of the building with Mrs. Branceer and went in the rear entrance. Mrs. Branceer closed the door and asked Marshal Boutwell to follow her. They walked down the hallway and into the kitchen for a cup of coffee while they talked. James thanked Mrs. Branceer for her kindness and sat at a large table, removed his hat, and placed it crown down. James felt something rubbing on his leg, looked down, and saw an odd-colored cat.

Mrs. Branceer brought James a steaming cup of coffee, sat down across from him, and said, "That's just Peaches. She's kinda the mascot of the house. I seem to remember asking you how you got the idea Thelma's name was Goodson."

Marshal Boutwell smiled slightly and replied, "Mrs. Branceer, if you please, I'll ask the questions. Did Miss Goodrich have any enemies you know of? Perhaps a client she got crossways with?

Mrs. Branceer was thoughtful for a few moments and then said, "No. Not that I can think of offhand. I don't allow any drunks or rudeness in this establishment. It is primarily a gentlemen's social establishment and only men of some means can afford our services. We cater to their enjoyment and rarely have a problem. As far as I know, all the other girls liked Thelma well enough and I never saw or heard anything out of the way with the clientele."

James cleared his throat, turned slightly red, and said, "I raised her dress to see if there was evidence that she had been raped. Her undergarments seemed to be properly in place."

Mrs. Branceer smiled and asked, "And you're an authority on women's unmentionables?"

Marshal Boutwell ignored Mrs. Branceer's comment and plowed on. "I appreciate your need for discretion as pertains to your clients, but at some point, I must know who visited Thelma, or asked for her specifically. Was a man named Jonathan Scruthers one of her regular customers?

Mrs. Branceer said, "I'd rather not say. The names of my customers will have to stay private."

Marshal Boutwell looked at Mrs. Branceer and said, "Ma'am, a woman's dead. I don't think she left her room here and walked a few miles into the sage and held her breath until she died, if that were even possible. I stumbled onto this by accident while doing my job. Now I have no choice but to investigate and attempt to find who killed this woman. I don't want to make life unpleasant for you, but I'm not one of the local yokels. You and I can do this informally, or I can get with the attorney general and probably get unlimited powers. If it comes to having to contact the attorney general, my first action will be to lock your doors until you decide to help me. Do we understand each other?"

Mrs. Branceer looked defiant, but said, "I understand. I'll help you any way I can and trust you to keep the information confidential." The conversation was over for the moment. James got up, thanked Mrs. Branceer for the coffee, and promised to stop by the next day for a list of Thelma's regulars.

Chapter 6

Marshal Boutwell got the horses from the stable, rode into Dallas, and stopped at the sheriff's office. The sheriff, J. L. Baggett, was in his office when James walked in. James told the sheriff that he could take control of the dead woman's body. The sheriff was angry and said, "Marshal Boutwell, I don't know who the hell you think you are but you're not doing any investigation in my county. Now butt out and stay out of my business."

James didn't say a word. He merely walked out of the sheriff's office and directly down the dirt street to the telegraph office. He walked up to the counter and said he wanted to dictate a wire. The telegraph operator said he would write it down and transmit the message.

"Honorable George W. Clark, Attorney General of Texas. Stop. Woman murdered in Dallas. Stop. Local officials obstructing investigation. Stop. Local citizens suspects. Stop. Request you instruct local law enforcement to stand down. Stop. Deputy U.S. Marshal James Boutwell."

James figured by going to the top, he would either get fired, or all the authority he needed to get his investigation done. James' father and George Clark had been childhood friends, before they went their separate ways. James' father moved to Missouri and George Clark went into politics and ended up in Texas. James had occasion to see and talk with

General Clark a few times and they were on good terms. Or at least he hoped they were on good terms.

James put his horse in the livery, brushed him down, and gave him a scoop of oats. After finishing with the horse, James walked up the street to the Dallas café and ate some beans spiced with chilies. After eating, he went to the Dallas House, got a room, and turned in for the night. The next morning, as he was eating breakfast at the Dallas Café the telegraph operator came running in and handed Marshal Boutwell a telegram.

"Deputy U.S. Marshal James Boutwell. Stop. You have full authority. Stop. George Clark, Attorney General, Texas" James turned to the telegraph operator and said, "Have you shown this to anyone else?

The telegraph operator shifted his feet and said, "Well kinda. Sheriff Baggett, Marshal Framington, and Mayor Scruthers were all in the telegraph office when the wire came in."

James smiled and said, "Good. That'll save me the time of telling them."

Marshal Boutwell got his horse out of the livery and rode to Maggie's Pleasure Palace, tied the animal to the hitching rail, and walked in the door. Mrs. Branceer met him at the door and said, "How about a cup of coffee, Marshal."

After talking about nothing of consequence for a few minutes, James got down to brass tacks. "Mrs. Branceer, I don't want a list of everyone who visited your facility. As I mentioned yesterday, I'm only interested in those men who regularly visited Miss Goodrich. Mrs. Branceer slid a piece of paper with some names on it across the table to Marshal Boutwell. James glanced at the list. The first name that jumped out at him was Jonathan Scruthers. James folded the note and put it in his vest pocket. He looked at Mrs. Branceer and said, "Ma'am, this is mighty fine coffee, mighty fine. I'm used to making my coffee. I guess I could use some tips." Mrs. Branceer just nodded, smiled, and said nothing.

After finishing his coffee, James excused himself, got up, and walked out of the building.

Mrs. Branceer followed James out the door, stood on the porch, and asked, "Does this mean I can stay open, Marshal Boutwell?"

James looked at Mrs. Branceer and replied, "Ma'am, who am I to hinder a lady who is providing a public service. I may come by one evening and have one of your T-Bone steaks. I've heard they are mighty good."

Mrs. Branceer smiled and said, "My cook starts cooking steaks at 5 PM by the order. Come out and I'll stand you to the first dinner."

James thanked Mrs. Branceer again for the coffee and the list and rode off. He made his next stop at the office of Mayor Johnathan T. Scruthers, Esq. James walked his horse into Dallas, stopped a man on the street, and got directions to Scruthers' law office. James hitched his horse to the rail and walked into the small office. Attorney Scruthers was sitting at his desk and nearly fainted when Marshal

Boutwell entered his office. The lawyer attempted to stand up and almost tipped over his chair.

James said, "Mind if I sit down? I've got a few questions to ask you."

Scruthers blanched and mumbled, "Yes. Yes, have a seat."

Marshal Boutwell just looked at Scruthers for a couple minutes to see how much he would squirm. Once James was confident the man was suitably nervous, he began questioning him. "Mayor Scruthers, you told me on the trail when we found the girl that her name was Goodson or Goodrich, or something like that. You left the impression that you didn't know the woman well enough to be sure of her surname. I've been doing a little checking, and you were on a first name basis with Miss Goodrich. In fact, I understand that you knew her in a biblical sense and were a frequent visitor to Maggie's Pleasure Palace. My question to you is this: why would you pretend that you just slightly knew her?"

Scruthers squirmed and sweat broke out on his forehead, and he said, "Marshal, I'm a man of some standing in Dallas, and I'm married. If my voters or my wife discovered I was consorting with a known prostitute, I'd be in trouble. The good people of Dallas might not understand, and my wife might leave me and go back east."

James waited a few seconds and responded, "I suppose that is true. But that doesn't answer my question. I was just delivering a prisoner. Why would you care whether I thought you knew the woman or not? If I wasn't going to arrest you for interfering with a peace officer, why would you intentionally misrepresent your knowledge of the dead woman?"

Attorney Scruthers pulled up a little courage and said, "Now see here, Marshal, what difference does it make whether I used the woman's correct surname? Perhaps I merely couldn't remember her surname or was in shock when I saw her dead."

James considered Mayor Scruthers' response for a few seconds and said, "Perhaps, any of those could be true, but there are also lots of other possibilities. For instance, you could know something about the woman's murder. Or, Miss Goodrich could have been with child, and was going to name you as the father. Or, Miss Goodrich could have threatened to tell your wife about your philandering if you didn't give her money. It has been my experience that people kill other people for some stupid reasons. Perhaps you had more reason than most: your reputation, your marriage, your law practice, or your job as mayor. I don't try to understand why people do the things they do; I just bring them to justice."

Marshal Boutwell was concerned that Mayor Scruthers was about to have a heart attack or stroke. Beads of sweat appeared on the man's forehead and he became pale. James decided he had pushed Scruthers enough for one day, got up, and said, "We'll talk again, Mayor. You have a nice day."

It was difficult to gauge Scruthers because he was a nervous individual by nature. He could have merely been reacting to the stress of being questioned, and perhaps he was guilty of the murder, or knew who was.

James took his horse's reins and walked towards the Dallas Café. As he was walking along, an older man came up to him and gestured towards his horse's rear leg. When James looked at the horse's leg, the man said, "There ain't nothing wrong with your horse. I just don't want people to know I'm feeding you information. You might want to talk to the Reverend Simon Smith over at the Methodist Church about the disappearance and murder of that young woman." With that, the older man walked off to the other side of the street.

James went into the café, ordered lunch, and sipped his coffee. He pulled the list Mrs. Branceer had given him out of his pocket. There was no Simon Smith on the list! He wondered if the old man was trying to send him on a wild goose chase, or had Mrs. Branceer left the reverend off the list by design, or did she simply forget? As he ate his ham steak, biscuits and redeye gravy, James began to wonder if everyone in Dallas had something to hide. The sheriff didn't want him investigating the murder, the mayor was evasive and misleading, and now Mrs. Branceer may have been less than forthcoming with him.

As James was finishing his second cup of coffee, Sheriff Baggett walked up to his table. He looked at James for a couple moments and said, "I guess you think by going to the Attorney General of

Texas you're the bull of the woods around here. I don't like you prying into a local affair. But I won't stand in your way, and I'll help when and if you ask."

James smiled and replied, "Here is some free advice for you, Sheriff. I wouldn't enjoy being rooted out any more than you. Just don't do anything to obstruct my investigation in any manner, and you and I will get along fine. Killing a woman, no matter her station in life, is a dastardly act. I intend to find out who killed her. You know most everyone in the county. I'm sure you could be helpful. But that's up to you."

James got up, placed some change on the table to pay for his lunch, and walked out of the café leaving Sheriff Baggett to stew in his own juices. He didn't really want to go back to Maggie's Pleasure Palace and talk to Mrs. Branceer, but he needed to explore what the old man had told him about the Reverend.

James rode out to Maggie's Pleasure Palace again, went inside, and found Mrs. Branceer sitting in the foyer like she had been waiting for him to arrive. Mrs. Branceer said, "Back for more of that good coffee, Marshal? Or is this something other than a social call?"

James smiled and said, "Do I need an excuse to visit a pretty lady and have a cup of coffee? I'm here following up on an anonymous lead. Well not anonymous, but the man didn't give me his name. I'm wondering if there was some reason that

Reverend Simon Smith wasn't on the list you gave me."

Mrs. Branceer's eyes gave her away for just a second. She got up and got James a cup of coffee and had recovered her composure when she got back to the table, and said, "Why would I put the good reverend on the list? Is there some reason you think he should be on the list? He has come here a few times on Sunday morning to lead our Bible study before he conducts his church service in Dallas."

Marshal Boutwell looked at Mrs. Branceer and replied, "You're avoiding my question. Let me be specific. And you need to understand that, even though I admire your coffee, failing to answer my questions could be an obstruction of justice and end you up in jail. Has Reverend Smith ever visited Thelma Goodrich in the biblical sense?"

Mrs. Branceer avoided James's eyes for a few moments and then replied, "I made special arrangements for Reverend Smith to visit Thelma. He would only come late at night and always left his horse in the stable behind the building. He would come in the back entrance, go through the foyer, and directly to Thelma's room." Mrs. Branceer paused for a few moments and continued, "Reverend Smith is a good man. His wife has been an invalid for some years now. He has creature needs like the rest of us. Thelma filled his needs. Please don't involve Reverend Smith in this investigation. He is truly a decent man."

James thanked Mrs. Branceer for her honesty and promised to talk to the Reverend on the pretense of getting general information and perhaps even spiritual advice. He got up, thanked Mrs. Branceer for the coffee, walked out, and mounted his horse. This was getting more tangled than a Gordian Knot!

Chapter 7

James had allowed the day to get away from him, so he decided to go to the Dallas Café and get a bite to eat. After ordering, he was sitting deep in thought savoring his cup of coffee when Amos J. Pickwell, MD came walking with purpose into the café and marched straight to his table. The doctor asked Marshal Boutwell if he could sit down and have a word with him. James reached over, slid out a chair, and asked the doctor to sit down.

Doctor Pickwell began "I went by Sheriff Baggett's office to discuss this matter with him and he referred me to you, saying you were overseeing the investigation of Thelma Goodrich. Is that correct?

James looked at the doctor for a couple seconds trying to get a read on him and then said, "Yes, the Attorney General appointed me to do the investigation. What's on your mind?"

Doctor Pickwell took a deep breath and dove in. "When you brought Miss Goodrich's body to Dallas and turned it over to Sheriff Baggett, he brought the body to me. I did an examination of the body and made an interesting discovery. Actually, it was two discoveries. Miss Goodrich was pregnant, probably between two and three months. The second thing is that whoever killed her, strangled her to death, probably with the scarf around her neck." After a few moments of silence, Doctor Pickwell went on and said, "There was no evidence of a struggle, no skin under her fingernails, and no bruises on her body. It was as if she just stood or lay still and let someone strangle her to death. From a medical standpoint, how she was killed is simple. How it was accomplished is mystifying. The larynx was fractured. That tells me that the killer was strong. Also, the amount of pressure applied was more than necessary. It was as if the killing was done in anger."

Marshal Boutwell asked, "Spare me the gory details if there are any, but how did you determine she was pregnant. Please tell me in layman's terms if you will."

Doctor Pickwell said, "Maggie, excuse me, Mrs. Branceer, has me check all the girls who work in the brothel every two weeks for gonorrhea. To do this, I must do an interview and pelvic examination. I keep records of each examination. When I examined her body postmortem, I noticed changes in Miss Goodrich's uterus and cervix. Both changes indicated pregnancy. About two weeks ago when I did the last gonorrhea examination of the girls at Maggie's, Miss Goodrich complained of a bad cold and I postponed her checkup. In a month a pregnant woman's uterus and cervix can change. I may have been able to have noticed the change two weeks ago and perhaps not. A month between examinations made it obvious. Now that I think about it, the bad cold could have been morning sickness."

James looked at the doctor and said, "Is there anything else that would be helpful for me to know concerning Miss Goodrich?" The doctor seemed a little nervous regarding the question but denied observing anything else that was remarkable when he did his examination. Marshall Boutwell thanked the doctor, told him to keep his findings to himself, and bid him good day. The doctor said he was glad to help, got up, and left the café.

James' mind was in a whirl. What did the doctor's information do for the investigation? How did the two facts get him any closer to finding the killer? A prostitute would have a difficult time identifying the father of her unborn child. And, James agreed with the doctor, how a woman could be strangled without any struggle was a mystery. After drinking another cup of coffee and getting nowhere with his thought process, he went to his room at the Dallas House, washed up, and tried to clear his mind. He was hoping he could relax enough to get some sleep. He planned to go back and visit Mrs. Branceer the following morning and get her thoughts on this new information.

James tossed and turned and finally drifted off to sleep somewhere around midnight. Around 2 AM he was awakened from his slumber by a crashing sound. Or at least when he gained his senses, he realized it was a crashing sound. On the floor was a fist-sized rock with a piece of paper secured with twine attached to it. James took his pistol out of its holster, put on his boots to make sure he didn't step on glass with his bare feet, and looked up and down the street. Whoever had thrown the rock had deserted the street.

Marshal Boutwell picked up the rock, untied the twine, and opened the paper. Printed in block letters was "*Go back to Austin. If you continue with this investigation, you'll die here.*" As he finished the note, there was a knock on his door. He walked over with the pistol still in his hand and opened the door. The hotel clerk almost fainted when he saw the barrel of the pistol!

In a couple moments the clerk recovered and asked, "Are you all right, Sir? I heard the loud noise and wanted to make sure you were alright."

James said, "How did you know it was my room that the sound of the broken window came from?"

The clerk said, "Begging your pardon, Marshal, but your room is the only one on the street side of the hallway that is occupied."

James felt as stupid as a box of rocks and merely mumbled to himself "Guess that makes sense." Once the clerk confirmed that James was all right and rather stupid without coming right out and saying so, he excused himself, and went back downstairs. After another hour of tossing and turning, James drifted back off to sleep.

He awoke early, washed his face in the plain white Minton wash bowl in his room, used the chamber pot, got dressed, and walked down the stairs into the lobby. He thanked the clerk for checking on him and headed for the Dallas Café. After eating some biscuits and molasses and one cup of coffee (he would visit Mrs. Branceer again and he wanted a cup of her coffee), he walked to the stable, got his horse, and headed for Maggie's Pleasure Palace.

James arrived a little after 8 AM, tied his horse, and walked in the door. Mrs. Branceer was sitting in the foyer drinking a cup of coffee and reading a magazine from back east. She looked up when she heard the door open and said, "Well, my, my, you're becoming a regular around here. If I was charging you, you'd go broke." Mrs. Branceer smiled, got tickled, and laughed at her own joke. James' face turned a slight pinkish color. About that time, Peaches started rubbing against his leg, and weaving in and out between his boots. Peaches sure was a strange-looking cat!

Marshall Boutwell began. "Mrs." And that was as far as he got.

Mrs. Branceer stopped him and said, "If you're gonna visit me every day; the least you can do is call me Maggie. I don't allow many people to call me by my given name, but I kinda like you. In fact, you make me wish I was twenty years younger. I suppose I like you because you're a persistent cuss. Mrs. is appropriate because I'm a widow, but I don't like the term."

James turned pink again and started over, "Ma'am, Maggie. Doctor Pickwell visited with me yesterday evening and gave me a couple bits of information that are puzzling to me, or at least, one thing he told me is puzzling. Miss Goodrich was pregnant, and someone strangled her with her own scarf without her offering any resistance."

Maggie looked at Marshall Boutwell, smiled, and said, "Which part is confusing you and which part do you want me to explain to you? How she got pregnant or how she got strangled to death?"

James turned red this time, and said, "Well, if you've got an idea of how someone could kill Miss Goodrich without her fighting back, I'd love to hear it. I think I understand the other."

Maggie looked at James and asked, "Have you been shot lately, Marshal? Unless you're out in the wilderness someplace, a doctor would give you chloroform or ether to put you to sleep before he started cutting on you. I expect Doctor Pickwell keeps a supply of one or both on hand in case he needs to do surgery. I expect that Ike Turnbull, owner of the Bar T, keeps some of one or the other on hand in case a drover gets hurt or they need to work on a horse or cow. And I suspect that some other ranchers might keep some on hand. I doubt that the anesthesia is hard to come by."

James sat there feeling as dumb as he had regarding the only room on the street side of the hotel. He seemed to have a gift for missing the obvious. He had read about chloroform and ether but hadn't associated it with this crime until Maggie suggested someone might have used the anesthetic. Dumber than a box of rocks! That's how he felt, dumber than a box of rocks!

Maggie said, "Are you thinking about something, Marshal?"

James just shook his head and said, "I don't think I'm doing much thinking. Everything has always been fairly cut and dried with me. When someone breaks the law, I go and arrest him. If he doesn't want to be arrested, I shoot him. The killing of this woman is a lot more complicated. I'm not at all sure I'm well suited for this type of investigation."

Maggie said, "I think you're selling yourself short, Marshal. I suspect you are out thinking yourself. A human killing another human being is straightforward. Once you figure out what motivated the killing, the killer won't be all that hard to identify." Maggie took a sip of her coffee and continued, "If I were trying to figure this out, I would look at everyone who had contact with Thelma in isolation. Take the person who you have some reason to suspect and work on that individual until you are satisfied you have the right person, or you have eliminated him."

Maggie impressed Marshal Boutwell with her common sense. This was one smart woman, and no doubt a real looker when she was a few years younger. He wondered to himself if she had been a big eastern city detective or worked with the Pinkertons before opening the sporting house. James asked, "How did you come about this ability to understand crimes?"

Maggie replied, "I have a lot of free time on my hands and I've ordered and read a lot of books:

The Trail of the Serpent, Armadale, and other mystery novels. I guess reading them helped me understand how to untangle plots. Do you want another cup of coffee, Marshal?"

James smiled and said, "Only if you stop calling me marshal. My name is James. James Boutwell." James and Maggie sat and chatted for more than an hour. He really liked her and wished she was about twenty years younger.

After they had kinda worn out anything else to talk about, James excused himself and said he thought he would have a chat with the preacher. He wasn't looking forward to that conversation, but the interview had to be conducted to assure himself that the reverend wasn't a suspect.

James mounted his horse, rode back into Dallas, and went to the Methodist Church. He dismounted, tied his horse to a rail, and walked to a side door and knocked. He waited for a couple minutes and knocked again. A voice said, "If you're a looking for Reverend Smith, he ain't here. He went to look in on the widder Jameson." James turned towards the sound of the voice and saw an older man who was working in the garden beside the church. The man went on to say that the woman was down with the lumbago and the reverend went to sit and pray with her. He should be back in a couple hours.

The man doing the talking was the same man who had stopped him on the street and suggested he should talk to Reverend Smith. James wanted to ask the man some questions but decided he would let the inquiries keep until he had an opportunity to interview the reverend. James thanked the man and acted like he had never seen him before.

James mounted his horse and walked the animal to the Dallas Café. This just kept getting better and better. He thought about going to Maggie's that evening and getting one of her famous T-Bone steaks but didn't want to wear out his welcome. He ordered a bowl of chili and some chopped up onions. He liked to mix onions in with his chili. It seemed to give it more flavor. As he was eating, he had an epiphany. Maggie had said that Ike Turnbull would have chloroform or ether on his ranch. If he was going to disqualify people, he thought he might as well ride out to the Bar T and have a little chat with its owner.

After paying for his meal and getting directions, James walked out, mounted his horse, and headed for the Bar T ranch. About forty-five minutes later, after riding through an opening that displayed a large bar and a T on a horizontal post over the opening, he arrived at a rustic ranch house.

Chapter 8

The Bar T wasn't a large ranch by Texas standards, perhaps 700 acres of rolling grassland, scrub, arroyos, and standing timber about twenty miles north of Dallas. The ranch was situated just south of Richardson, a tiny settlement which was built on 101 donated acres of land alongside the Houston and Texas Central Railway tracks. There wasn't much in Richardson, just a building which was part store and saloon, and a few houses. The Bar T hands would go to Richardson for a few drinks and maybe a card game. If they wanted adult entertainment in the form of soiled doves, they would ride to Dallas and use one of the bawdy houses.

When James pulled up in front of the ranch house, a large man wearing chaps, a slouch hat, and carrying a pistol met him. With no greeting, the man said, "Who are you and what do you want? We have all the help we need in case you're looking for work." The man hadn't looked directly at James. When he shielded his eyes from the morning sun and looked up, he saw the badge. The man said, "A U. S. marshal. What the hell has one of my drovers got himself into now?"

Marshal Boutwell looked at the man and said, "As far as I know none of your hands are in trouble. I'm here to see Isaac Turnbull, are you him?"

The man looked James over and replied, "You found him. Climb off your horse and come in for a cup of coffee and tell me what's on your mind." James tied his horse to a rail in front of the ranch house, dismounted, and followed Turnbull into the house. The interior of the house was rustic but clean. The décor didn't appear to have the refinement a woman would lend to the surroundings. James sat down at a table and Turnbull poured him a cup of coffee.

As James was sipping his coffee, a young man walked into the room. The man was clean shaven and dressed like a fop. He walked over to the table, extended his hand, and said, "Hello there. I'm Marcus Merriweather, and you are?" When James shook hands with the young man, it sufficed to say that the man didn't offer a manly handshake. The man offered no grip and extended his hand as a female might. James replied that he was Deputy U.S. Marshal James Boutwell.

James noticed that Turnbull didn't seem particularly happy with the man giving attention to his visitor and said, "Marcus, don't you have some chores to attend to?" The young man smiled demurely at Turnbull, smiled at James, and sauntered out of the room. Turnbull sat down, looked at James, and said, "Well, Marshal, what can I do for you this fine morning?"

Marshal Boutwell was just a little perplexed. Maggie hadn't told him anything about Isaac Turnbull which would have prepared him for the meeting. Most of the questions he had in his mind probably had no application where Turnbull was concerned. Homosexuality wasn't an acceptable lifestyle in the 19th century and some places had laws that prohibited sexual activity between two men. However, none of that was James' concern or interest. On the other hand, presuming could get one into a lot of trouble. So, James asked Turnbull the same questions he would ask any other man. He looked at Turnbull and said, "This is merely routine, but have you ever used the services of Maggie's Pleasure Palace? More specifically, if you have used the facility, was it with Thelma Goodrich?"

Mr. Turnbull bristled a little but replied, "Yes, I have used the services of Maggie's place, but not in the way you are implying. I go there occasionally for a drink or two and one of Ling's great T-Bone steaks. I don't use the services of the girls as you might have figured out if you were paying attention."

James didn't respond directly, thanked Turnbull for answering his question, and asked, "Do you keep chloroform or ether here on your spread? Perhaps you would use one of them when treating an injured cowhand, horse, or a cow?"

Turnbull said, "Yes. I keep a bottle of chloroform to help calm down our horses while we geld them or do anything else that would cause them pain. It's better than getting a drover hurt with an animal thrashing around. You have to be careful with the stuff so only I or my foreman uses it."

James nodded his understanding and asked, "Do you know exactly how much you have on hand?

71

Would you be able to tell if some had been removed or used for some other purpose?" Chloroform was packaged in twelve-ounce bottles which would be a little large to carry around, but not impossible.

Turnbull replied, "I bought a twelve ounce bottle some time ago. It doesn't go bad if the cork is inserted tight after use. We can check and make sure the bottle is in the tack shed. I would have no way of knowing if some of the chloroform had been transferred to some other bottle. It's not something I would keep track of. Why are you asking about chloroform?"

James looked at Turnbull and said, "I'd like for you to check and see if the bottle is still in the tack shed. I'm asking about chloroform because a woman was killed in Dallas and the use of chloroform in the crime is a theory I'm considering."

Turnbull said, "Yes, my foreman told me that a drover was in Dallas and had said someone had killed a woman. Let's go check the tack shed." They got up from the table, walked out of the house, and to the tack shed. Turnbull opened the door and walked inside. James stood just outside the door where he could watch. Turnbull took a bottle off a shelf, pulled the cork, held the container away from his nose, and sniffed. He turned to Marshal Boutwell and said, "Yep, it's still here, but I have no idea if some of it might be missing."

James couldn't think of anything else to ask Isaac Turnbull, so he thanked him for his time, walked to his horse, mounted, and rode off. He had ridden perhaps four or five miles when he felt a sting on his right shoulder and immediately heard the report of a rifle shot. He rolled off his horse and took cover behind the animal. There was a small copse of trees around 150 yards to his right. Other than the trees, James couldn't see anyplace else the shot could have come from. He kept his horse between him and the trees and began walking towards a desert willow tree which would give him some cover. The tree was blooming and exhibited some white trumpet-like flowers. He got his horse behind the tree, pulled his binoculars out of his saddlebags, and looked towards the copse of trees.

James had long since learned to look for movement. He didn't try to find a solitary object hiding in trees or foliage. Most outdoorsmen wore drab colored clothing and were difficult to see while hiding, unless they moved. He waited for a little more than thirty minutes and continuously scanned the tree line. He saw nothing move. Satisfied that the drygulcher had left, he mounted his horse and headed on to Dallas. The bullet wound was only a scratch and had merely nicked the skin and tore his shirt. There was a little blood but nothing serious. First the rock thrown through the hotel window and now this, someone didn't want him poking around into the murder of the girl.

After riding a mile or so, a man rode up towards James on a dun-colored horse, pulled up near him, and asked, "I heard a gunshot over this way. Did you shoot at something?"

James looked at the man who was well dressed and in clean clothes, wore a slightly soiled slouch hat, sported well-maintained boots, and wore a cross-draw holster containing a pistol. The dun was a fine-looking animal and seemed spirited. James replied, "No, I didn't shoot at anything, but someone took a shot at me from a copse of trees about a mile back. Nicked my shoulder but did no damage."

The man said, "I'm Mark Johnson, the ramrod of the Bar T. I heard from a drover that someone killed a girl and that a marshal was looking into the murder. Judging by your badge, I guess you're that marshal. I worked for the Texas Rangers for a spell, and I don't envy you your job. Judging by your line of travel, I guess you saw Mr. Turnbull. You're barking up the wrong tree there. Turnbull has an arrangement with Merriweather and has never indicated any interest in women per se. He goes by Maggie's place once or twice a month, but only to have a whiskey and maybe eat a good steak. He pays me well, lets me do my job, and I mind my own business."

James looked at Johnson and asked, "You got any idea who might take a shot at me?"

Johnson laughed and replied, "How the hell would I know? Maybe you're making somebody nervous. Maybe you're getting too close to the truth about who killed the girl. I haven't been off the ranch the past few days, so I haven't heard the town gossip. All I can tell you is that Isaac Turnbull would have had no interest in the girl who was killed."

In for a penny, in for a pound, so James asked, "How about you? Were you one of Thelma Goodrich's customers?"

Johnson bristled a little and said, "I've been to Maggie's Pleasure Palace if that is what you're asking. And I've seen the Goodrich girl there, but I never had the pleasure of sampling her wares. She was a real looker though. Yes Sir, a real looker. A blond-haired girl as I recall. When I feel the urge to satisfy my needs, I visit with another girl at a different brothel. Maggie's place is a little out of my price range."

James plowed on, "When you were visiting Maggie's did you see anyone with the Goodrich girl, anyone in particular who seemed taken with her?"

Johnson pulled out paper and tobacco and began rolling a cigarette. He said nothing for a few minutes, as if he was deep in thought. He looked at James and said, "The men who visit Maggie's are there for a good steak, a few drinks and soothing music, or to spend some time with one of the girls in a biblical sense. Anyone who wanted to satisfy their sexual needs would be charmed with any of the girls I saw there. Why just that female? No, I saw nothing I thought was out of place, but I only went to Maggie's a couple times and never got past the bar, so I'm no authority on who frequents the place or what goes on in the establishment."

James smiled and asked, "And you're sure you've never sampled the wares of Thelma Goodrich?"

Johnson said, "I answered your damn questions. No, I've never been with the dead girl. I saw her at Maggie's, but I was never alone with her or any other girl at Maggie's. And Marshal, I'm not accustomed to answering a question twice."

James told Johnson he meant no offense, thanked the foreman for checking on him and taking the time to answer his questions. It was getting on towards noon, so he decided to get a bite to eat when he got back to Dallas. He had some new information to chew on and had eliminated at least one man from his list of suspects. Well, not entirely, just because a man favored men in a sexual way didn't mean he couldn't or wouldn't sample the wares of a female from time to time. He'd have to chat with Maggie to make sure Isaac Turnbull was telling the whole truth. James was no authority on the subject but had read that some men liked to have sex with men and women.

James allowed his investigation was taking more twists and turns than a mountain stream. He decided, since he was going to have another chat with Maggie, he would see if he could get one of her T-Bone steaks for lunch. He rode through Dallas and arrived at Maggie's Pleasure Palace. He tied his horse to the hitching rail and walked inside. Maggie had seen him ride up and greeted him when he walked in the door by saying, "You are becoming a regular. To what do I owe the pleasure of your company today?"

James said, "Well, I need to ask you a few more questions, and since I was coming to see you anyway, I thought I'd buy one of your T-Bone steaks."

Maggie looked at James, grinned, and said, "You're a little early for a steak. We don't start cooking steaks until 5 PM, but I'll have my cook, Ling, prepare us some lunch and we can chat while we're eating."

In a few minutes the Chinese cook placed two steaming bowls of stew on the table, a loaf of warm bread, a slab of cow butter, and two cups of coffee. Maggie said, "Now. What do you want to ask me about today?"

James filled Maggie in on his talks with Isaac Turnbull and Mark Johnson. He needed confirmation that Johnson had never been with Thelma Goodrich, and that Turnbull had never visited her establishment to sample the wares of her girls.

Maggie was thoughtful for a few moments and said, "Mark has been here a few times, but as best I recall, he never visited Thelma or any of the other girls. I think he is sweet on another girl in Dallas. As to Turnbull, he's been here a few times, but just had a steak, a couple drinks, and then left. He's never visited one of the girls. There was a theatre troupe that came through here a year or so ago. Turnbull went to one of the plays, was smitten with an actor named Marcus Merriweather, and took him home to live on the ranch. As far as I know, Merriweather is still out there."

77

The stew was excellent, and James thanked Maggie for her hospitality. He allowed he still needed to talk to Reverend Smith, so he would be on his way.

As James rode off, he thought to himself, "*Some of this is coming together, or at least I'm narrowing down the suspects.*"

Chapter 9

It was early afternoon and James was hoping he could catch Reverend Smith in his office, so he rode to the Methodist Church. When he arrived at the church, he saw the same older man working in the garden. He dismounted and knocked on the side door of the church. A man wearing a clerical collar opened the door and greeted James.

Reverend Smith was in his fifties, short, balding, and pale of skin. Obviously, the reverend spent most of his time indoors. James introduced himself to Reverend Smith and told him that he needed to ask him a few questions. Sweat broke out on Smith's forehead. He became nervous and said, "What about? Have I done something wrong?"

James looked at the reverend, noticed his obvious discomfort, and said, "As you may, or may not know, I'm investigating the murder of Thelma Goodrich. I received an anonymous suggestion that I needed to talk to you. Mrs. Branceer had given me a list of her clients, and you weren't on it. I went back and talked to Mrs. Branceer again, and after some prodding, she reluctantly acknowledged she had made special arrangements for you to meet with Miss Goodrich more than once. That, Sir, is why I'm here. Perhaps I'm naïve but I thought it just a little strange that a minister would use the services of a prostitute." It concerned James that the reverend might have a heart attack. James had discovered his indiscretion and perhaps a lot more. The reverend was turning paler by the second and large beads of sweat appeared on his face.

When Reverend Smith opened his mouth to speak, the words came out in little more than a squeak. "I knew this would come out eventually, I just knew it. The old axiom that '… and be sure your sin will find you out' Numbers 32:23 is true. My sin has found me out.''

James said, "Reverend Smith, I have no desire to cause you any trouble. I just need to fill in some details of your relationship with Miss Goodrich. Other than your sexual relationship with Miss Goodrich was there anything more involved? Did you want a relationship away from the brothel?

Reverend Smith cleared his throat and said, "This is not an excuse, but my wife has been confined to a wheelchair since a freak accident left her paralyzed. We can't come together as husband and wife. I chose not to just dry up and blow away, so I planned with Maggie to come to the brothel late at night, use the back door and stairs, and go straight to Thelma's room. Other than the cat, Peaches, I don't think anyone ever saw me."

James said, "I'm not here to judge you on this or any other matter, but I need for you to answer my questions. A young woman has been murdered. Someone killed her. I need to explore every avenue which could lead me to that killer."

Reverend Smith fidgeted in his chair, a pained look came on his face, and he replied, "Yes, I fell in love with Thelma, but nothing could come of it. I'm a minister and a married man. I couldn't leave my wife because of her condition and my vocation as a minister. And I'm not sure that Thelma would have been interested in any relationship with me outside of business, anyway. I'm not exactly a handsome man and have little to offer."

Marshal Boutwell thought Reverend Smith's explanation made sense, or as much sense as one could expect from his situation. Marshal Boutwell looked at Reverend Smith and said, "I only have one more question. Was Thelma Goodrich blackmailing you?"

The reverend shook his head and said, "Heavens no. She mentioned nothing like that."

James followed up. "You're sure Miss Goodrich never threatened to tell your wife about your indiscretions? Never asked for money?" Reverend Smith just shook his head. James thanked the minister for his time and assured him he wouldn't mention their discussion unless it became necessary. James suggested to Reverend Smith that he should stay away from Maggie's Pleasure Palace.

Reverend Smith agreed, but said, "If I stop doing the Bible Study on Sunday morning, people, especially my poor crippled wife Emma, might get suspicious. So, I'll continue with that." James just replied that Reverend Smith should do as he thought best. James went away wondering how a reverend could afford the services of an expensive prostitute.

As James was riding through Dallas, he noticed an uproar at the jail. He turned his horse towards the jail and saw the crowd of people were hollering and screaming. James asked a man near him what the hullabaloo was about. The man told him that an Indian, a half-breed, had been arrested for the murder of the prostitute. James dismounted, tied his horse to the hitching rail, went to the jail, and walked in the door. Marshal Framington was grinning like a Cheshire cat. Sheriff Baggett just stood to the side and said nothing. Marshal Framington looked at James and said, "I guess we didn't need all your big shot power to catch the murderer. Apache Fred was in the saloon and tried to use a piece of the jewelry that had belonged to the Goodrich woman to pay for a drink. The bartender sent a man to tell me, and I arrested the Indian."

Marshall Boutwell looked at the marshal and the locket, and said, "That's it. All you have is the fact that the man had a piece of jewelry. Do you even know for sure that it's Miss Goodrich's jewelry? Has he confessed to killing her?"

Marshal Framington said, "We need no more evidence. This here's Dallas, we don't hold with all these highfalutin legal requirements you folks in the marshal service use. We know when a man is guilty, and this Indian will hang just as soon as a jury of townspeople finds him guilty. You can get on your horse and go back to Austin now."

Marshall Boutwell walked over to the cell and looked at the Indian. Only he wasn't an Indian, or at least he wasn't a full-blooded Indian. The man had green eyes and dark brown hair. James looked the man in the eye and said, "I need to ask you some questions. I would suggest you answer them truthfully. Where did you get the locket, you used to buy the drink?"

The half-breed looked at Marshal Boutwell and said, "Aren't you eager to put a noose around my neck like this Dallas law dog? What difference does it make what I say? You're gonna hang me either way!"

James looked at the man and said, "One thing for sure. If you don't talk to me, you're sure gonna hang. Think about it, I'm probably your only hope. I'll be by to see you tomorrow." With that James turned to Marshal Framington and said, "I'll take that locket if you please. Mrs. Branceer can probably confirm that it belonged to Miss Goodrich." Marshal Framington made no response; he just flipped the locket to Marshal Boutwell. James left the jail and rode over to the Dallas House, washed up, combed his hair, and rode to Maggie's Pleasure Palace. It was about 6 PM when he arrived, and he could smell steaks being cooked by Ling.

As usual, Maggie saw him ride up and met him at the door. After they greeted each other James said, "I've been thinking about a big T-Bone steak all day. Medium rare would be just about right and a cold beer would wet my whistle." Maggie led him to the kitchen area, closed the door leading to the foyer, and ordered him a beer. She didn't want the marshal in the dining room because it might just make her customers nervous to see a man wearing a badge in her establishment. James reached into his vest pocket, took out the locket, handed it to Maggie, and asked her if she would show it to the girls and see if any of them recognized it.

About the time he finished his beer Maggie appeared, closed the kitchen door which led to the foyer, and sat down at the table. Maggie said, "A medium rare steak will be ready in just a couple minutes." As predicted, a Chinese man appeared with an enormous steak, a large helping of fried potatoes, a couple pieces of warm bread, and a cup of coffee on a serving tray.

After one bite, James was sure this was the best steak meat he had ever put in his mouth. Most steaks tasted bland. Ling has seasoned this piece of meat with something which enhanced the flavor. The fried potatoes had caramelized onions mixed in with them. James shook his head. He thought to himself, "My gracious, even without the girls this place could make a fortune!"

After James finished the steak and potatoes and two cups of coffee, Maggie reappeared with a giant piece of fresh apple pie. James said, "Maggie, if I eat all that, I won't be able to get back to the hotel. I'm already as stuffed as a Christmas goose." He got through the large slice of excellent pie and had another cup of coffee. When Maggie appeared again, he asked her if she or any of the girls recognized the locket.

Maggie looked sad and replied, "Yes, two of the girls said they had seen Thelma wear the locket around her neck on a gold-colored chain. She had told them it was a gift from her mother and had a strand of her mother's hair in it."

James said, "Well that cuts it. A half-breed tried to buy a drink at the saloon with the locket. Unless he has a real interesting story about how he came by the jewelry, he's gonna hang in a few days. So far, he won't talk to me. Unless he changes his mind, I guess he'll hang." James was thoughtful for a few moments and said, "The thing I don't understand is why Miss Goodrich would pack up her things, and leave in the middle of the night to meet a half-breed Indian she probably never saw before in her life? I suppose she could have been planning on meeting someone else and the half-breed picked her up. Or she could have bumped into the half-breed, but if she was meeting someone, wouldn't that someone pick her up, here at your establishment, probably with a buggy? Something just doesn't smell right about this half-breed. It's all just a little too convenient to suit me."

Against her protests, James paid Maggie for the drinks and steak, bid her good night, mounted his horse, and rode to Dallas. After getting the horse squared away in the livery, he went to the Dallas Hotel, took his boots off, and went to bed. He was tired and stuffed.

According to his Elgin pocket watch, it was 2 AM when the gunfire woke him up. He pulled on his boots, ran down the stairs, and headed for the jail where a few people were standing around. The night jailer was there and when he saw Marshal Boutwell said, "I don't understand it. The cell door had to be unlocked because Apache Fred just walked over to me, took my pistol, and said to be quiet. I checked the cell door when I came on duty and it was locked. I only left the jail long enough to use the privy. As soon as he walked out the jail door, I heard gunshots. Then I heard hoofbeats." As the jailer was finishing his story to Marshal Boutwell, Marshal Framington walked into the jail.

Marshal Framington's hair was slicked back, and he didn't appear to have just gotten out of bed. Framington said, "What's going on here? Where's the half-breed?

James had been born, but not yesterday. Something about this jail break smelled to the high heavens. He walked over to Marshal Framington and removed his revolver from its holster. Framington said, "Now see here."

James made no response, checked the cylinder, and saw it had fired two shells, and when he smelled the barrel, fired recently. James tossed the pistol back to Marshal Framington and said, "Marshal, I don't know what's going on here, but this half-breed didn't pick the lock on the jail cell. And since he didn't harm the jailer, we can presume he isn't the cold-blooded killer you want everyone to think he is. And since you took a couple shots at him, either you're a piss poor shot, or you weren't trying to hit him."

James continued, "I'll go after the half-breed in the morning. I doubt you could find the city limits sign and I don't need your help anyway. So just stay out of my hair. If Sheriff Baggett shows up, tell him he's welcome to ride along if he wants."

James walked back to the hotel, took his boots off, and climbed back in bed. He would ask around tomorrow morning. Someone would know where Apache Fred lived. Unless the half-breed headed for the Oklahoma Territory and tried to blend in with reservation Indians, he shouldn't be too hard to find. He closed his eyes to get some rest; he had a half-breed to track down and arrest. Maybe if he could find him, he could get some answers.

Chapter 10

The next morning James was up at daybreak, walked to the Dallas Café, had breakfast, and headed for the livery stable. Generally, hostlers know horses, so James wanted to find out what the livery man knew about the horse the half-breed rode out of Dallas. The hostler was evasive and said he really didn't know what the man had ridden away on. Marshal Boutwell looked at the hostler and said, "In case you don't know, I'm Deputy U. S. Marshal James Boutwell. I'm asking you a question regarding a murder I'm investigating. Withholding evidence or lying to a federal agent can get you into a lot and trouble and maybe even some time in jail. Would you like to start over with your answers?"

The hostler swallowed hard and said the horse was a bay roan gelding and was wearing an old Mexican saddle. Someone had stolen the horse and saddle from the livery.

James said, "Now we're getting somewhere. Who told you to saddle the horse? And don't tell me someone just slipped in saddled the horse, led it out, and you didn't hear a sound. Don't even think of trying to tell me that."

The hostler said, "No one told me to saddle the horse. Someone suggested that I go up to the saloon and have a beer."

James said, "OK. Who told you to go have a beer? Let me guess. Could it have been Marshal Framington?"

The hostler looked down and nodded his head. James said, "I'm going to need a pack horse and panniers. I'll get supplies for a few days' journey before I leave town. Now, tell me about Apache Fred. I want to know everything you know about the half-breed."

The hostler told James that Apache Fred lived in an old abandoned line shack at the northwestern edge of the Bar T ranch. He hired out to local ranchers to hunt and kill wolves. The animals were killing a lot of the younger and weaker stock, so they paid him so much per hide to get rid of the critters. The hostler said, "You heard none of this from me about the horse and saddle. I have to live in Dallas."

Around 8 AM James had gotten provisions at the general store and was on his way to the Bar T ranch. He skirted well shy of the ranch house and headed for what he figured had to be the northwest corner of the ranch. About an hour later he arrived at the shack. There was no bay roan. In fact, there was no horse at all in the corral.

James rode slowly to the shack and hollered. He got no reply. He dismounted and walked to the cabin with his pistol drawn. When he opened the door, it almost fell off the leather hinges. There was no one in the shack, but it showed signs of recent occupancy. There was a skillet on the stove and a metal plate on a roughhewn table. Both had food leavings and no sign of mold. That meant they were left recently.

James went out and walked around the area. About ten minutes later he found the tracks of a single horse headed north. Dennison, Texas, was close to the Oklahoma border and was about a seventy-five-mile ride. It would be a comfortable two-day jaunt. Apache Fred might or might not have gone to that town. He could have just headed straight for the border, crossed into Oklahoma Territory and blended in with reservation Indians. James figured his best bet was to catch the half-breed before he crossed the border.

The tracks of the horse were easy to follow, and James kept his horse at a canter. The trot was eating up miles while still allowing him to follow the trail and allow his horse to stay fresh. James kept at it until it got too dark to see the trail. He figured he had made up some time. Apache Fred had stopped at the line shack and eaten before heading north, so James figured he was only four or five hours ahead. And if the half-breed was traveling slowly, he could well be closer. James decided not to make a fire. There were still a few Apaches roaming around, he didn't need them to see his fire and visit him. And Apache Fred might see his fire and light out, then James might never catch up with him.

James took the saddle off the horse and the panniers off the packhorse, picketed both animals, spread his ground cover, took off his boots, and quickly fell asleep. When the sun peeked over the horizon, James was awake. He wanted a cup of coffee but didn't want to waste the time brewing it, so he saddled his horse, put the panniers on the packhorse, and set out at the same ground eating trot.

Right after 10 AM, James saw a small mesa in the distance. As he got near the butte, he saw a small canyon that ran to his right of the hill. He could make out the outline of horses in the distance, and as he got closer, he saw four men. One of them appeared to be Apache Fred!

Marshall Boutwell didn't know what he was riding into. He knew Apache Fred wasn't a man killer because he hadn't harmed the jailer. If these were his friends, James presumed they wouldn't try to kill him. When James got to within about 100 feet of the men, he saw he would have a problem, and it wasn't Apache Fred. The three men had Apache Fred tied and were punching him and trying to make him lose his balance and fall. James held his horse to a walk. The men saw him approaching but paid him no mind.

When he got to within thirty feet of the men, they all turned towards him. Apache Fred was bleeding from his mouth and their blows had swollen his face. The three men looked rough. They were wearing well-worn clothes which displayed a fair amount of tobacco stains and dirt. They were all carrying side arms but none of them looked to be pistoleros. They wore Mexican hats but looked more Anglo than Mexican. After years in the harsh sunlight and weather it was difficult to tell.

The man to James' right spoke up and said, "Can we help you, Marshal? We caught us a half-breed while he was takin a dump and was having a little fun before we drag him to death. Apaches killed my brother and I aim to get me some revenge on this devil."

Marshal Boutwell said, "I reckon not. I'm trailing this man. He's wanted for murder in Dallas. I'll be taking him back." With that James pulled his pistol and aimed it in the general direction of the three men.

The talker said, "Now see here, Marshal. Are you taking the side of a redskin over three white men? I don't think you can kill three men before one of us puts a slug in you."

James looked at the talker and said, "I'm not taking anyone's side. I told you, I'm taking him back to Dallas to stand trial. You may be right. I may not kill all three of you, but you'll never know because I will kill you first."

The talker turned away from James and pulled his pistol. James shot the man in the side, turned slightly and shot the man standing in the middle of the three, and caught a bullet from the man on his left. James fired as he fell out of the saddle and hit the last man in the brisket. All three men were down, dead or dying but at a price. Marshal Boutwell had a hunk of lead in his left shoulder just beside the ball and socket. Luckily, the bullet hadn't hit the bone. The gun the shooter had used was an old cap and ball Paterson and probably hadn't been charged in weeks. The weapon only burned half the powder, which reduced the speed and penetration of the bullet. Still James was bleeding and hurting and a long way from civilization and medical help.

While Marshal Boutwell was trying to keep his wits about him, Apache Fred crawled over and took his revolver out of his hand. James tried to get up but fell over. The half-breed was beaten badly and wasn't very spry either. The half-breed looked at James and said, "Well, we're two poor looking specimens. I can't sit a horse to ride away, and you couldn't get on your mount to follow me if I could leave. So, I guess we're stuck with each other for a little while at least.

With a great deal of effort, Apache Fred got to his feet, walked over to James' horse, removed his canteen, and took a long drink of water. He walked over to James and handed him the canteen. After James took a pull from the canteen, Apache Fred extended his hands and said, "If you'll cut these thongs, I'll get a fire started and see about digging that bullet out of you. Seems it is the least I can do after you saved my life." James cut the thongs and the half-breed got the saddle off James' horse and the panniers off the packhorse and picketed both animals. He looked through the panniers, found a coffee pot and coffee, and put the pot next to the fire to boil some coffee.

He looked at James and said, "If we're going to be friends for a few days how about calling me Fred." Fred walked over to one of the dead men and relieved him of his knife. He checked the blade and found it had a good edge. The man might not have been a gunfighter, but he knew how to put an edge on a knife. Fred put the knife in the fire's edge to kill any varmints that might live on the blade. He handed James a piece of wood and told him to bite down on it so he wouldn't break his teeth when the whittling started.

James thought he was ready, and sure wished he had some of Isaac Turnbull's chloroform. He wasn't ready and after the first probe, passed out. When he awoke, Fred was sitting by the fire drinking a cup of coffee. There was a bandage on James' shoulder. He looked at Fred and asked, "Did you get the bullet out?"

Fred said nothing, just flipped him a piece of lead. In a couple minutes Fred said, "You lost a lot of blood while I was digging around trying to find that hunk of lead. I was afraid you might go into shock and die. Guess you didn't."

James said, "My shoulder feels like you used a hatchet and crowbar to work on it. I appreciate you getting the bullet out. I suppose we're even now. I saved your life, and you saved mine. I think I'll try to get some sleep now. I still need to ask you some questions, but it can keep." Within a minute James was fast asleep.

The morning sun woke James, and he looked around. Fred was heating coffee and cooking some bacon. Fred turned towards him and asked, "You ready for a cup of coffee? I'll have us some breakfast ready in a few minutes."

James took the cup and thanked Fred. After they had eaten, James said, "I need to ask you some questions now. I know you're not a killer, or at least not a man or woman killer. First, tell me how you got out of your cell."

Fred said, "A noise woke me up from my sleep and I saw the cell door was ajar and the jailer was missing. When he returned, I took my weapons and walked out of the jail."

James smiled and said, "I figured it was something like that. Now tell me how you came by that locket."

Fred said, "I had been hunting wolves south of Dallas and was going into town to buy a few provisions before going back to my cabin. When I got close to Dallas, I came upon buggy wheel markings in the sage. I followed the wheel marks and, in a bit, saw the locket lying between the wheel marks. I figured it was just a man and woman heading south and got off the trail so the female could make sure she had privacy when using the privy. And after taking care of her bodily functions, they would get back on the trail. So, after finding the locket, I saw a pile of dung, so didn't follow the wheel marks any further. Guess it could have been something other than human dung, but that would sure have been a coincidence. I figured the woman had got the necklace hung on something and didn't realize the locket had fallen."

James was thoughtful and after a couple minutes said, "A buggy you say. Was it one horse or two? Traveling fast or slow?"

Fred replied, "One horse traveling fairly slowly. Funny, the buggy stopped a few times like the driver was looking for some special place to stop for whatever purpose. Like I said, after I found the locket, I quit following the buggy tracks."

That confirmed what James had thought. Someone driving a buggy had picked up Thelma Goodrich, and that someone was an individual she trusted. Finally, something he thought had proven to be right. Now all he had to do was find the person who was driving the buggy.

Chapter 11

James and Fred stayed in the camp for two more days. As bad as James felt, Fred looked worse. He had taken quite a beating. Fred had an eye swollen completely shut, a split lip, and his face was a mass of dark bluish contusions. James was sure Fred had a broken rib or two to go along with his obvious injuries. James was on the mend and getting up and walking around some. The steady diet of bacon and beans caused a lot of gas, but he was getting his strength back. The black coffee that could melt a horseshoe didn't hurt either.

When Marshal Boutwell got back to Dallas, he would have to lock Fred in the jail cell until he sorted out the mess and the real killer was identified. Now James was relatively certain the killer was someone who either owned or had access to a buggy. He hadn't seen a buggy at the livery, but that didn't mean the hostler didn't have one to let. James hadn't been thinking in terms of a buggy and hadn't looked for one at the livery.

James told Fred that when they got close to Dallas, he would have to place manacles on him. The circuit judge wouldn't be in Dallas for a few days. And James would make sure there wouldn't be a trial until he arrived and held court. Marshall Boutwell assured Fred that there wasn't any evidence against him to lead to a conviction. However, he would be safer in jail than any other place. Fred didn't like the jail but understood the need. If he was free, some drunken idiot might kill him just because the simpleton Framington had arrested him.

There had been a T handle shovel on one of the dead men's saddles so James and Fred, mostly Fred, had dug one shallow grave on the second day, rolled the three bodies in the hole, and covered them with dirt. They had gone through the dead men's pockets and found nothing that would identify them. Between the three, they had twelve dollars and fifteen cents, one pocket watch, one pocketknife, and the knife Fred had used to remove the bullet. The dead men each had a Paterson pistol and old Sharps rifles. Their saddles were well worn, and the saddle bags contained only some powder, shot, wads, hardtack and beans. Their horses had no markings. Two of the horses were dun and the third a pinto.

Right after sunup James and Fred set out for Dallas. James led two horses' tail tied one behind the other and Fred led the other two. At James' suggestion, Fred had taken the pinto to be his mount. They spent one night on the trail, not because of distance, but because they were both still under the weather and tired easily. James was recovering from the bullet wound and Fred from the beating. When they neared Dallas, James placed the manacles on Fred. Before starting their horses again, James asked, "Fred, what's your surname? Everyone calls you Apache Fred, but that's not what your parents named you at birth."

Fred said, "My father was an Anglo buffalo hunter named Allen Benton. My mother was an Apache named Cocheta. I suppose my surname is Benton. A man killed my father in a knife fight in a saloon. After he died, my mother and I went to live on a reservation in Oklahoma Territory. My mother died of diphtheria when I was fourteen, I've been on my own ever since. That's more than you asked, but that's who I am."

When they arrived at the jail, they dismounted and walked inside. The same jailer was on duty. Fred said hello to the jailer, and the jailer returned the greeting. James removed the manacles and Fred walked into an empty cell. James turned to the jailer and said, "It's your responsibility to see that Mr. Benton doesn't escape again. You need to make sure you lock the cell door, not necessarily to keep Mr. Benton in, but to keep others out. Do not, under any circumstances, leave Marshal Framington alone with Mr. Benton. I'm holding you responsible." The jailer allowed he understood.

James walked out and led the horses to the livery. The hostler came out, looked at the string of horses and said, "Looks like you got yourself some horseflesh since I saw you last."

James said, "The pinto and the saddle on him are the property of Mr. Benton. The other horse with the old saddle is yours, as is the packhorse. You call Mr. Benton Apache Fred. His correct name is Fred Benton. I appreciate the use of the packhorse and panniers. Please store the panniers and provisions. I may need to use them again. The other two horses are now mine. Make me a price on the two of them."

The hostler scratched his chin, looked the two horses over carefully, and said, "I'd go $200.00 for the both of them."

James looked at the hostler and said, "Part of my job is arresting men for stealing. You're in grave danger of being arrested right now."

The hostler laughed and said, "OK, I'll go $300.00."

James smiled and replied, "I was thinking $400.00, but I found these goods, so I'll make you a deal. How about you do $350.00 and give me free boarding for my mount while I'm in Dallas?"

The hostler slapped his knee and said, "Marshal, you're a good haggler, done." He shook James' hand and walked to an old desk and started counting out bills.

James collected the greenbacks and walked off to the Dallas Café to eat some decent food. After walking a few steps, James turned and walked back to the hostler and asked, "Do you have a buggy to let?" The hostler said that he did. It was in a shed behind the livery. James said he needed the hostler to make a list of people who had rented the buggy within the last week or so. He turned and started for the café again. After eating, James walked to the jail and handed Fred $175.00 and said, "The horses were as much yours as mine." He then walked out and went to the Dallas Hotel and lay down on the bed in his room. The ride to Dallas had tired him out.

After taking a nap, James went to the barbershop, got a bath, his hair trimmed and a shave. He had his trousers cleaned, his boots polished, and put on a clean shirt. He was feeling somewhat normal. He walked to the livery, saddled his horse, and rode to Maggie's. He had another of her T-Bone steaks in his mind. Either Maggie had a sixth sense, or she was always looking out the window because she greeted James when he walked in the door.

After they exchanged greetings, she noted he looked a little peaked. Maggie led him to the kitchen and went to the bar and got him a cool beer. She left for a couple minutes. When she returned, she said that Ling was searing a T-Bone steak for him and frying up some potatoes. She allowed that he looked like he could use some red meat.

Maggie sat with James as he was eating and told him about Thelma Goodrich's funeral. They had buried her while James was out tracking Fred Benton. Reverend Smith had conducted the funeral and had some difficulty keeping his composure. All in all, the funeral went as well as could be expected and several townspeople showed up.

James felt he could confide in Maggie and filled her in on what had happened with the capture of Apache Fred, Fred Benton, and told her the man's explanation of how he found the locket. Maggie didn't have much to say other than she agreed the buggy tracks implied someone had picked Thelma up from Maggie's Pleasure Palace during the middle of the night of her disappearance.

James asked what time the girls would be up and around the following morning. He wanted to question each of them individually and see if any of them could add anything that might help him find the killer. Maggie said she would have them up, fed, and ready to meet with him starting at 9 AM.

James thanked Maggie, paid for his beer and steak, walked out, mounted his horse, and rode to the livery. By the time he finished at the livery it was full dark. As James was walking along the wooden sidewalk towards the Dallas Hotel a bullet struck the building right beside his head followed by the crack of a rifle being discharged. He lay down and stayed in the shadows. He couldn't see anyone and then he saw movement from the alley across the street. He hadn't been able to tell anything about the shooter. Just a momentary movement and then the drygulcher disappeared into the darkness.

Marshal Boutwell saw no logic in crossing the street and going down a dark alley after whoever had taken a shot at him. The shooter had missed. If he went down the dark alley, he might not miss again. As James thought about it, either the shooter was the worst marksman in Dallas, or meant to miss and was just giving another warning to leave. James got up and went into the saloon for a rye whiskey to settle his nerves before going to bed.

When James entered the saloon, the sounds of hoots and hollers greeted him. James walked over to see what all the commotion was about and saw four men pushing Marcus Merriweather back and forth between them. James said, "What's going on here?"

A man replied, "We're just having some fun with the sweetie pie."

James said, "I see. Marcus, are you having fun?"

Marcus looked at James pleadingly and said, "No, not at all. I came to town to get a couple things at the mercantile. I thought I would get a drink before heading back to the ranch. These horrible ruffians started abusing me."

James looked at the men and said, "You've had your fun. Go back to your business." The men drifted back to the bar and ordered drinks.

James said nothing and Marcus went on. "Ikie can go to town and do what he wants, but any time I go on my own, I'm treated horribly. It isn't fair. I hate these people, especially the whores Ikie sees when he goes to town."

James said, "Life's unfair sometimes. If I were you, I would head for the ranch." Marcus thanked James and headed out the saloon doors. James watched him go and just shook his head. Sometimes people made their own problems, or perhaps life just dealt some folks a poor hand.

James ordered a rye whiskey, gulped it down, and walked through the bat-wing doors just in time to see Marcus Merriweather drive off in his buggy. James watched the buggy go down the street and said to himself, "*Nah*." He went on to his hotel room and turned in for the night.

The next morning James went to the Dallas Café for breakfast and then walked over to the jail to check on Fred Benton. Marshal Framington was at the jail. James looked at the city marshal and said, "Framington, I don't know how you figure in all this yet, and rest assured, I'll figure it out. But let me make this very clear to you. If there are any more shenanigans concerning my prisoner, I'll nail your hide to the wall." With that James turned and walked out. As he walked by the jailer, he noticed the man had a slight smile on his face.

When James arrived at Maggie's, she had eleven girls waiting in the foyer. She walked Marshal Boutwell into the kitchen and he sat in his customary place at the table. Maggie slid a piece of paper across to James with eleven names on it: Abby, Beverly, Camila, Daisy, Edie, Faye, Gabi, Jenny Lee, Joyce, Mary, and Polly. Maggie had even been nice enough to list them alphabetically. He started calling the girls one by one and asking each of them if they knew of any problems Thelma had with a customer, or if she mentioned intending to run away with a customer. Jenny Lee mentioned that Thelma had been sick a couple mornings but had attributed it to a bad cold she had been battling. Each of the girls denied knowing anything helpful.

James was sitting sipping a third cup of coffee when a beautiful raven-haired young woman walked into the kitchen, poured herself a cup of coffee, and sat down at the table. James looked at his list and saw he had missed no one. He supposed

Maggie had just forgotten and neglected to put the woman on the list. He looked at the woman and said, "What's your name?"

The young woman looked at James for a couple seconds and replied, "Rhonda." James thought to himself, "*Yep, Rhonda would come after Polly. Maggie forgot sure enough.*"

James began his questions. Had the woman seen anyone threaten Thelma? Had she seen Thelma paying more attention to one customer than another? Did she know of anyone who might want to harm Thelma? The woman, Rhonda, smiled demurely, and replied no to each question. Finally, Rhonda said, "I really didn't know Thelma Goodrich at all. In fact, I don't think I've ever met her." As James was asking Rhonda the last question, Peaches came into the kitchen and began rubbing against his leg and walking in and out between his feet. Rhonda smiled and said, "Well, it looks like you have one female admirer. Peaches normally doesn't like men."

James got a puzzled look on his face, ignored the cat and the comment, and said, "Miss, you work here, and you didn't know Thelma at all?"

As he was finishing his question Maggie walked into the kitchen and said, "There you are. I was wondering where you had gone off to when you weren't in your room." Maggie walked over to the stove, picked up the coffeepot, and poured herself a cup of coffee. She looked at James and Rhonda and asked, "Either of you want your coffee reheated before I put this back?" Rhonda just shook her head and James sat there with a bewildered look on his face.

Maggie sat down with the two of them and asked, "What are the two of you talking about?"

Rhonda replied, "Oh, nothing important really. Marshal Boutwell was just questioning me regarding Thelma."

Maggie giggled, then doubled over with laughter, and almost fell out of her chair she was laughing so hard. Rhonda got tickled and then couldn't control her laughter either. James wasn't in on the joke and didn't understand what was going on.

When Maggie got control of herself, she looked at James, started to say something, and burst out laughing again. James said, "What's so darn funny?"

Maggie said, between outbursts of laughter, "This is my daughter Rhonda. She's been in Denver attending school and just came home while you were off chasing that Fred fellow."

James turned as red as a beet and said, "Miss Branceer, Rhonda, why didn't you tell me who you were so I wouldn't make a fool of myself. You're your mother's daughter, no doubt about that! She loves to have fun at my expense anytime she can."

Maggie looked at James, and said, "The way the two of you look at each other, I'll have to keep an eye on you, James Boutwell. I wouldn't want you trying to take advantage of my little girl." This time both James and Rhonda turned beet red!

106

Rhonda recovered, looked at James, and said, "Pay no attention to my mother. She loves to try to shock people. She's just a big tease. I'll be here in Dallas until September, if you aren't busy stop and see me. Maybe we can find something to talk about other than your investigation."

James felt like a whipped puppy. He had absolutely no chance with these two women. He excused himself and said he would drop by and see Rhonda if she was agreeable. She smiled and said, "Please do."

After James left, Rhonda said to her mother, "He seems like such a nice man. You would think, as a lawman, he would be less refined."

Maggie replied, "Yes, I'm quite fond of James Boutwell. He is a fine young man. He must have had a good mother. You might want to try to corral him before someone else does."

Rhonda blushed and said, "Oh, Momma."

Chapter 12

When Marshal Boutwell rode into Dallas, he saw a group of people congregated in front of the bank. He pulled up his horse, tied him to a hitching rail, and walked inside. Sheriff Baggett and Marshal Framington were in the bank questioning people. Elmer P. Jones, the president of the bank, was on the floor with a fair amount of his head missing and a large pool of blood gathered on the floor.

When Sheriff Baggett saw James, it was as if he had somehow been transformed. Suddenly, the sheriff was looking at James with new eyes. He looked at Marshal Boutwell and said, "We've had a bank robbery. Four men came in here, took the money from the teller, forced Mr. Jones to open the safe, and cleaned it out. The bastards shot poor Mr. Jones as they left. Two men were in the bank during the holdup and identified one man as Emmitt "Snake Eyes" Bishop. They didn't know the other three men. One man said that Bishop seemed to be in charge and said that Bishop was the person who killed Mr. Jones." James made no comment.

Sheriff Baggett began again and said, "Marshal Boutwell, I'm about to form a posse, and was hoping you would come along with us."

Marshal Boutwell looked at Baggett for a few seconds before responding, and then said, "Sheriff, it's been my experience with a posse that some members are a help, and some just get in the way.

Why don't you select one deputy, and you, he, and I go after the bank robbers? But this is your county you do it the way you want. I'll ride along whatever you decide."

Sheriff Baggett was thoughtful for a couple seconds and replied, "Marshal Boutwell, you've got a good point there. Posse members have slowed me down and I've had to send men back home a couple of times. All right, just the three of us will go after them. I'll take Deputy Blevins along. How soon can you be ready?"

James said, "Are we taking your pack horse or mine? If mine, it's in the livery, as are the panniers. All we'll need is a few more provisions for you and the deputy."

Sheriff Baggett said, "If yours can be ready to travel quickly, let's take him. I'll meet you at the general store as soon as we can get our gear together and you get the panniers on the horse."

Ten minutes later, James tied his two horses to the hitching rail in front of the store. Sheriff Baggett and Deputy Blevins came out of the store at about the same time. Each had an arm full of provisions. They stuffed the provisions in the panniers and mounted their horses. Sheriff Baggett said, "We need to hurry along, my jurisdiction ends once we cross the Irving County line. The bandits headed due west. Irving County would be right on their route."

Marshal Boutwell said, "Sheriff, I don't think that's gonna be a problem. Both you and your deputy

109

raise your right hands." James swore them in as deputy U. S. marshals and flipped each of them a badge. James said, "Just put the U. S. marshal badges in your pockets, and if we leave Dallas County, just swap badges."

Sheriff Baggett looked at James and said, "I'm starting to like you better all the time. Maybe I judged you too harshly."

James smiled and said, "My charm takes a while to grow on people. But so does ringworm." They all had a good chuckle and headed out of Dallas at a fast trot. As they took the trail west, they met people headed east towards Dallas. They stopped and asked them if they had seen four men riding fast towards the west. They had. Marshal Boutwell and the other two men picked up the pace. The bandits were headed straight towards Fort Worth. There wasn't much there, just a growing cow town suffering a downturn in the cattle market. But the bandits might stop. There was no way of knowing what men on the run might do.

The lawmen held their horses to a ground eating canter and arrived on the outskirts of Fort Worth in late afternoon. Sheriff Baggett allowed that if the bandits stopped in Fort Worth, it would have been at a saloon. They headed for the Stockyard Saloon with Sheriff Baggett leading the way. They stopped about fifty feet before the front doors of the saloon, dismounted, and tied their horses to the hitching rail. Sheriff Baggett pulled a double barrel shotgun out of its scabbard and said he and Deputy

Blevins would go in the front door and James could go around back and find a rear entrance. If there wasn't a rear door, he could come back and join them.

When Baggett and Blevins entered the saloon, they saw four men sitting at a table with a bottle of whiskey and four glasses. James saw the men as he came through the storeroom and opened the rear door into the saloon. When the bandits saw Sheriff Baggett, they drew their pistols, and all hell broke loose. Baggett fired a load of 00 buckshot pellets into the man nearest him. People started running and trying to get out of the way. There was no way James could get a clear shot because eight to ten people were between him and the bandits and ducking and dodging around. In all the confusion, a bandit shot Deputy Blevins. They also shot two saloon customers. Baggett grabbed a table, turned it over, and took cover behind it.

The bandit Sheriff Baggett had shot with the scattergun was graveyard dead. One customer was dead, another wounded, and Deputy Blevins was bleeding like a stuck hog. The other three bandits used the saloon customers for cover and fled through the saloon doors!

James ran to Blevins, looked at his wound and applied hard pressure to get the bleeding stopped. The bullet had hit Blevins on the inside of his left arm and missed the bone. Unfortunately, the bullet had severed the brachial artery. The pressure James was applying was slowing the bleeding but

111

without a doctor getting to the man soon, and clamping off the artery, he would bleed to death. Within five minutes, Deputy Blevins was dead. When a major artery is severed, there is little that can be done without a trained physician to get to work immediately.

Sheriff Baggett looked at Blevins and said, "This was a shite storm. Once I got inside the saloon, I knew we had a mess on our hands. There were just too many people in the saloon. Blevins had a wife and baby daughter, and I got him killed."

James knew what the sheriff was going through. He had seen friends killed. It wasn't a fun experience. He looked at Sheriff Baggett and said, "You didn't get him killed. A bandit killed him. It was an unfortunate happening. If the bullet hadn't hit the artery, he would have been fine and kept riding with us after getting his arm bandaged." Sheriff Baggett knew Boutwell was right, but that didn't lessen his sense of loss or guilt. He would have to tell a young wife that she would have to raise a child all on her own.

The city marshal of Fort Worth came running into the saloon, saw the dead and wounded, and said, "How in the hell did all this happen?" He recognized Sheriff Baggett and said, "J. L., what are you doing outside Dallas County?" You've got no jurisdiction here. I'm gonna have to hold you for a coroner's inquest into the man you killed."

Marshal Boutwell said, "No. You're not going to hold Deputy Marshal Baggett for anything.

I deputized him as a deputy U.S. marshal. What he did was in self-defense and we don't have time to wait around for you to dot I's and cross the T's. Take Deputy Blevins to the undertaker, have him prepared for burial, and take his horse to the livery and have it attended to. We'll go to the telegraph office and make the arrangements to have his body picked up and taken back to Dallas."

The town marshal said, "Now, see here." And that was as far as he got.

Marshal Boutwell said, "I have neither the time nor inclination to have a debate with you. I'm leaving to catch the three remaining bandits. I expect my instructions to be followed to the letter. To the letter or you'll wish you never met me! Do you understand?" The city marshal nodded his head and stepped out of the way.

Boutwell and Baggett walked out of the saloon and asked bystanders which direction the three men had taken. Everyone pointed west. Sheriff Baggett walked to the telegraph office and sent a wire concerning Deputy Blevins. James and Sheriff Baggett mounted their horses, James took the lead of the packhorse, and they took off west at a brisk trot. As they rode along, Sheriff Baggett said, "Seems I remember seeing that charm of yours in Dallas. You have a way of cutting to the chase and stopping the nonsense." James didn't respond.

This was all new territory for James. Dallas was the farthest he had been to the north of Austin. Normally, his duties took him east, south, or west.

Sheriff Baggett said that Weatherford was the next settlement of any size. There were a couple way stations for the overland stage to stop to change horses and allow passengers to use the privy and get a bite to eat, but nothing other than that. It was about thirty miles to Weatherford. Since it was late afternoon, they couldn't get there until the following day unless they rode all-night. Neither Baggett nor Boutwell were eager to ride into an ambush at night, so when it started getting dark, they stopped and made camp.

Baggett started working on a fire and James unsaddled the horses, took the panniers off the packhorse, and picketed the animals. When he got finished, Baggett had a good fire started and had the coffee pot water about ready to boil. James said, "Baggett, you're gonna make someone a good wife with your domestic skills."

Baggett smiled and said, "You know what you can do. I'm just not gonna watch." They both had a good chuckle. When Baggett got the bacon and beans ready, they filled two metal plates and went to work on the food. The food and coffee made James miss being at Maggie's place. Her coffee and food put this to shame, but it was food.

After they finished their meal and cleaned their plates, they leaned back on their saddles and had a second cup of coffee. James looked at Baggett and asked, "What do the initials J. L. stand for?"

Baggett said, "Why are you so interested?"

James said, "Well, if we're gonna be trail buds, I would like to know your name."

Baggett replied, "Well if you must know its Janosch Lamarcus, and that's why I use J. L. My dad was an educated man and wanted me to have distinctive names. I have no idea where he came up with the monikers, probably from Greek literature, I suppose. Anyway, when I was a boy, I took a good bit of ribbing over those names, so I started just using my initials."

James smiled and said, "Well, I'm impressed. I've never known even one person with one fancy handle, let alone two."

Baggett took the ribbing in stride. They lay back on their saddles and talked about things and got to know more about each other. Baggett was married and had two daughters. One daughter was married and the other engaged to a local farm boy outside Dallas. James had never been married. He had been involved with a girl in Austin when he first got there, but her family had moved away, and he never saw her again. He'd never been closely involved with another woman. He was always on the road, delivering or picking up prisoners, chasing outlaws, or serving warrants. He was rarely in Austin long enough to form a relationship.

Baggett allowed he understood. After coming back from the Civil War, he had vowed to his wife that he wouldn't be gone from home again for long periods of time. She had raised two girls by herself for most of three years. Even though the girls were grown, he didn't plan on leaving his wife, Evie, alone again for any prolonged absences. Life was just too short.

James only half heard what Baggett was saying, his mind had drifted to a raven-haired beauty he had met a few days before. He had to be ten years older than her, and no doubt she had a beau at the school she attended, or one from the Denver area. If Maggie had enough money to send Rhonda away to boarding school, it obviously wasn't in her plans for her daughter to marry a poor deputy U. S. marshal. But he was getting way ahead of himself; he had only just met the girl.

Baggett and Boutwell drifted off to sleep. They had three bandits to catch.

Chapter 13

James and J. L. were up at dawn. James got the horses ready to travel while J. L. started a fire and got the coffee going. After they both had a cup of coffee, J. L. dumped the grounds out of the pot and put it in the panniers along with the cups. They mounted their horses and headed out to Weatherford, Parker County, Texas. Weatherford, Texas, has an interesting history.

****

Cattle baron Oliver Loving is buried in Weatherford's Greenwood Cemetery. Loving was killed in an Indian attack in New Mexico in 1867. Loving's dying request to his friend, Charles Goodnight, was to be buried at his home, Parker County, Texas. Goodnight brought Loving's body back 600 miles by wagon for burial. Goodnight's commitment to his friend's dying wish served as Larry McMurtry's inspiration for the story of Captain Woodrow Call taking Captain Augustus McCrae back to Lonesome Dove and burying him beside the river in his novel of that name.

Bose Ikard was a Negro who worked first with Oliver Loving, and then after his death with Charles Goodnight. The character of Deets in Lonesome Dove was loosely modeled after Ikard's association with Loving and Goodnight. I also modeled my character Wil Byrd in my novel The Cattlemen after Ikard. Bose Ikard died January 4, 1929 and is buried in Greenwood Cemetery in Weatherford near the man he so admired.

****

     James and J. L. arrived in Weatherford around noon and went directly to the Parker Saloon. When they walked in every eye in the room turned and looked at them. Both men had their badge exposed for the entire world to see. James walked up to the bar and said loud enough for the entire room to hear "We're looking for Emmitt Bishop. Some folks call him Snake Eyes Bishop. He and three men robbed a bank in Dallas and killed the banker for no good reason other than the killer is part skunk. One of his associates is in a box in Fort Worth. Since skunks tend to stay together, the other two are probably still with him. Have any of you seen three men who may have come into this saloon?"

     No one said anything, and most returned to their card games or drinking. An older man walked to the bar and ordered a beer. When the bartender walked away to draw the beer the man leaned over to James and said, "They were here this morning. They had a couple drinks and left. I overheard one of them say something about going to Abilene." The bartender came back with the man's beer. The man threw some change on the bar and walked off.

James looked at J. L. and asked, "Do you believe him?"

J. L. thought a few moments and replied, "It kinda makes sense. Abilene is a cow town. It would be a good place to hole up or maybe get on with a cattle outfit and get out of the state."

James thought about what J. L. had said and responded, "I don't know. There was a Texas Rangers detachment camped on Palo Pinto Creek, which is on the southern route to Abilene. Or at least the rangers made their camp there the last communique I read."

J. L. replied, "Well I don't know if that's common knowledge. I didn't know it til now. But let's presume they took the northern route. The Buchanan Trading Post and the small settlement of Picketville are on the way. I suppose they could cut south, and it would come out about the same distance wise. I'm no authority on this area, but I've been there."

James said, "So, which way do you want to go, southern or northern route?"

J. L. was thoughtful for a few moments and said, "Let's presume Bishop knows this part of Texas. And let's presume he knows that Texas Rangers have their camp on Palo Pinto Creek. If they ran into the rangers, they could be in big trouble. Word of the bank robbery and the killing of Mr. Jones would be on the wire. I'm thinking they would have taken the northern route." With that settled, they mounted their horses and headed for Picketville.

It was about seventy miles to Picketville, so they would need to spend one night on the trail. There were scarcely anyplace the bandits could have gone down the northern trail other than Picketville or perhaps Buchanan's trading post. There were a few isolated outposts that sold rotgut whiskey and a meager amount of supplies. They could check them quickly and continue. So, they saw no reason to hold their animals back. They let the horses set their own pace hoping to close the gap between them and the bandits. At dusk, they had covered more than half the distance to Picketville. They stopped and went through their established routine, ate supper, and settled in for the night.

The following morning, J. L. got the coffee going, they had a cup, and got on the trail about thirty minutes after sunup. They allowed their horses to set the pace again and arrived at Picketville around 2 PM. There was one small combination store/brothel/saloon in a rustic building that appeared to have been constructed in haste.

When they neared the building, they saw three well-lathered horses hitched outside the building. James and J. L. looked at each other, and James said, "Maybe we got lucky." He walked around back of the building and returned in a couple minutes. There wasn't any entrance other than the front. There would be a few moments before their eyes became accustomed to coming out of the bright sunlight into the darkened building. They would be most susceptible during that transition period.

J. L. looked at James and said, "I have a lot of free time on my hands and read a lot. I read something sometime back that claimed if you were in bright sunlight, you could keep your eyes closed for a couple minutes, and they would adjust faster to a dark room. Let's stand on either side of the door, close our eyes, and wait for a couple minutes before we go inside. I don't know if it'll work, but it can't hurt. I'll count to 120 slowly and when I stop counting, we'll go through the door together. You go right and I'll go left."

What J. L. had said sounded silly to James, but why not give it a try? He stood beside the door with his eyes tightly closed and waited for J. L. to finish counting. When J. L. said 120, both men burst into the room. It worked. They could see well enough to suffice. There were eight men in the saloon. The bartender, four men standing at the roughhewn bar, and the three men they were looking for sitting at a table in the back of the room.

James moved to his right, which put him alongside the bar. J. L. moved to his left. They were far enough apart that a shooter would have to half-turn to get a shot off at either man after shooting at the other. The conditions were as favorable as they were likely to get.

J. L. said, "Emmitt Bishop, you're under arrest for bank robbery and murder. You can surrender or try my young friend and me, your choice."

121

None of the three men moved. They just sat and looked at J. L. In a couple minutes the man who was the leader, presumably Bishop, said, "I don't think the two of you can take the three of us on and come out still kickin. As I recall it didn't go well for you in Fort Worth."

James spoke up and said, "I couldn't get a shot off in Fort Worth because of people in my way. That won't be a problem in here. I'm always more than willing to take men in alive, but that's your choice. If you pull on me, you'll die, it's that simple." The man nearest James was getting fidgety, the man in the middle was stoic, and the man farthest away looked bored. James hoped J. L. could take care of the man who looked bored. Of the three, he was the one to be concerned about and he was the farthest away from James.

J. L. had his scattergun in his hands with both barrels cocked. He waited a few moments and said, "Last chance. This ain't Dodge City and I don't want to play gunfighter. Either take your pistols out easy or I'm gonna blow your guts all over this room, your choice." The fidgety man slowly stood and took his pistol out of its holster with his thumb and forefinger and let it drop to the floor. James told the fidgeter to get on his knees and put his hands atop his head. The man complied.

The man with the dead eyes went for his pistol and there was a deafening roar from J. L.'s Purdey double-barrel shotgun. The impact of the 00 buckshot pellets forced the man back, out of his chair, and against the wall. The man in the middle raised his hands and said, "Don't shoot. I surrender, don't shoot." J. L. opened the breech to eject the spent shells, and the man drew his pistol. James' pistol belched fire, and the bullet caught the man in the left side of his head. The slug made a small hole in the man's temple and exploded out the back side of his head.

James walked to the man who was kneeling and placed manacles on his wrists. He then turned to J. L. and said, "If I didn't know better, I might think you were enticing Bishop to draw by opening the breech of the scattergun." J. L. didn't respond.

After getting the bracelets secured on the bandit, James said, "What's your name and what's the names of the two dead men? I also need to know the name of the man that we killed in Fort Worth." The man said the man James had shot was Emmitt Bishop, the man J. L. had shot with the scattergun was Wiley Sproutt, and his name was Emil Harmon. The man killed in Fort Worth was Samuel Johnstone.

Other than Bishop, James didn't recognize the names of the other men. J. L. said, "Word has it that Wiley Sproutt was a gunfighter who had killed several men. I've heard of him, but never saw him before."

James picked up the bandits' saddlebags off the floor, opened both sides, and found them stuffed full of greenbacks. James asked, "Where is the rest of the money from the bank robbery?" Harmon said that it was all in the saddlebags except for some they had spent on drinks on the road. They hadn't split up the money yet.

James walked to the bar and said to the bartender and the four men who had moved to the end of the bar. "You heard the names. I'll write a short statement. Each of you will sign the paper or make your mark. Any of you have a problem with that?" With all the blood and gore all over the back of the saloon, they would have gladly signed anything.

After they signed the statement, James turned to the bartender and said, "I want the two dead men to receive a funeral. It doesn't have to be fancy but get them in the ground." J. L. walked up holding two Model 1873 Colt revolvers and about $7.00 in coinage. James told the bartender to use the $7.00 to bury the two men and slid the money across the bar. J. L. put one of the Colt revolvers in his waistband. Sproutt, the gunfighter, had got his hands on two of the new Colt revolvers, not that they did him a great deal of good. J. L. handed the other pistol to James.

They now had six horses. The prisoner rode one, and they tail-tied the dead men's two horses behind the pack horse. The hostler would be happy to see two more horses and saddles to sell or let. James took his revolver out of its holster and replaced it with the newer Colt model in the 44.40 caliber. It was nice to have the same bullets for his pistol and rifle and the Colt 1873 was a vast improvement over older models of the Colt revolver.

It was only 3 PM, so James and J. L. thought it prudent to put some miles behind them before it got dark. It was 130 miles to Dallas, give or take. J. L. wanted to get back to his family. James' mind was on a raven-haired beauty he was hoping to get to know better. Maybe something would come of it and maybe not, but it was time to get on the trail back to Dallas.

Chapter 14

James, J. L., and the prisoner had traveled a little over fifteen miles when J. L. suggested they camp for the night. They got off the trail perhaps fifty yards, picked a likely spot, and made camp. James got Harmon cuffed to a tree, removed the saddles and panniers, and picketed the horses.

When the food was ready, James undid Harmon's manacles and followed him to the campfire. After eating, the three men sat by the campfire and drank coffee. James looked over at Emil Harmon and said, "What inspired you to rob a bank? And why did you kill the bank president? You already had the money."

Harmon replied, "I can't speak for the other three men, but I fell on hard times. My wife and baby daughter died of cholera. After that I took to drinkin and lost our farm. I ran into Bishop in a saloon and he invited me to join his gang. I had no prospects, so I went along with them. But I didn't shoot the man in the bank. Sproutt, the gunfighter shot him just to add to his total of men he had killed. It was cowardly but done before Bishop could stop him."

James and J. L. looked at each other and just shook their heads. The man seemed sincere in what he was saying, and they suspected he was telling the truth. Harmon's story conflicted with the eye-witness accounts that claimed Bishop had killed the banker. The sad truth was that it made little difference which bandit killed the banker. Harmon would probably be hanged when they got him back to Dallas. Some poor decisions lead to lasting consequences.

James got Harmon situated with his saddle, ground cover, and blanket, cuffed him to the tree again, and went back to the campfire. Out in the wilds, using trees were about the only remedy to keep prisoners from running off during the night or opening your head with a rock while you were sleeping. He had some questions to ask Sheriff Baggett and hoped he had built up enough trust and goodwill with the man to get his allegiance and cooperation. James looked over at Sheriff Baggett and said, "Sheriff, J. L., I need to ask you some questions. I know we got off on the wrong foot in Dallas, but the attorney general appointed me to investigate the murder of the Goodrich woman. I'm hoping you will help me sort through this quagmire to find the killer."

J. L. said nothing for a couple minutes, and just sipped his coffee. Finally, he looked up at James and said, "When you got the attorney general to assign you to investigate the murder, it was an affront to me and my office, and I didn't appreciate it one bit. After spending some time with you, I realize you are a competent peace officer, and only did what you thought was right. I'll help you any way I can."

James said, "Thanks. My first question is how do you think Apache Fred, Fred Benton, escaped from a locked cell in the jail? I always hate to think a lawman is corrupt, but I have my suspicions about Marshal Framington. Something about his part in all this just doesn't smell right."

J. L. replied, "I've known John Framington for a few years. He's more of a politician and opportunist than a lawman. I have a theory about why he let Benton out of the jail, but I could be wrong. John Framington and Jonathan Scruthers are thick as thieves, so to speak. When Scruthers tells Framington to jump, John only asks 'how high.' I'm certainly not ready to say that either of them killed the girl, but it somehow involves them in trying to cover up something relating to the murder. Why Framington made it possible for Apache Fred to escape is beyond my understanding. Of course, the intent could have been to make him look more guilty, or get him killed while trying to escape, or both.''

James said, "I agree. Framington allowed Apache Fred to escape. I confirmed that a horse was waiting for him. I don't think Framington wanted Fred Benton killed during the escape. I checked Framington's revolver. He had shot it twice as Benton escaped. More likely, he wanted him to get away and continue going. Once he rode away, never to return, he could be blamed for the murder of the Goodrich woman, and they could put the entire killing to rest. The problem is that I'm convinced that Benton didn't kill the girl. In fact, I doubt he has ever laid eyes on the girl in his entire life. He isn't the sort who would visit an expensive brothel. So how would he have known Thelma Goodrich?"

J. L. replied, "I've known Apache Fred Benton for a few years. He's a good sort, and I've never known him to get into any trouble. The puzzling part to me is how did he come upon the locket?"

James explained what Fred Benton had told him about finding the locket and added that it made perfect sense to him. James went on to say, "The only thing is, whoever was driving the buggy wasn't looking for a place to use the privy. That individual was looking for a place to dump Thelma Goodrich's body. I've put that much together in my mind. Unless Miss Goodrich was attempting to blackmail someone, I just can't for the life of me figure out why someone would want to kill the woman."

J. L. said, "It seems you have hit a dead end. James, I think unless someone has a severe case of a guilty conscience, you've got a problem."

James replied, "Doctor Pickwell looked me up and informed me that Thelma Goodrich was a couple months pregnant. That could be a strong motive if Miss Goodrich was threatening to tell his wife, or if the father thought she might tell a wife. And even if a wife would forgive and forget that doesn't mean voters or members of a congregation would if you get my drift."

J. L. said, "Are you implying that Mayor Scruthers or Reverend Smith might be the guilty party?" Without giving James time to respond he went on "I'm married, and I stand for reelection every four years. That would give me motive if I were the father."

James replied, "I think I have it narrowed down to one of two people but, I could always be wrong. Crimes of passion seldom make much sense. Oh, by the way, does Mayor Scruthers or Reverend Smith own a buggy?"

J. L. replied, "As a matter of fact they both do. And I own a buggy, as do several people in Dallas. Wives tend to get rather grumpy if we ask them to ride a horse to church on Sunday morning." James didn't make any response. The conversation ebbed, and James and J. L. turned in for the night.

They arrived in Dallas on July 3 and got Emil Harmon locked up in jail. After taking the horses to the livery, James went through the haggling routine with the hostler, and walked away with the same $350.00 again. James walked to the sheriff's office, handed J. L. $175.00, and went to the barbershop, got his hair trimmed, a shave, and bath. He then went to the Chinese laundry and got his two clean shirts and headed for the Dallas Hotel. When James got to his room, he changed shirts, brushed off his boots, and headed back to the livery. He saddled his horse and set out for Maggie's. He wanted another big T-Bone steak, and kinda hoped he would see a certain raven-haired girl.

When he arrived at the brothel, he hitched his horse and walked in the front door. Maggie wasn't in the foyer, but Rhonda was, and seemed delighted to see him. She said, "Well it took you long enough to catch those bandits. Momma told me you were an expert at catching criminals."

James laughed and replied, "I'm only an expert at catching colds. Sometimes I get lucky, but for the most part I just slog along until someone hunts me down, confesses, and surrenders."

Rhonda laughed and said, "When I saw you riding up, I asked Ling to put on a steak for you. Medium rare, I think? Mom told me that was the way you like your steak."

James replied, "Yes, medium rare is fine. By the way, where is your mother? I have something I need to talk with her about."

Rhonda smiled and teasingly said, "It's a little premature for that don't you think?" James turned as red as a beet. These Branceer women seemed to delight in trying to embarrass him. She laughed and said, "Well, if you are weary of my company, I'll go fetch her."

James said, "No, no, don't do that, there is no hurry. I have been thinking about your company for the past few days and have missed talking with you." James polished off the giant T-Bone steak, fried potatoes, two chunks of bread, and was working on his second cup of coffee when Peaches started rubbing against his leg. He wasn't much on cats, but this creature sure seemed to like him. As he was trying to decide if he wanted to pick up the cat, Rhonda got up and took his plate away.

She said, "I'm going out back to enjoy the sunset. Would you like to come along? I'll get you a fresh cup of coffee if you like." They sat together looking at the sunset, and after a few minutes Rhonda took his hand, smiled, and said, "It's beautiful out here. Whenever I come home, I'm reminded of how wonderful the sunsets are." They sat, talked, and the evening got away from them.

Maggie came walking up and said, "Hey, you two, its 10 PM. Do the two of you plan to sit out here all night?"

James said, "No, I didn't realize it was that late. I've some questions for you, but it can wait until tomorrow if you are too tired. After all its 10 PM, and mature women need their rest." Maggie allowed she could probably struggle through a few questions if they didn't last more than an hour. They all three laughed. James and Rhonda said their goodnights, and she walked into the building.

James looked at Maggie and asked, "Is there any chance that Apache Fred could have known Thelma Goodrich? Was he ever a customer here at your place? I know it may seem a little farfetched, but I need to cover every possibility. Marshal Framington seems awfully eager to see him swinging at the end of a rope. I don't think Fred Benton had anything to do with this killing but, unless I can come up with something, the good people of Dallas may have their scapegoat even if there is no evidence."

Maggie said, "To answer your question, Fred Benton has never been in my place of business to my knowledge. I know him, but not well, and I agree he isn't a killer. People can't pick their parents. Fred's father took up with an Indian woman and he was their offspring. When they died, he was pretty much on his own. To answer the other question, I don't think Thelma Goodrich knew Fred Benton at all. But that is merely an opinion on my part. She could have seen anyone she wanted on her trips to Dallas. It's possible she could have met him away from my place, but I doubt it."

James asked, "What's your opinion of Marshal Framington? Would he have the wherewithal to have killed Miss Goodrich? He was one of her customers."

Maggie said, "I'm afraid my comments regarding Marshal Framington would be just a little biased. I have nothing good to say about the SOB, and for good reason. When I first opened this establishment, Marshal Framington appeared in the foyer and informed me that if my girls didn't service him once each week, he would close me down. I reminded him that Maggie's Pleasure Palace was located outside the city limits of Dallas and he had no jurisdiction. He backed down and said he had just been joking. If he had it in his mind to shake me down for services, he might just be shaking down some Dallas merchants for money or something else. In my estimation, Framington is just a crook wearing a badge."

James took a deep breath, smiled, and said, "I'll take that as a firm, maybe. Based on what little I've seen out of him, I have little regard for Framington either, but I'm not sure he has the

133

wherewithal to kill anyone. I suppose we are both good judges of character, or lack thereof." He thanked Maggie for suffering his questions again and bid her good night. He rode back to Dallas deep in thought, stabled his horse, went to the hotel, and went to bed. He needed some rest to soothe his troubled mind. Tomorrow was another day.

Chapter 15

It was the fourth of July 1874. James went to the Dallas Café and was having breakfast when the telegraph operator came trotting in and stopped at his table. The man was out of breath, but managed to say, "I have a telegram for you, Marshal Boutwell."

James opened the wire and read, *"Whore found dead in Ft Worth last night. Stop. Need you to investigate. Stop. Marshall Danford, Ft Worth."* James rubbed his chin and thought to himself, "This rips it. Maybe I'm chasing shadows on the Goodrich murder."

After he finished his meal James walked to the livery, saddled his horse, and rode to Maggie's. Rhonda was in the foyer again and met him at the door. They walked into the kitchen and Rhonda poured him a cup of coffee. James explained that he would be gone a few days. There had been a killing of a prostitute in Fort Worth, and the marshal of Fort Worth had asked him to come and investigate. They chatted for more than an hour, and James said he would think of her often while he was away.

Rhonda looked at James and he noticed her eyes were wet. She said, "Be careful. I'll be thinking of you too while you are away." With that she leaned over, kissed him on the cheek and walked out of the room. James went out and got on his horse and set out for Fort Worth. It was about an hour and half ride, so James saw no reason to take the packhorse. When he arrived, he went directly to the marshal's office.

When he walked in Marshal Danford was sitting at his desk. The marshal neither got up nor greeted James, but that was to be expected since Marshal Boutwell had dressed him down when they last met. Danford looked at James and said, "I want you to know this isn't my idea. The town council told me to notify you and give you any help you needed. If it was up to me, you would be in Dallas minding your own business."

James looked at the marshal and replied, "Marshal Danford, if it was up to me, I would be in most anyplace but Fort Worth. But this is my business, so I don't have a choice. Tell me what you know."

Marshal Danford looked pained and began, "The woman, Marie LaPierre was found in an alley near the brothel she worked in by a couple citizens who were walking to the feed mill to start their shift. It seems they always use the alley as a shortcut. They came to the jail and reported what they had found. The deputy came to my home and woke me. I got dressed, saw the girl, and had her body taken to the undertaker. That's about it."

James asked, "Did a doctor examine her? If so, I need to talk to him. Let's go see the body."

Danford sent a deputy to fetch Doctor Grimes and led the way down the street to the undertaker's office. James looked at the body and immediately noticed that the dead woman kinda resembled the

Goodrich girl. Other than the Goodrich girl had light colored hair, and the LaPierre woman had dark hair, they had the same general features. In a few minutes, Doctor Grimes arrived and said, "What can I do for you, Marshal?"

James asked, "Did you examine the body?"

Doctor Grimes said, "Yes, I did, and determined she was dead. That's required for a death certificate."

Marshal Boutwell said, "You don't say. I didn't know that. Could you be more forthcoming please? Did you determine a cause of death other than she stopped breathing? And did you by chance determine if she was pregnant?"

Doctor Grimes ignored James' sarcasm and replied, "There were no marks on the body. Whoever killed her apparently came up behind her and strangled her with her own scarf. She struggled, but with the killer behind her, she could do little. The killer busted her windpipe, so whoever strangled her was strong. Her blue scarf was tight around her neck, so there is little doubt that the killer used it to strangle her. I had seen Miss LaPierre in my office about ten days ago. She saw me complaining of painful urination. I suspected gonorrhea and did a pelvic examination. All I saw was some vaginal irritation, probably caused by an infection of the bladder. There was no indication that she was pregnant. I told her to drink lots of water and she should be fine in a couple days. I never heard from her again, so I suppose she got over the infection. Is there anything else I can help you with, Marshal?"

James thanked the doctor and asked him if he could approximate the time of death. The doctor was thoughtful and said, "Only slight rigor mortis had set in when I started examining the woman. Let's see, I got to the undertaker's around 8 AM, so I suppose she died somewhere between 9 PM and early morning sometime. I wouldn't think any later than maybe 3 AM at the latest." James thanked the doctor for coming and told the undertaker he could cover the body.

James had Danford take him to the brothel, and he talked to the other women who worked there. They didn't know of anyone who had been angry with Marie, and no, she had said nothing about running off with anyone. She had said that she had saved almost enough money so she could go to San Francisco and find some other line of work. None of the women knew of anyone who would want to harm Marie. They knew of no regular who might have become involved with her outside the brothel.

James talked to the madam. She was a portly woman named Margaret Dever, and he got little if any helpful information from her. She only parroted what the brothel women had told him.

****

The population of Fort Worth had taken a sharp decline since the Panic of 1873. The financial

138

crisis caused a mild depression that lasted from 1873 until 1879. It hit the cattle business hard, and many who worked around the stockyard left Fort Worth to find work elsewhere. In fact, Fort Worth was so impacted by the financial crisis that the railroad suspended the laying of track around thirty miles outside the town. Things got so bad that a newspaperman said he had seen a panther sleeping in the street outside the courthouse. People used Panther City to describe the town for a time. The Texas and Pacific railroad renewed the laying of tracks, and once completed, the cattle market rebounded, and by 1879, Fort Worth became known as The Queen City of the Prairies.

****

Miss Dever had said that the decline in population influenced the number of men who could afford to visit the brothel. Business had been slow but was picking up. She went on to say that most of her customers were men of some substance. Not necessarily rich, but not the run-of-the-mill cowhand either. Any cowboy who visited the brothel would leave a good bit of his month's wages. The local men she knew. People from outside Fort Worth might not even use their correct name, and she couldn't help beyond knowing the regular local crowd. James hadn't found out anything which would help him find a killer.

James stayed in Fort Worth two days interviewing men who Miss Dever had told him regularly visited Miss LaPierre at her brothel. None of them seemed to be the type that would kill Miss LaPierre. All the brothel's clients except one were married men and didn't want any publicity regarding their visits. James had come up with nothing, left on July 7, and rode back to Dallas. He had found nothing to lead him to believe that anything connected the two murders.

When he got back to Dallas, he went by the hotel, cleaned up a bit, and put on a clean shirt. He then rode out to Maggie's to purchase one of her famous T-Bone steaks. Rhonda saw him ride up, opened the front door, and hugged him when he walked up on the porch. She led him to the kitchen and asked Ling to get a steak cooking on the spit. She poured James a cup of coffee, set it on the table in front of him, and took a chair directly across the table where she could look at him face to face.

Rhonda wanted to know what he had found out during his investigation of the murder in Fort Worth. And she wanted James to know that she had missed him. James told her what he had discovered, which amounted to nothing. He suspected someone had just seen the woman and killed her. He couldn't understand why there weren't any marks on the woman other than the strangulation marks. He hadn't found anything to connect the two murders other than both young women had been strangled with a scarf. It was possible there could be a connection and it could just be a coincidence and a random killing. A random murder with no witnesses was almost impossible to solve. And he certainly hadn't solved this one!

James' steak arrived, and he went to work on it. Rhonda watched him eat. James was a man. He ate like a man, talked like a man, and acted like she envisioned a man should act. After he finished eating, he and Rhonda left the building and went for a walk and just chit chatted. When they stopped under a large tree, James kissed her. Rhonda didn't resist at all and then started taking part in the kiss. When the kiss finished, she said he could do that anytime. This relationship with Rhonda was moving way too fast for James' liking, but he couldn't deny his feelings for the young woman. They walked back to the building and went inside.

Rhonda got James another cup of coffee. As he took a sip, Maggie walked into the kitchen and said, "Well, what have we here? What have the two you been up to?" James flushed but said nothing. Rhonda just smiled and winked at her mother.

Maggie asked James how his trip to Fort Worth had gone and if he caught the killer? James confessed again that he had discovered nothing of importance.

When he finished, Maggie looked at him and said, "Did you run into Mayor Scruthers or Reverend Smith while you were there?"

Maggie's question surprised James, and he said, "Why would I have seen them there? Are you saying they were in Fort Worth on the 4th of July?"

Maggie explained that there was a church get-together in Fort Worth and Mayor Scruthers and Reverend Smith had gone for the three-day meeting. It seemed Scruthers was a deacon at Smith's church and was required to attend the gathering with the reverend.

This got Marshal Boutwell's attention. He looked at Maggie and said, "How do you know all this?"

Maggie said, "I went with Ling to the railroad depot to pick up a shipment of beefsteaks and saw Scruthers and Smith getting on the train going to Fort Worth. Seeing Reverend Smith get on the train wasn't anything unusual as he goes to Fort Worth every few months for a church meeting thing. I know little about churchy things so I can't tell you exactly what the meetings are about. I thought it a little strange that Mayor Scruthers was going with him until I remembered that he was a church official."

James said, "That's mighty interesting and opens up some possibilities. It's probably nothing more than a coincidence that Scruthers and Smith were in Fort Worth when the prostitute was killed, but it sure is interesting. When did they leave and get back?"

Maggie said, "Let's see now, you left on the 4th, so I guess they left on the 2nd. I can check my shipping form if it's important."

James said, "It might be. But you're sure they left a couple days before I got the wire?"

Maggie said, "Yes, I'm certain. I remember thinking it strange that Mayor Scruthers would miss our 4th of July celebration. The old windbag loves to give a speech on Independence Day!"

Neither James nor Maggie said anything for a few moments and then Maggie said, "I guess both Mayor Scruthers and Reverend Smith's wives wanted to see Fort Worth. You should have seen them trying to get Mrs. Smith's wheelchair on the train. It took four men to lift her and the chair and get it on the train. Mrs. Smith is a stout woman. Mrs. Scruthers is a tiny little snip of a woman. Before Mrs. Smith's accident, they looked like a giant and midget when you saw them walking together."

Chapter 16

James looked at the ceiling, took a deep breath, and exhaled. Just about the time he thought he had things figured out, a new twist appeared. He excused himself and told Maggie and Rhonda that he needed to go back to the hotel. He had lost track of time. Suddenly, James felt exhausted and just wanted to go to sleep and forget about dead women and who might have killed them.

When James awoke it was already muggy, and it was only 7 AM. He shuddered to think how hot it would be before the day was over. He knew he had two people to interview and knew a lot depended on how candid these people were. He could verify some things, some things he couldn't. He decided the best place to start was with a hearty breakfast. So, he finished getting dressed and headed for the Dallas Café. Five biscuits, several spoons of blackstrap molasses, and two cups of coffee later, James was ready to tackle the world. Actually, he felt ready to tackle a nervous mayor and minister.

James pulled Maggie's list out of his vest pocket and looked at the names. There were two left that he hadn't interviewed. The mayor and reverend would keep. He decided he would ride to the Lazy J ranch and talk to Melvin Jacobson. According to Maggie, he hadn't exclusively used the services of Thelma Goodrich, but he preferred her when she was available. He stopped by and had a cup of coffee with

J. L. and asked him what he knew about Melvin Jacobson.

J. L. allowed that Jacobson was a rough character and could be difficult. He had come to the Dallas area some years before and started his ranch. Apparently, he was a good cattle breeder and businessman because his herd had grown, and he always seemed to know the right time to sell. More often than not, the price of beef on the hoof seemed to drop not long after he completed a drive and sold some cows. The Lazy J was located, or at least most of it was situated, in Irving County, so J. L. had few dealings with Jacobson. Most of what he knew about Jacobson was second hand.

Before James left, J. L. cautioned him that Jacobson was notorious for having a terrible temper and had almost killed one of his ranch hands over some money that went missing from the ranch house. Apparently, Jacobson was capable of most anything during a fit of temper. James thanked J. L., walked to the livery, got his horse, and set out for the Lazy J ranch.

It was the better part of twenty miles to the ranch house. The oppressive heat had soaked James with sweat by the time he arrived. There was just no escaping the scorching rays of the sun or the extreme heat. The heat had his horse in lather even though he hadn't pushed the animal. James rode up to the front of the Jacobson ranch house, tied his horse to the porch rail, and loosened the cinch on the animal.

145

Before he got to the door, a man walked out and said, "You must be the U. S. marshal who's turning every rock over trying to figure out who killed the whore. Who put you on me?"

James knew Jacobson was trying to use bluster to put him on the defensive and said, "Who suggested it might be good to talk to you is of little importance. The questions I have for you and your answers are what are important. Can we go inside the house or do you want to talk out here in the heat?"

When Jacobson saw that he hadn't been able to intimidate Marshal Boutwell, his attitude changed somewhat. But he was still far from charming and said, "All right, you can ask your questions, but I have things to do and don't have time to waste."

James wanted to establish who was in control and said, "Mr. Jacobson, if I've caught you at a bad time, I offer my apologies. Perhaps you'd rather ride over to Dallas in the next couple of days when you're not so occupied and we can cover my questions there at the sheriff's office. You don't have to answer questions today."

Jacobson realized the marshal had outfoxed him and said, "Come on in the house."

The inside of the house showed a woman's touch but lacked the refinement one would expect of a person with Jacobson's wealth. They sat down at the kitchen table and James began. "Mr. Jacobson, I know you are busy, so I'll get right to it. How often do you visit Maggie's Pleasure Palace, and how many times would you estimate you used the services of Thelma Goodrich?" James could tell that his questions infuriated Jacobson, but the man was trying hard not to show his anger.

Jacobson replied, "I don't keep a damn log of visits to a whorehouse or how many times I see a particular female. My wife died in childbirth about seven years ago with our first child. I saw no reason not to continue my life. I suspect I have gone to Maggie's about once a month for the past six years, excluding times when I was taking cows to market, or tied up with other matters. As far as how many times I saw Thelma Goodrich, she hadn't been at Maggie's all that long. When she was available, I saw her. She was my favorite. Sometimes female companionship is as important as a poke. Thelma was a good listener. I hate it that someone killed her."

James asked, "When you visited Maggie's did you ride a horse or drive a buggy? I assume you have a buggy?"

Jacobson said, "Yes, I have a buggy. I bought it for my wife but, I've found as I have gotten older, it is more comfortable than riding horseback. I suspect I drove it to Dallas on each visit. I even use it some here around the ranch to check stock and see what my drovers are doing. Why do you ask?"

James ignored Jacobson's question and said, "Do you recall if you visited Maggie's on the 20th of June?" James could see Jacobson's temperature rising and was looking for an outburst.

Jacobson kept his temper in check and said, "Yes, I was at Maggie's on the 20th. That was a

Saturday, and I went to Dallas on business that day and then stopped by Maggie's for a T-Bone steak and a couple glasses of rye whiskey. I probably left about 8 PM and didn't use the services of the girls. I was probably back to the ranch around 10 PM and went to bed. Unless you are getting around to accusing me of something, I need to get to work."

James thanked Jacobson for his time, walked out to his horse, tightened the cinch, and led the animal to the water trough. After the animal drank his fill and James soaked his head with water, he mounted the horse and headed back to Dallas.

When James got to within five miles of Dallas, he met two men riding toward him on the trail. As the men approached, James began to get a funny feeling on the back of his neck. Something just didn't seem right. When the two men got nearer, they stopped their horses. James reined in his mount and said, "Is there something I can do for you, fellas?" One man had dead eyes and was wearing two pistols in a cross-draw fashion. The other man seemed a mite nervous but was trying to cover his nervousness with bluster.

The nervous man said, "Marshal, someone hired us to do a job. This is nothing personal." With that, both men went for their guns. James rolled off the right side of his horse and drew his pistol all in one motion. The impact of hitting the ground threw off his aim a mite, but he still got off an effective shot. The bullet hit the man with two guns slightly above the mid-section and he rolled out

148

of the saddle and hit the ground in a heap. James fired again and hit the nervous guy in the chest. Unfortunately, the nervous guy got off a shot before James got off his second shot.

The assassin's bullet hit James a glancing blow in the side, broke a rib, and exited leaving a sizable hole in the left side his back. The bleeding didn't seem to be all that bad, but the wound sure hurt. With a great deal of effort, James got up and walked to each of the men. The nervous man was dead, and the two-gun man would be dead soon. He searched both men and found four twenty-dollar Liberty Head gold pieces and two 1870 Liberty Head ten-dollar Gold Eagle in each man's pocket. Someone had paid the two men to make sure James didn't get back from the Lazy J. The only person James could think of who knew he would see Jacobson was J. L. It was possible that whoever hired the men could have seen him ride out and paid the men to kill him. One thing was for sure: the two men wouldn't provide any information.

James put the $200.00 in gold coins in his pocket, took the two Colt 1873 revolvers the cross-draw assassin had been carrying, and put them in his saddlebags. There was no way he could load the two bodies on their horses, so he ground picketed their animals. With some effort, James got on his horse, and started out for Dallas. Every stride of the horse jarred him and made his rib bark. When he got into town, he headed for Doctor Pickwell's office. As he rode by the general store, Maggie and Rhonda were coming out. They saw him and Rhonda dropped her packages and ran to his horse. She said, "James, what's happened. My God, someone shot you?"

James replied, "Yes, two men tried to kill me right before I got to Dallas. I need to get to Doc Pickwell's and see about this rib. Maggie, can you find Sheriff Baggett please?" He continued riding his horse towards the doctor's office and Rhonda walked alongside the animal. When James stopped in front of the doctor's office, Rhonda lent him some support as he dismounted and walked with him into the office.

Doctor Pickwell got James on an examination table, unbuttoned his shirt, and looked at the wound. Pickwell said, "Well, you're lucky. The bullet hit nothing vital, but it cracked a rib, and you're gonna have a handsome scar where the bullet exited. You're gonna be out of action for a few days until that rib bone mends. If you get hit or fall, the rib bone could completely fracture, enter your lung, and you would no doubt die. I'll clean the wound and wrap your chest to support the rib bone, but you've got to stay down for at least three days."

Rhonda said, "Momma's got a couple empty rooms. I'm sure she will have no objection to him staying with us until the rib mends. When you get finished, I'll bring the wagon over and he can ride in it to our place."

Sheriff Baggett walked into the office and said, "What the heck happened to you James?"

James told J. L. that someone had hired two men to assassinate him, but he had gotten lucky. He told the sheriff where he could find the bodies and the horses.

About the time the doctor finished his work, Maggie walked into the office, and said, "You don't seem to make a good impression on the good people of Dallas. People throw rocks at your window, people shoot at you from an alley, and now this. We'll get your horse tied to our wagon and you can lie in the back. I've got a vacant room next to my private quarters. You can stay in it until you mend. That is, if you think your reputation can stand being in my establishment overnight. People may get the wrong idea. And of course, I must check and see if anyone wants to attend to you."

Rhonda said, "Oh, Momma, you know very well that I will take care of James. Quit teasing, he's hurt, you know."

James grinned through the pain and replied, "I don't see that I have a great deal of choice regarding where I stay. I'm not concerned about what people might think. I appreciate your kindness. I hope that I'm not a burden."

Maggie and Rhonda helped James climb into the back of the wagon and got his horse tied to the rear. Maggie drove the wagon slowly to her establishment, got James out of the wagon, and helped him in the rear door. Maggie unlocked a door and James stepped into a very impressive room. James smiled and said, "Maggie is this room reserved for the president or something. I've never seen anything this fine." Maggie didn't respond and walked out of the room.

Rhonda pulled his boots off and he lay down on the bed and tried to relax. Every breath reminded him that he was alive and how lucky he had been.

In a few minutes Maggie returned with a serving tray containing a cup of coffee and some fancy piece of cake. She smiled and said, "As long as you're in the presidential suite, I guess you might as well enjoy the stay. Ling will fix you a steak and your favorite fried potatoes. I guess Rhonda will bring the food if she can leave your side long enough to go get it." Maggie laughed and walked out of the room.

Chapter 17

James started feeling better after staying in bed for a couple days. Rhonda waited on him hand and foot, brought his meals to his room, and sat and talked with him when he wasn't sleeping or reading. Maggie looked in on James occasionally, but mostly just allowed Rhonda to attend to him.

On the 9th of July, J. L. stopped by and visited with James. After exchanging greetings and a little small talk, J. L. handed James $350.00, laughed, and said, "The hostler said to tell you he couldn't afford any more horses for a while." J. L. rolled a cigarette, lit it, and said, "The two men you killed were kinda new to the area. Martin Halstead was the fella who wore the two guns. According to the word I have received, he was a gunman for hire and proficient at what he did. He supposedly killed five men, all in gunfights. I guess his ego wouldn't allow him to drygulch you. He reportedly had killed other men at long range with a rifle. Some people want to build on their reputation as a gunman. Guess Halstead guessed wrong about being able to take you on. Scanty Blevins was the other man's name. He was a no account who hung out at saloons in Dallas, but he was a fair hand with a pistol. I suspect someone hired him to make sure Halstead killed the right man and provide back-up if needed. Guess whoever did the hiring should have hired three killers. Since you killed Halstead in a fair fight, you must be a fair hand with a pistol. I knew you could shoot; I just didn't know how fast you could get your pistol into service til now. I'm impressed."

James smiled and replied, "I don't consider myself to be a gunfighter. But sometimes I'm forced to protect myself. There are men who want lawmen dead for whatever reason. I spend some time practicing and guess I have gotten better over the years." Neither man said anything for a few moments. James asked, "Did you tell anyone that I was going to the Jacobson ranch? These two men obviously knew I would ride back on the trail to Dallas and were waiting for me."

Before J. L. could respond, Rhonda brought a pot of coffee and two cups, spoke to Sheriff Baggett, excused herself, and went back out the door. J. L. looked at James and just smiled.

After a few moments, J. L. said, "No, I don't recall even talking to anyone where your name came up. Anyone could have seen you ride out towards the west. It seems most everyone in Dallas knows who you are, and I'm sure when you go to the privy, people know." J. L. and James talked for a while, and the sheriff excused himself and left.

The following day, James started getting up and felt much better. On the morning of the 10th he told Rhonda that he was going to his room at the hotel. He had some loose ends to tie up. She made a fuss and told him to be careful. The rib was still mending. James stopped and thanked Maggie for putting him up while he recovered. She allowed it was her pleasure, asked if Rhonda took good care of him, and then started laughing. James turned red and excused himself. He walked to the stable, saddled his horse with some difficulty, and rode to the hotel. After checking to make sure his possibles were still in the room, he went back downstairs, mounted his horse, and rode to the Methodist Church.

When he arrived, the same older man was working in the garden. Since the man seemed to know something about the killing, James decided it would a good idea to talk to him. He dismounted and walked over to where the man was standing. James said, "You told me a few days ago that I needed to talk to the reverend. What's your interest in all this?"

The man said, "I'm Elmer Goodrich, Thelma was my niece. A drunken cowboy killed my brother Simon in 1872 while he was minding his own business and drinking a beer in a saloon. His wife had died while trying to deliver their second child. The baby also died. He would turn over in his grave if he knew his only daughter had turned to prostitution." Goodrich paused for a few seconds, seemed thoughtful, and continued. "I just want to see my niece's murder avenged. You're barking, but so far, you're barking up the wrong trees. I'd tell you what's going on, but I want to see people sweat. You'll figure it out."

James walked to the side door of the church and knocked. Reverend Smith opened the door in a couple minutes and invited Marshal Boutwell in. After chatting for a couple minutes about the heat and both wondering when it would let up, James decided it was time to get to the point. He looked at Reverend Smith and said, "I understand you were in Fort Worth on the 2nd of July. I also understand Mayor Scruthers and both your wives went with you."

Reverend Smith was nervous but worked to keep his composure and said, "Yes. Yes, I was there and Mayor Scruthers and our wives went along. It was a church function, don't you see. I go to Fort Worth three or four times a year for meetings regarding Methodist Church business."

James asked, "Does Mayor Scruthers normally go with you? What about your wife? Does she normally go with you or stay in Dallas?"

Reverend Smith said, "These trips take three days. We have an evening get-together on the evening I arrive, then meetings pretty much all the next day, and then I come back to Dallas on the third day. They're not very exciting trips. I'm afraid just business. I get one of the church members' wives to look in on Emma two or three times each day I'm gone, and they bring her meals."

James said, "That's interesting, but you neglected to answer my questions. Does Mayor Scruthers normally go with you? And does your wife normally go with you?" James already knew the answers from talking with Maggie but wanted to see what Reverend Smith would say.

Reverend Smith said, "No, Mayor Scruthers had never gone with me before. I invited him a time or two, but he always begged off. On this event, the church requested that we bring at least one deacon. Mayor Scruthers didn't want to attend because he would miss the 4th of July ceremony, but Amon Blunt, the other deacon, was down with his back, so that left Mayor Scruthers."

As Reverend Smith finished his comment, there was a knock on the inside office door. Reverend Smith got nervous, got out of his chair, and opened the door. There was a rather large woman sitting in a wheelchair with a light blanket covering her knees and lower legs. Reverend Smith turned to James and said, "Marshal Boutwell this is my wife Emma. Emma, this is Marshal Boutwell. He is here asking me some questions regarding some Dallas citizens. He is trying to find out who killed that poor woman."

James stood, tipped his hat, and said, "My pleasure, Mrs. Smith. How are you today?"

Mrs. Smith smiled and replied, "I'm well considering my situation, I suppose. I'm wondering if this horrible heat is preparing some folks for the hereafter." She had looked at Reverend Smith when she made that comment. Mrs. Smith continued. "It's nice to finally meet you, Marshal Boutwell; you're the talk of Dallas. I sure hope you catch whoever murdered the whore. I'm sorry to have bothered you, Simon. I didn't know you were in a meeting. I'll talk to you later."

James thought the use of the term "whore" was a little tasteless for the wife of a minister to use. It almost seemed that there was a hint of resentment

157

in her tone. But women sometimes were very judgmental of those who drank or engaged in the world's oldest profession. After Mrs. Smith departed, James got back to his conversation with Reverend Smith.

James said, "You were about to tell me about the wives accompanying you and the mayor."

Reverend Smith said, "Yes. Yes, I was. Please pardon the interruption. Mostly, Emma can take care of herself but some things I must help her with. Emma had shown no interest in taking the Fort Worth trips with me after the accident, but when she learned Mayor Scruthers was going, she insisted that she and his wife accompany us. Normally, she doesn't like to go much of anywhere because of the problems with the wheelchair, but she was insistent."

James said, "You told me that Mrs. Smith was crippled in an accident. If you don't mind my asking, when and how did that happen?"

Reverend Smith looked away for a couple moments and then said, "It was three years ago, actually. Emma was crossing the street in front of the general store to buy some material for a dress she wanted to make. I'm afraid she was inattentive regarding traffic in the street and walked in front of a cargo wagon. The horses knocked her down and one stepped on her. A couple men who saw the accident took her to Doctor Pickwell's office." Reverend Smith stopped and seemed to be deep in thought. After a minute he continued, "Doctor Pickwell said that Emma's spine seemed to be unharmed, but she hasn't walked since the accident. Her legs respond to stimulant, but she can't stand without support and can't walk at all. Doctor Pickwell attributes the loss of the use of her legs to nerve damage. The doctor said that she might recover the use of her legs but so far she has made no progress."

James didn't respond and sat in his chair deep in thought. He would have expected Mrs. Smith to have referred to Miss Goodrich as "that poor soul" or perhaps "that unfortunate woman" but she had instead used the term whore. And what was puzzling James was that Mrs. Smith's response seemed almost resentful, but he put it aside and attributed it to prudishness. He thanked Reverend Smith for his time.

Reverend Smith thanked Marshal Boutwell for not mentioning anything about his knowing Miss Goodrich. James left and went to the Dallas Café to have a bite of lunch. While he was eating, the telegraph operator walked in and handed him a wire. Marshall Boutwell opened the paper, "*Austin circuit court. Stop. Your appearance at trial on 13th required.*" James looked at the telegraph operator and said, "Send them a response. I'll be there."

After finishing his lunch, James went to the hotel and packed his few items, checked out, and told the desk clerk that he would be gone for a few days. He rode to Maggie's and found Rhonda in the foyer. They sat and talked for a few minutes and James told her he should be back by the following Saturday.

Besides testifying at the trail, he needed to check in with the court and see what was going on during his absence. All plans are great when they work; this one didn't.

James kissed Rhonda and headed back to Dallas, put his horse in the livery, and caught the 3 PM train to Austin. When he arrived, he went to his office and checked his messages. He had been gone for over two weeks, so there was a sizable stack of "to do" items. James walked down to the judge's office, knocked, and walked in. After chatting about the upcoming trial and explaining what luck he was having with the investigation, the judge said, "Once this trial is over, I'm afraid you're gonna have to go to Arizona and pick up a prisoner. I expect your killer in Dallas will still be there. If this pickup wasn't important, I wouldn't bother you with it."

The trial started on Monday morning at 9 AM. James was the third witness called by the prosecution. About halfway through the questions, James was wondering why they had brought him all the way from Dallas for the trial. Other than describing the details of Sam Brightwell's arrest, he really didn't have much of anything to offer. After several minutes on the stand, the prosecutor said, "I'm finished with this witness." The man who was defending Brightwell just smiled at Marshal Boutwell, apologized for the court wasting his time, and said, "I have no questions your honor." The judge scolded the lawyer for his comment but seemed to agree in principle.

The judge looked at Marshal Boutwell and said, "You're excused, Marshal. I believe you have somewhere to go. Don't let me hold you up." The judge laughed and said, "I guess I should have said 'detain you,' good luck on your trip." James got up and walked out of the courtroom. What a colossal waste of time his testimony had been. The prosecutor was young, maybe he would get better at his job.

James looked at the extradition order and saw it was for one Jack J. Taylor. Taylor had held up a stagecoach near El Paso is 1873 and shot the driver who recovered and identified him.

Before boarding a train for Tucson, Arizona, James stopped at the telegraph office and sent a wire to Rhonda. *"Gone to Tucson. Stop. Back soonest. Stop. James."* James knew Rhonda would be expecting him back and would presume the worst when he didn't show up. He waited around for about an hour and got on a train headed for Tucson. He wouldn't be back in Dallas on the 18th. Such was the life of a lawman.

Chapter 18

James got on the train at 9 AM on July 14 and tried to get comfortable in the Pullman car. He hated trains. They jostled, squeaked, rattled, and the Hopper toilets were nasty. The horrible part was that if everything went like clockwork, he would be on the damn train for around thirty-six hours. The problem with trains was that they never worked as designed. If you arrived on the day you were scheduled, they considered the train on time. Considering train changes, the trip would take at least three days going and three days on the return trip. Almost a week of miserable travel!

When Marshal Boutwell got to Tucson, Arizona, he went directly to the jail to make sure that Jack J. Taylor was locked in one of its cells. James looked at the man and said, "I'm U.S. Marshal James Boutwell. The State of Texas has assigned me to take you to Austin, Texas, to stand trial for robbery of a stagecoach. I've transported several prisoners through the years, so I'll give you some advice. Just enjoy the ride. If you give me any problems, you may well ride in the baggage car with a tarp covering you." With that, James walked over to the jailer and said he would be back to pick up Taylor at 8:30 AM the following day to get on the 9:14 AM train headed towards Austin, Texas. James could only suppose the court wanted to hold the trial in the Texas capital for political purposes.

James checked in at the Tucson House, had dinner, and then went upstairs to his room. He got a good night's sleep and felt refreshed when he woke up. Riding on a train didn't allow one to get much rest and even less sleep. After eating breakfast, James headed for the jail. When he opened the jail door, the jailer was lying on the floor, the cell door was open, and Taylor wasn't in his cell.

Marshal Boutwell didn't know beans about Tucson and hadn't the slightest idea of where to look for Taylor or even who to notify that he wasn't in his cell. James checked on the jailer who was recovering his senses. He had a large knot on his noggin but was sitting up with a little help from James. Marshal Boutwell asked, "How did this happen?"

The jailer said he really didn't know. Taylor had called him, and he walked over to the cell to see what the prisoner needed, and the lights just went out. Obviously, he had forgotten to lock the jail door when he returned from the privy. Someone came into the jail and hit him on the head. He had seen no one so he couldn't help with who had hit him, and he had no idea where Taylor might have gone after his escape. In a couple minutes, Sheriff Mark Wonlers walked in the jail door, saw the empty cell, and went into a fit of anger. When Wonlers finished exercising his frustrations with some colorful metaphors and berating the jailer for being an idiot, he looked at James and said, "Well, I guess we had better go get him. I know exactly where he went." Wonlers walked to the rifle rack, unlocked it, and took out a

Greener coach gun. He stuffed a half dozen 00 buck shells in his vest pocket and put one in each chamber of the scattergun.

Sheriff Wonlers asked, "Marshal, do you want to borrow a shotgun or a rifle?"

James looked at the sheriff and said, "Where are we going? Is this going to be close in work or long gun work? I'm not crazy about using a rifle I haven't proven. If a shotgun fires, I guess it will be fine." Wonlers took another double-barrel shotgun out of the rack and handed it to Marshal Boutwell. James looked at the firearm and saw "R. Richards-Belgium" engraved on the back of the action.

Wonlers handed James a box of .12-gauge 00 buckshot shells and said, "Help yourself, Marshal."

James said, "You said you know exactly where Taylor went. I know nothing about Tucson, but I would like to know where we are going. Is this in town or do I need to get a horse?"

Sheriff Wonlers said, "It's within walking distance. Taylor's brother owns the feed mill. I'm betting he broke his brother out of jail and we'll find Jack hiding somewhere in the mill until they can smuggle him out of town. It's a dirty place where they process, and sack grain so keep your eyes open. There are a lot of nooks and crannies in that place for a man to hide." James put a shotgun shell in each chamber and stuffed six more in his vest pockets, three in each side.

Sheriff Wonlers and Marshal Boutwell walked down the middle of the street towards a large building that sat all alone. Gawkers started following them, but at a distance. By the time they walked the half-mile to the mill, there were around twenty people following them perhaps fifty yards behind. James wondered what these people were thinking. No one, or at least no one with good sense, wanted to be anywhere close to where he was trying to arrest someone. Anything could go wrong and could cause a real mess with some civilians getting hurt.

Marshal Boutwell looked at Wonlers and said, "Shouldn't you break up that crowd. If something goes wrong, someone could get hurt."

Sheriff Wonlers laughed and said, "Ain't much in the way of excitement in Tucson. These people aren't likely to miss out on our arrest of Taylor."

James said, "If you're so all fire sure Taylor is just going to surrender, why are we carrying shotguns? My experience is that if things can go wrong, they will. I just don't want to see a civilian get hurt. And being distracted by the crowd could get me hurt." Sheriff Wonlers just ignored James and continued walking towards the mill.

When they walked in the mill office door, the room was empty. Wonlers opened the door leading to the mill proper and hollered, "Michael Taylor. This is Sheriff Wonlers. You need to come out and bring Jack with you. I will not shoot or arrest you for breaking your brother out of jail. You'll just pay a fine for hitting my jailer on the noggin. The problem is, I've got a U.S. marshal with me. He doesn't know what a fine fellow you are or that you felt compelled to help your worthless brother. He may shoot you if something goes wrong. Come on out now, Michael."

There was no response. Sheriff Wonlers looked at Marshal Boutwell and said, "I guess we're gonna have to do this the hard way. Michael Taylor ain't a bad fellow but be careful. He may do something stupid trying to protect his brother."

When Wonlers and James entered the mill proper, the sheriff went to the left and James to the right. The place had a great deal of dust in the air and everything was coated with powder and grain debris. It was all James could do to get a lung full of air. James pulled his scarf over his nose and mouth, stayed near the wall, and slowly walked along scanning for movement. The sheriff had been right. There were many places for a man to hide. There were stacks of grain filled bags, piles of empty sacks, pieces of some type of equipment, and a couple wagons inside the building. As James moved along, he saw a grain chute ahead. It was above and on the edge of the building. Below the shoot was a large pile of some type grain.

James stopped and surveyed the building. He couldn't see around the mound of grain and didn't really want to poke his head around the edge to see what was on the other side. That could be a good way to lose his head! James shouted, "Jack Taylor. This is Marshal Boutwell. I've ridden on a train for two days and now I'm in this nasty mill. I've got no patience for this nonsense. You need to come on out before you get hurt or killed." There was no response.

James eased around the grain pile and saw movement to his left behind some piece of equipment. He knew it wasn't Sheriff Wonlers, so he fired a load of buckshot at the piece of equipment. Pellets ricocheted around, and the boom of the shotgun was deafening. A man came out from behind the machine with his hands raised in the air, but it wasn't Jack Taylor.

James said, "Who the heck are you?"

The man replied, "I'm Michael Taylor, Jack's brother. Helping him get out of jail is one thing; eating a load of buckshot is quite another. I've had all I want of this. If I had any sense, I would have left him in jail."

James said, "Get down on your knees and put your hands behind your head. Is your brother armed? If you lie to me, you need to know that I'll shoot you after I deal with him. If he's armed, you would be just as guilty of trying to kill me as him."

Michael Taylor said, "No, Jack's not armed. The guns in the jail were locked up in the rack so he couldn't get one, and the jailer wasn't armed. I hit the jailer in the head with a club I kept in my office in the mill. I swear he's not armed." Marshal Boutwell had Michael Taylor put his hands behind his back, placed manacles on his wrists, told him to lay flat on the floor, and stay in that position. James could finally see Sheriff Wonlers across the giant room. He was pointing in the direction James was walking.

When James had walked another thirty feet, he saw another pile of grain. He almost broke out laughing. A pair of boots was sticking out of the grain pile. James hollered. "I see a pair of boots. I think I'll put a load of buckshot in the one on the right and see what happens." Jack Taylor came crawling out of the pile of grain and husks with his arms in the air. James put his other pair of manacles on Taylor and started walking him out of the building. He stopped long enough to get Michael Taylor up and moving along with them out of the building.

James was sure happy to get out of the mill. It had been sweltering hot, dust filling the air, and sticky grain pieces flying everywhere. Sheriff Wonlers came out the door shortly after James got outside. They walked the Taylor brothers to the jail and locked them in separate cells.

James looked at Jack Taylor and said, "You've cost me a day because the train for Austin has already left for today. If I have any more trouble from you, it will be because you tried to escape, and it forced me to shoot you. I'm not a very good shot with a pistol so I'll just aim at the middle of you and shoot two or three times to make sure I hit you. After that, you can ride back to Austin in the baggage car with a tarp over you."

Marshal Boutwell had absolutely no problems with Jack Taylor on the train ride to Austin and arrived on July 22nd. On the day of the trial, they discovered that the stagecoach driver had quit the job and left the territory, or at least no one knew where to find him. Since there was no one to identify Jack Taylor, the charges had to be dropped. James was less than happy. This was the same idiot prosecutor who had called him to Austin for no good purpose. Now he had allowed his only witness to leave town. Marshal Boutwell thought about arresting the young prosecutor for being stupid but knew the judge would probably let him off.

****

Jack Taylor was a member and supposed leader of a gang of train robbers and killers who roamed Arizona and New Mexico looking for opportunities to rob and kill. The Jack Taylor Gang robbed a train near Nogales, Arizona, but escaped unscathed even though there were a few shots fired at them. During the gang's string of train robberies, they killed three train workers, one engineer, and a couple passengers. Texas John Slaughter tracked down and killed or arrested most of the Taylor gang. Finally, in 1888, Mexican Rurales captured Jack Taylor. He received a life sentence for train robbery and died in a Mexican prison.

Chapter 19

James delivered Jack Taylor to the Austin jail and made sure the jailer securely locked the bandit up. James went to his office in the courthouse and saw a note from the judge. Since he wasn't in the mood for more bad news, he stuck the piece of paper in his vest pocket and headed down the street to get a meal at the Capital Café. Whatever the judge might want, it needn't ruin his meal, and it would wait.

****

The term "extradition" was imported to the United States from France, where the *decret-Loi* of February 19, 1791, appears to be the first official document to have used the term. We do not find the specific term in treaties or conventions until 1828. The French Treaties with Wurtemberg (a German state which existed from 1805 until 1918) of March 26, 1759, and of December 3, 1765, incorporated the equivalent terms of "restituter" (to restore or hand-over) and "remettre" (to send back, restore or hand-over). Extradition applies to those who were tried and convicted and have subsequently escaped from custody, or to those who have been convicted in absentia.

Extradition does not apply to persons merely suspected of having committed an offense but against whom no charge has been laid or to a person whose presence is desired as a witness or for obtaining or enforcing a civil judgment. Often extradition was a political, as opposed to legal, effort between countries and could require, at times, years to resolve. The French Third Republic was the system of government adopted in France in 1870. On May 23, 1873, Patrice de Mac-Mahon began his term as president of France.

****

After he had finished eating, James opened the note. It read, *"The Attorney General, George W. Clark would like to see you as soon as possible."* James thought, I guess the attorney general is second guessing himself on allowing me to solve the murder of the prostitute in Dallas County. I suppose I'm about to get fired. James walked the 200 yards to the capital building, went to the attorney general's office, and told the receptionist the Attorney General had summoned him. After getting James' name, she asked him to have a seat. In about five minutes the woman said, "General Clark will see you now, Marshal Boutwell."

When James entered the well-appointed office, Mr. Clark stood and extended his hand and introduced himself. James did likewise and General Clark asked to him to please sit and asked if he would like a cup of coffee. James declined, and Mr. Clark said, "All right let's get right to this then." There was a pause of a few moments and then Mr. Clark began, "Marshal Boutwell, I will walk you through this

171

entire circumstance so you will appreciate the gravity of the situation and the position my superiors have put me in. President Ulysses S. Grant gave his Attorney General George Henry Williams a very delicate task to perform. George Williams and I go way back a long way, so he notified me I was to perform a very delicate task for him. I thought about it and started checking up on you. I was pleased with the feedback I got from the trial judge and some of my contacts regarding your professionalism during your tenure as a deputy U.S. marshal. Therefore, I have tasked you with a very delicate mission."

James scratched his chin whiskers and asked, "If I may, Sir, what kind of delicate task? I'm not known for my tact. In fact, people have accused me of thinking tact was something to hammer into a wall."

Mr. Clark laughed and said, "Well, you come highly recommended. You're a man of some education and sophistication and have earned the respect of influential people, so I suspect you will be fine. You're also your father's son, so I know the good stock you come from."

Marshal Boutwell said, "Sir, could you give me some idea of what I will be doing?"

Attorney General Clark turned gravely serious and replied, "Marshal Boutwell, you're going to Paris, France, to escort a man and his wife back to the United States. Curtis and Marissa Breedlove are their names. They are being housed in a hotel in Paris by the French government. I'm not at liberty to tell you what their status is, or why you are to escort them to the United States. However, I need to tell you that there are powerful people who don't want Mr. Breedlove to come back to the United States or to testify before congress. The gravity of this mission should prepare you to act as much as a bodyguard as an escort. About all I can tell you is that Mr. and Mrs. Breedlove are returning to the United States of their own accord, extradition isn't a factor in this case. But the French government must approve their exit from France, so you will have to go through them and satisfy their concerns to secure Mr. and Mrs. Breedlove's release."

Marshal Boutwell said, "How exactly am I expected to protect Mr. Breedlove? I don't think the French authorities would be very excited about me coming off a ship with a pistol strapped to my hip."

Mr. Clark responded "And that's why I selected you for this assignment. You're resourceful and intelligent. I'm sure you will come up with a solution to this problem. If any harm should come to Mr. Breedlove, my buttocks will be in a bind and my political career will be over. I think it goes without saying that you shouldn't expect advancement in the marshal service if you fail. And, if the situation deteriorates into a crap storm perhaps you might want to look for other work. Do you understand?"

Marshal Boutwell said, "Yes, Sir. I only see one problem. Mr. Breedlove is traveling with his wife. There is no way that I can protect them both. I suspect she will need some time alone to attend to her personal hygiene needs. I can conceive of how someone could snatch her and use her for leverage against Mr. Breedlove. I will need a female to accompany Mrs. Breedlove wherever she goes on the ship on the return trip to the United States. Am I to presume there are American agents protecting them until they board the ship?"

Attorney General Clark responded "Yes, your protection responsibilities won't start until the Breedlove's board the ship. But you will be required to meet with French authorities before boarding. You've got a legitimate point regarding a female traveling companion. Unfortunately, I don't have a female that I feel would be competent for the task."

James said, "If you'll make the arrangements for two cabins, next to the Breedlove's cabin for the crossings, I'll get the female. When do I need to be underway?

Attorney General Clark said, "Today's the 24th. Why don't you go on back to Dallas and snoop around some more on your murder investigation and I'll make the travel arrangements for you and a female associate. I'll send you a wire and give you plenty of time to get to the port and catch a ship. By the way, tell your dad I said hello when you next see him."

James went back to his office, tidied up, went by the gun shop he used, and barely made it to the train depot in time to catch the 3:15 PM headed for Dallas. With stops for water and wood, the train arrived in Dallas a little after midnight. James went to the Dallas Hotel and got the same room, took off his boots, and stretched out to get some sleep.

The next morning James was up early, washed up, and headed for the Dallas Café. After eating, he went to the barbershop, got a hair trim, and bath. While he was bathing, he had his boots shined. The woman cleaning his clothes beat most of the dust off his pants, and he put on a clean shirt. He walked to the livery and got his horse and set out for Maggie's Pleasure Palace.

When he arrived, it was just after 9 AM on 25 July. He took his horse to the stable behind the building, loosened the cinch on the animal, and walked in the back door of the building. When he had taken a couple steps inside the door a voice said, "Thought you could sneak in the back door huh." James looked in an open door and there sat Maggie behind a desk covered with papers. He walked in and said hello. Maggie returned the greeting and asked him what he had been doing. After a brief description of his trip to Austin, leaving out his latest assignment, he asked, "Where's Rhonda? Normally she has a sixth sense about when I'll ride up."

Maggie said, "She was in the kitchen. I suppose you need to check there." James walked down the hallway and into the foyer. He gazed into the kitchen and saw Rhonda sitting at the table with her back to him. He tip-toed in and nuzzled her hair with his chin. She jumped, recovered, got up, and embraced him. She stood back and looked at him.

Rhonda said, "I've missed you. It seems like you've been gone a month." Rhonda threw her arms around James and kissed him. About that time Maggie walked in, pretended not to notice what was transpiring, and poured the three of them a cup of coffee.

They sat and chit-chatted for a few minutes and then James said, "Actually I need to talk to both of you and I suppose now is as good a time as any." Both Maggie and Rhonda looked apprehensive and puzzled. James hesitated and said, "I've got to make a trip and I need a female to accompany me to help chaperone a man's wife. The government will pay all the expenses. And I figure the exposure to danger will be minimal. The trip, start to finish should be close to a month, give or take."

Maggie said, "Are you getting around to asking my daughter to take this month-long trip with you? I'm quite fond of you but I won't have my daughter's virtue compromised and perhaps be the source of gossip. She has to endure enough loose talk due to my owning this business."

James said, "I appreciate that, and I would do nothing improper to compromise Rhonda. She would always have her own accommodations, and mostly, would be in the company of another lady, who would be a chaperone for Rhonda as much as Rhonda would be a companion to her. I'm responsible for the safe delivery of the lady's husband and I merely need a female to be a travel companion to the wife."

Rhonda said, "You two are talking like I'm in another room. I'm of age and able to make my own decisions."

Maggie said, "I'm aware that you are an adult. And I respect James discussing this with both of us. And the decision is yours and yours alone. But a month is a long time and a lot of things can happen in that length of time."

Rhonda looked at James and asked, "If I can be so bold as to ask, where would I be going on this trip?"

James said nothing for a few moments, swallowed hard, and then replied, "France. Paris, France, to be more specific."

Maggie exclaimed, "James Boutwell, you want to take my daughter to France. You want to get on an ocean liner and take my daughter to France." Rhonda smiled, looked at James, and waited for her mother to calm down.

James just ignored Maggie's outburst and didn't reply directly but alternately looked at Rhonda and Maggie and said, "I figure it will take five or six days by train to get to New York. We would have to go from Dallas to New York City to catch the steamship to France. Rhonda, you would have your own room on the train coming and going. You would have your own cabin on the ship. The crossing will take eight days. Once I get the man and his wife onboard the ship for the return voyage, it will take eight more days to sail back to New York. Then I may be required to escort the gentleman and his wife to Washington, D.C., or other marshals may pick them up to escort them on. I don't really know. The details weren't entirely clear on that point. They have told me that my responsibilities start when the couple gets on the ship and end once they disembark at New York harbor. On the short side it would be thirty days, and it could stretch out to more like thirty-five or forty days if we have transportation issues. I understand it is a formidable undertaking." James turned and looked at Rhonda and said, "If you have any misgivings at all about taking this trip, then you shouldn't go. I will try to find someone else to be a companion to the woman. But logically, I think it has to be a female." James then looked at Maggie and said, "If I have to go to Washington, I could put Rhonda on a train to Dallas. But, I would rather she is gone a few extra days than travel that distance by herself." Maggie seemed in a daze and didn't respond.

Rhonda said, "This is a lot to swallow in one bite. Let me sleep on it tonight, discuss it with Momma in the morning over coffee and breakfast, and see if she has any serious misgivings. She's upset right now and not recognizing this as an opportunity. Why don't you come by for lunch tomorrow and I'll give you my answer?" Maggie excused herself and walked out of the kitchen and towards her office. Rhonda asked, "Will I need to take a weapon?"

James was thoughtful for a few moments and said, "It wouldn't be a bad idea. I doubt you would need it, but it's better to have a weapon and not need it than it is to need a weapon and not have it. I secured two pistols for the trip."

Rhonda sighed and said, "Something else to sleep on, I suppose." She got up from the table, leaned over, kissed James lightly on the lips, and said she would see him tomorrow. James sat at the table alone wondering to himself if this was a horrible idea. Not entirely alone, Peaches appeared and began rubbing against his boot. James went to the stable, got his horse, and set out for Dallas.

When he got to Dallas, he stabled the horse and went to the hotel, read a book, thought about the trip, and finally tried to get some sleep. With his mind in a whirl, he doubted he would get much rest.

Chapter 20

James was up early and nervously tried to fill his morning with something to kill the time before going to Maggie's and getting Rhonda's answer. James was just a little apprehensive regarding Rhonda's decision. A month was a long time to be on a trip with a man you had scarcely known a few weeks. There also was an element of danger, be it ever so slight. James doubted anyone would try to hurt Mrs. Breedlove, but there was always that possibility. He wouldn't blame Rhonda at all if she refused to accompany him.

James cleaned his pistol, and then his rifle, ate breakfast, and got waterlogged with coffee. He got his horse from the stable, saddled him, and rode to Maggie's. After getting his horse stabled, he walked in the back door of the building. Maggie was in her office, looked up, and waved as he walked by her door. The large clock in the foyer chimed 10 AM as James walked into the waiting room. Rhonda was sitting in a parlor chair sipping a cup of coffee and waiting for him to arrive. When she saw James, she placed the cup on a side table, stood, walked over, and kissed him lightly on the lips. Rhonda said, "Let's go into the kitchen. It's more private there."

When they got situated and Rhonda had poured James a cup of coffee and sat down, she said, "I've given this proposed trip a great deal of thought. In fact, I had a lot of difficulty sleeping because it is such an overwhelming situation. Momma doesn't want me to go. She hasn't said that in so many words, but I can tell she's concerned. As a matter of fact, I'm concerned too. I've never been on a boat in my life. I'm worried about getting seasick and looking after the woman is a lot of responsibility. I've been away from home, but I could always communicate with my mother. A letter could reach her within days. In an emergency, we could reach each other within hours by telegraph. And, if I had a problem in Denver, there were people who could help me. If something happened to you on this trip, I would be in a real mess. On this excursion, you and I will have no contact with the United States until we return. I'm not easily scared, but this is a little frightening to me."

James could only say, "I understand completely. It's a big challenge and lots of things could go wrong. I'll let the attorney general know and he will just have to get someone to go on the trip with me."

Rhonda said, "Oh, no, I'm going. I just wanted you to know that it was a big decision."

James smiled and said, "I'm happy about your decision. I picked up two Webley Bulldog pistols in Austin and I think we should get used to them before we leave. Have you ever shot a gun?" Rhonda replied that she had shot a rifle but never a pistol. James said he would come back in the late afternoon with the pistols and they would get in some practice so she would feel comfortable with the weapon.

Later that afternoon James came back with the two pistols and they practiced shooting at a stump behind the stable. James showed Rhonda how to aim the revolver with both hands held in front of her body. If she had to use the pistol, she would shoot from less than ten feet so there was no reason to go through a lot of aiming or shooting positions. The main thing was that she couldn't be afraid of the weapon. After going through perhaps a half box of .44 rimfire, Rhonda was getting the weapon out of her purse, squaring her body with the stump, extending her arms straight in front of her body before firing, and getting a shot off in a reasonable amount of time. She was aiming the pistol with her body and arms. She had excellent hand to eye coordination and took to shooting like a duck to water.

****

The Webley Bulldog pocket revolver was a small, powerful handgun which experienced considerable commercial success. Philip Webley & Son, Birmingham, England, introduced the weapon in 1872. The weapon was designed to be small and compact so that it could be concealed in a coat pocket or even a woman's purse. The pistol was chambered in .44 rimfire short, .442 Webley, and .450 Adams. Charles Guiteau used a Webley Bulldog to assassinate President James Garfield on July 2, 1881. Garfield contracted a massive infection from the bullet wound and died. They executed Guiteau in 1882. The pistol was placed in the Smithsonian Museum but disappeared. The .44 short version was all that was available in Austin and plenty powerful for what James needed.

****

Once he was confident Rhonda could use the pistol, he took both revolvers back to Dallas to the hotel and cleaned them. He would take the second pistol back to Maggie's so that Rhonda could work on getting it out of her purse and become accustomed to having it in her hand. She would pack one and he the other for the trip. The pistols wouldn't be needed until they began escorting the Breedloves.

On July 29, the wire James had been waiting for arrived. They were to board the SS Baltic in New York City harbor on August 4, 1874. The SS Baltic was an ocean liner owned and operated by the White Star Line.

They were to make the return voyage on the SS Celtic which was to sail from La Havre, France, on August 16, 1874. Since the Breedloves were traveling first class, the tickets for Marshal Boutwell and his traveling companion would also be for first class cabins.

As soon as James finished reading the wire, he went to the livery, got his horse, and set out for

Maggie's. He stabled his horse and went in the back door. Rhonda and her mother were both in Maggie's office. James knocked and walked through the open door. He got right to the point. He and Rhonda would have to leave the following morning in order to get to New York City in time to catch the ocean liner to France.

James cautioned Rhonda not to carry any more luggage than was necessary. The more pieces of luggage they carried, the more space they would take up on the train and the small rooms on the ship. Rhonda allowed she understood.

James told Rhonda he would pick her up at Maggie's at 7:30 AM sharp the following morning. That should give ample time to get to the station and board the 9:10 out of Dallas headed east. James got his clothes together, packed his pistol and ten cartridges for each firearm, and had everything ready before he went to bed on the 29th. James was up at 6 AM, ate a bite at the Dallas Café, walked to the livery and got a horse and general-purpose wagon. After placing his two small grips in the wagon's bed, he headed for Maggie's. He parked the wagon in front of the porch and walked into the foyer. Rhonda had five valises stacked in the middle of the room. James said, "I'm sure you said you understood that we were to pack as light as possible for this trip?" James was happy he had got a wagon rather than just a buggy. If he had brought a buggy, the valises wouldn't have fit.

Rhonda replied, "James, we will eat in the first-class dining room with people of some substance. I simply won't be embarrassed by being underdressed. I suggest, if you didn't pack a nice suit, you stop at the hotel and get one or buy one at the mercantile or in New York City. The red caps got Rhonda's luggage on the train, the porter assigned them their sleeping berths, and they settled in for the journey. They arrived in New York City on the morning of August 2, 1874, caught a horse-drawn taxi to a hotel near the harbor, got separate rooms, and got freshened up to have lunch.

****

Nothing could have prepared either James or Rhonda for New York City. The city was teeming with immigrants. The streets were crowded with beggars and street vendors. In 1874, nearly sixty-one percent of all U. S. exports passed through New York harbor.

The post-Civil War period in New York City was known for the corruption and graft for which Tammany Hall had become synonymous. On the other side of the coin, the Metropolitan Museum of Art, Metropolitan Opera, and the American Museum of Natural History were all erected.

One of the most striking things of interest to a stranger visiting New York City was the ocean steamers in the harbor. There would be thirty to forty of these huge floating structures alongside the docks

185

in the harbor. They would also anchor ships in the mouth of the Hudson River, and at the confluence of the East River flowing into it from the Sound. There were vast basins of deep water, well sheltered, where ships of any size and number could lie anchored in safety. The different shipping lines ran to different ports in England and Scotland, to Germany, France, and to the Isthmus of Darien where they connected with other lines from Panama. Sometimes eight to ten of the steamers might leave the port in New York on the same day.

It was amazing just to watch the coal being loaded on the giant ships. For the two neophyte travelers headed to France, who had never been out of the western prairies and mountains, James and Rhonda were amazed when they observed the sights and sounds along the harbor.

****

After eating lunch near the harbor, Rhonda asked to take a walk and look at some of the sights. James said, "Ok, but let's go back by the hotel and let me get my Webley. There is a lot of crime here and I don't want to have to defend us with only your purse as a weapon." After getting the pistol, they walked up 5th Avenue to the Metropolitan Museum of Art and spent the afternoon looking at paintings and artwork. Rhonda did most of the looking and James just kinda tagged along. The only art appreciation he had was in admiring the lines on a fine horse. Rhonda's idea of art was just a little more sophisticated.

When they returned to the hotel, the concierge stopped them, and said, "Madam, if I may be so bold, we have a couple lightly used steamer trunks. You could purchase one and cut down on the number of valises you would have on the ship. After looking at the trunk and discovering that it contained room to hang most of her clothes, and drawers for her other personal effects, she thought it was a wonderful idea. The steamer trunk was designed for ocean travel, and eliminated three large valises, leaving Rhonda with just the one large trunk and two valises. Rhonda thanked the concierge, and James tipped him. The concierge said that he would store her valises and she could exchange the steamer trunk for them when she returned.

James and Rhonda had a nice dinner and went to a show in a large bar near the harbor. The singing and dancing were entertaining. They both had a drink and then walked back to the hotel. They only had one full day to visit the city. The SS Baltic was scheduled to depart at 7 AM on August 4. They planned to get their luggage on the ship and find their state rooms before 6 AM.

They arrived at the ship in a horse-drawn taxi with Rhonda's bags stacked all over the conveyance. The seamen loading the vessel started unloading Rhonda's valises and putting them on a skid to load into the ship's hold. Rhonda would have none of it. She said, "Those valises will go to my cabin. I've necessities in them for the ocean voyage." A couple able seamen struggled with the bags but got them onboard. They had no difficulty boarding the ship, followed the men carrying the bags, and were assigned cabins just a few doors apart. A few minutes after 7 AM, the SS Baltic started out of New York harbor. Rhonda was excited. This would be an adventure she would tell her grandchildren about. And hopefully they would also be James Boutwell's grandchildren as well.

The first day on board ship went well enough. They got settled into their cabins and then met for coffee in the ship's galley. After coffee they toured the ship, or at least the part of the ship the crew allowed them to visit. Being in first class had its benefits, but it didn't allow one to see much of the ship below decks. After a brief tour, they returned to their cabins, took a nap, and dressed for the evening meal. Rhonda was correct. There were a lot of "stuffed shirts" in the large dining room. Every man wore a dark suit.

When they finished their meal, they walked out to the rail of the ship and looked out over the ocean. There was a waning Gibbous moon and the reflection from the moon made the water seem to twinkle. James put his arm around Rhonda and said, "I'm sure glad you came. I wouldn't have wanted to have had to ask one of your mother's female employees to come with me." In a few minutes James' shoulder quit hurting.

Every so often they would see what appeared to be twinkling stars on the horizon. The next day when they asked about the twinkling lights, the second mate told them that the ship followed the coastline until it reached a point, beyond Newfoundland, where the coast trends westward before entering open seas.

Chapter 21

On the ocean liner, the great saloon served as a parlor, study, dining-room, drawing-room, and when necessary, as an invalid-chamber. Sleep was difficult because at all hours of the day and night the scream of the steam-whistle on deck would shock the passengers who were already struggling to sleep. The whistle blasted because the fog and darkness were so dense that the only safeguard to preclude a collision with other ships, or with fishermen, was in sounding the alarm. After sounding the ear-piercing whistle, there would be an interval while waiting for a response to warn them away. The possibility of striking an iceberg was an ever-present danger as the RMS Titanic was to discover in 1912.

After the first day on the ship, Rhonda was a nervous wreck. The steamer moved on through fogs, mists, and flying patches of rain. There was no hesitation, no slowing down, just the constant onward progress of the ship. James tried to reassure Rhonda. He told her that a woman of greater sensitivity and timidity would have been overpowered by the thrashing of the waves, winds, and possibilities that worried the mind. Rhonda looked at James and said, "Stuff it, Boutwell. That psychology won't work right now. I'm scared." Undaunted, James plowed on, and said, "In my opinion, you are a woman of character, nerve, and resolve." The truth was that James was as concerned as Rhonda, only he couldn't allow his worry to become obvious and increase her fear.

As if the voyage wasn't bad enough, when they entered the Gulf Stream, a fifty-mile-wide and 1,000 feet deep current of warm water, a confluence of forces met them. When the warm tropic water met the counter-current coming down from Baffin's Bay, it produced a stream of icebergs, ice-floes, and ice-cold water. Accompanying the ice was a perpetual succession of fogs, mists, and driving rain. Gales and squalls often accompanied these elements. It was as if something had thrown them in the grasp of some giant force that tested their spirit. While they would have taken umbrage with the suggestion, James and Rhonda were traveling at the best time of the year to make the voyage. May, June, and perhaps early July would have been far worse. They weren't aware of the most favorable traveling time and were a captive of their schedule.

On the fourth evening, James received a note inviting him and Rhonda to dine at the captain's table. James sent word that the Captain honored him by extending the invitation, but he had only brought a dark suit and no formal dinner attire (in fact he didn't own such a garment). He didn't want to embarrass the Captain or other passengers who would be properly attired for a formal dinner and asked to beg off. Around 2 PM local time, a young ensign walked up to Marshal Boutwell and said, "Captain Freberg's compliments, Sir. The captain would like to see you personally, if you would be so kind as to follow me." James followed the officer up a series of stairs and into a small room which contained a giant wheel, the function of which was to steer the vessel, and an assortment of different gizmos he had never seen and had no idea of their function.

When they arrived, the captain got up from his chair, walked over to James, grasped his hand, and said, "My second mate has informed me that you're concerned about your wardrobe regarding my dinner invitation. Your dark suit will do just fine. You will be my guest, and as such, will be welcomed. Anyone offended by your attire may move to another table of their choosing; it is, after all, a large room and they can find seating elsewhere. It is my table and reserved for those I choose to invite to dine with me. They told me you were on a diplomatic mission to escort some dignitary back to the United States, not serve as a clotheshorse for inspection of our snobbish first-class passengers. I will see you and your traveling companion at 6 PM." With that, the captain turned, walked back to his chair, and picked up his binoculars.

Obviously, the conversation was over, so James headed back to his cabin while trying not to get lost in the maze of catwalks. When he got to his cabin, he walked two doors down and knocked on the door of Rhonda's stateroom. She came to the door, smiled, and said, "My, my, Marshal Boutwell, what can I help you with, Sir?"

James didn't know whether Rhonda was out of sorts because of the turbulence of the sea or if it was something he had or hadn't done. With females it was often difficult to know. He ignored Rhonda's tartness and said, "Rhonda, you look lovely. We're invited, I suppose more accurately commanded, to dine with Captain Freberg this evening at 6 PM. You will no doubt turn every male eye in the great saloon and be the envy of every woman. Miss Branceer, it would be my pleasure and honor to escort you to the dinner."

Rhonda smiled and said, "You can be quite the charmer when the urge hits you. Come by at 5:50. That should give us time to get to the table fashionably late. If we get there too early, we will be constantly getting up and down to greet other guests." James made no comment other than to say he would pick her up at 5:50 on the dot.

James picked Rhonda up as promised. She wanted to look at the ocean. Actually, she wanted to time their entrance into the great saloon. They walked to the railing and gazed out across the sea. After a couple minutes, she looked at James, took his hand in hers, and said, "Let's go eat dinner." When they walked into the dining room, the ship's whistle announced it was 6 PM. Everyone was at the captain's table and had already seated themselves. They rose out of their seats when James and Rhonda walked up to the table. There were two unoccupied chairs and James slipped Rhonda's chair out and helped her get situated. He then sat down beside her.

After they had gotten seated, the captain said, "This is Marshal James Boutwell and his traveling companion Miss Rhonda Faye Branceer. Marshal Boutwell and Miss Branceer are going to France to escort a distinguished couple back to the United States." Everyone nodded to James and Rhonda and the waiters began serving food to the table occupants.

After a little chitchat between the table occupants, an older man who said he was a lawyer from New York City, asked, "Marshal Boutwell, what does a deputy U. S. marshal serving on the frontier get paid these days?"

James didn't say anything for a few moments, took a sip of wine, and then responded, "Actually, I don't get paid a salary at all. I do my job out of love for the country." No one said anything for a few seconds, and James added, "And for the $2.00 per warrant that I'm paid for each one I serve." Everyone at the table except the lawyer laughed.

The lawyer was still persistent and asked, "And how many warrants do you serve in the course of your work?"

James was thoughtful for a few moments and replied, "I guess that depends. Some weeks I may serve ten or more. Other weeks, I will serve as few as two or three. It depends on the simplicity of the warrant and the distance I am required to travel to serve it. If you are attempting to establish that I don't make a great deal of money, that's a given. If you are trying to establish that I'm not a proper fit for first class, that's probably also a given. I started life with nothing and still have most of it." Everyone, including the lawyer, chuckled. James continued on, "Good things and bad come with this job. I sometimes can't even control who I'm obliged to break bread with." Rhonda kicked him on his boot and dug her fingernails into his leg.

The lawyer, Marcus Peabody, replied, "I meant no offense, Marshal Boutwell. We must have men who will uphold the law, or our land would resort to violence. The men will have a glass of brandy and a cigar after dinner, would you care to join us?" James thought about telling the lawyer to go jump over the railing, instead, he looked at Mr. Peabody and said, "I would take pleasure in that. I enjoy a good cigar." James got up and followed the three men to the smoking area of the room. Rhonda and the other ladies retired to an area in the main saloon to chat.

As James, the captain, and the other men were enjoying their brandy, the lawyer said, "Marshal, I mean no offense when I say this, but I'm amazed at your obvious education. People have led us to believe western men are uneducated and rather obtuse. I find you to be just the opposite."

James paused a couple seconds and responded, "The west is probably no different from the east. There are educated men and illiterate men in the West. There are men who came west out of a sense of adventure or to make their fortune. And there are those who came to escape their past and get a new start. I suppose what I'm attempting to articulate is that people are people. Their relative wealth, clothing, and status may distinguish them, one from another, but we all share the human experience. In my case, I became self-educated for the most part. I read every book I can get my hands on." James paused for a few moments, and continued, "I wouldn't trade my lifestyle for yours, as I'm sure you would have no interest in trading yours for mine. I've heard it said that it is a lucky man who loves his work. If so, he never has a job. I love what I do and hope it makes a difference." The lawyer and the other men stood, clapped, and said, "Bravo. Well said." James stood, and shook hands with each of them.

Rhonda's confab with ladies went equally well. All the women were significantly older than Rhonda and there was some initial frostiness and resentment, but her wit and charm quickly won them over. All in all, it had been a most enjoyable evening for James and Rhonda. After the after-dinner drinks and a cigar, James and Rhonda strolled down the railing and watched the rolling waves. Rhonda tip-toed, kissed James, and said, "I'm so proud of how you handled yourself with those stuffed shirts. They were complimenting you as they picked up their wives. I know this isn't your cup of tea, but you held your own with this crowd."

The seas calmed somewhat, and the rest of the ocean crossing went well. They docked at La Havre and got Rhonda's two small valises and steamer trunk carried to the dock. A Gendarmerie nationale official, who spoke passable English, met them as promised. He had a small wagon with which to take them to their hotel. After getting them settled in, he said he would return the following morning at 8 AM to pick them up. James and Rhonda ate in the hotel dining room and went to their rooms to retire for the evening.

The next morning James met Rhonda at her door and said, "We need to get this little formality out of the way before we escort the Breedloves. I need to swear you in as a deputy U. S. marshal."

Rhonda laughed and said, "You have to be kidding."

James only replied, "Raise your right hand and repeat after me." After he had sworn Rhonda in, he handed her a well-worn deputy U.S. marshal badge, which she should always keep in her purse. He then said, "Technically, we have no authority until we get back on United States soil. But the status as a deputy marshal will protect you should you have to shoot someone."

The same gendarmerie official picked them up at the hotel at exactly 8 AM and took them to a government building. A distinguished-looking gentleman, wearing a fancy uniform, greeted them, and asked them to sit. It was August 13, 1874, and the ship was to leave for the United States the following morning. The official explained there was no formal extradition request or agreement as pertained to Curtis and Marisa Breedlove, they were returning of their own volition. They would have to reaffirm their decision to return to the United States before the French authorities would permit them to board the ship. With the formalities out of the way, the official said he would have the gendarmerie official take them to meet the Breedloves.

Chapter 22

The same gendarmerie official took James and Rhonda to the Hotel d'Angleterre where Curtis and Marisa Breedlove were staying while in Paris. The facility impressed James and Rhonda. They were awe-struck by the grandeur of the building. The gendarmerie official acted as a tour guide for a few minutes and told them some interesting information about the famous hotel.

****

The Hotel d'Angleterre is one of the oldest intact buildings in Paris. In the late 18th century, the building was the location of the British Embassy and took its name based on that function. The Hotel d'Angleterre was planned to be the location for the signing of the historic Treaty of Paris, which recognized the independence of the fledgling colonies from England. On September 3, 1783, Benjamin Franklin arrived to sign the document on behalf of the colonies, saw the Union Jack displayed, and refused to set foot on British sovereign territory. This required the signing to be moved to a neutral location. The treaty formally ended the American Revolutionary War.

****

James, Rhonda, and the gendarmerie official met the Breedloves in a sitting room off the main lobby of the hotel. The gendarmerie official made the introductions and left the room so that James and Curtis Breedlove could discuss the details of their trip back to the United States. Rhonda and Mrs. Breedlove, Marisa, sat at a sidebar. Rhonda explained to the lady that she was along to accompany her and serve as her companion while they were on the ship. Rhonda said that her function was to allow Marshal Boutwell to devote 100% of his attention to providing security for Mr. Breedlove. The Breedloves were in their sixties and appeared to be in relatively good health. Apparently, French food had agreed with them both, and they seemed to be just a little large for their apparel. Curtis Breedlove was a portly man with a round face. Marisa was small in stature, pleasant, but seemed slightly reserved.

Mr. Breedlove explained that there were individuals who didn't want him to appear in front of a congressional hearing and might well attempt to intercept him and do him harm. In fact, there had already been a covert attempt to kidnap him while he and Mrs. Breedlove were in Paris. United States marshals, who had been assigned to a protection detail, had thwarted that effort. Unbeknownst to Mr. Breedlove, the U. S. government had assigned two men to always follow him to serve as bodyguards. Only when they intercepted the kidnappers did they reveal their presence. While he appreciated the Americans interceding on his behalf, it was disconcerting to realize that there were forces which intended to prevent him from returning to the United

States. But, on the other hand, given the gravity of the information he intended to deliver to congress, they were correct to anticipate an attempt on his life. James never asked why Mr. Breedlove was so urgently needed in the United States and the gentlemen never offered an explanation.

James didn't think knowing what was so important about Mr. Breedlove would make any difference in his task, so he didn't ask. And in all likelihood, Mr. Breedlove wouldn't have told him. He asked Mr. Breedlove if the two men were around the hotel when he came through the lobby. Mr. Breedlove said there were four different men, two would be around, but unobtrusive, anytime he and Mrs. Breedlove were outside their hotel rooms and about in Paris. Satisfied that he had all the information he needed, James shook hands with Curtis Breedlove, and said he and Rhonda would be at the hotel at 7 AM to accompany them to the ship. James excused himself, and he and Rhonda left the hotel with the French official.

As they were riding back to their hotel, James asked Rhonda how her conversation with Mrs. Breedlove had gone. Rhonda replied, "Mrs. Breedlove seems like a nice enough lady. She is concerned about her husband and nervous regarding the impending ocean crossing. I assured her it was as bad as she feared but that we would weather the adventure."

James and Rhonda walked around Paris, or at least walked around within a few blocks of their hotel, had a nice lunch, and went back to the hotel. Rhonda said that she would need about twenty minutes to freshen up, and they would then catch a coach to the Louvre. Since they only had the one day in Paris, she felt that the Louvre would be the best thing to see. A horse-drawn taxi picked them up in front of their hotel and took them to the Louvre. They spent the afternoon looking and looking. James had been less than excited about visiting the museum, but he had to admit that they had filled the Louvre with interesting things. The paintings and other artwork were impressive. Perhaps Rhonda's sophistication was rubbing off on him.

When they finished their tour of the Louvre, they walked out of the museum, hailed a taxi, and went back to their hotel. They had dinner together in the hotel dining room and walked up the staircase to the corridor leading to their rooms. Rhonda looked at James and said, "Would you like to come into my room for a while?"

James smiled and said, "There is absolutely nothing I would rather do, but I won't. I care for you very much and if I enter your room, it will be as your husband, not your lover." He bent over kissed her lightly on the lips and said, "Good night. I'll call for you at 5:30 AM. By the time we have breakfast, it will be time to pick up the Breedloves and get to the ship."

Rhonda opened the door and entered her room. She wasn't sure if she was elated that James had rejected her offer or if she was insulted because he had refused her offer. But, if she had held any doubts about how deep her affection for James was, his most recent action convinced her. He loved her and cared more about her virtue than his physical needs or desires. He was the man she would marry. She had no doubt about that.

They were up at 5 AM, had Rhonda's luggage taken to the lobby, went into the dining room, and ate a light breakfast. The concierge had secured them a large carriage which would carry four people, all the bags, and two steamer trunks of Rhonda and Mrs. Breedlove. When they got to the d' Angleterre, the Breedloves were in the lobby. Mr. Breedlove wasn't traveling as light as James. Still, he only had three bags. Marisa Breedlove easily had as many bags as Rhonda, and with her steamer trunk, perhaps more. But this was basically a permanent move for them so naturally she would be taking most of her apparel. They got everything loaded in the carriage and entered the conveyance. James noticed two large men entering a taxi, obviously to follow their carriage.

When they got to the dock, seamen began carrying the bags and two steamer trunks aboard the ship. The two men who had followed them stood to the side and surveyed the crowd. As Mr. and Mrs. Breedlove started up the gangplank one of the two men walked over to Marshal Boutwell and said, "They're all yours now, Marshal. Good luck. They seem to be nice enough people, but someone doesn't want them to get to the states. Be careful."

After they got the Breedloves and themselves settled into their rooms, James looked at Mr. Breedlove and said, "I don't want to infringe on your privacy, but the U. S. government has entrusted me to make sure you arrive at New York harbor unharmed. To accomplish that task, I will have to ask you not to leave your cabin unless I accompany you. The same will go for Mrs. Breedlove. Miss Branceer will always need to be with her when she leaves your cabin. Obviously, we can't protect you if you go wandering around the ship without our knowledge. Again, we don't want to infringe on your privacy, and we'll give you both your space, but we must be fairly close to intercept anyone who might want to do you harm."

Curtis and Marisa Breedlove said that they understood and would do their best to make James and Rhonda's job as easy as possible. And they did with one exception!

On the third evening of the voyage, right after dinner, James and Rhonda escorted the Breedloves back to their room. Around 10 PM, James was uneasy, got up, opened the door to his room, and saw Curtis Breedlove standing by the railing smoking a cigar. As he was watching Mr. Breedlove, a large man came walking up and pulled out a knife. James lunged out of the door and rammed his shoulder into the man knocking him against the railing. The man attempted to get up and James pulled the Webley revolver out of his pocket and put a large dent in the man's head. Somehow the unconscious assassin rolled under the bottom restraining rope and fell into the sea. Mr. Breedlove looked at James but didn't say a word. James lit a cigar and said, "Beautiful night, Mr. Breedlove. I thought we agreed you would stay in your room and let me know if you wanted to take a walk."

Mr. Breedlove said, "My apology, Sir. I just never envisioned being attacked standing by the railing in front of my cabin door. I'm comforted by the fact that you are obviously accomplished at your job. You have my solemn word that I will knock on your door, day or night, if I want a cigar or to go for a walk. And I'll make sure Mrs. Breedlove contacts Miss Branceer if she wants to go outside the cabin for any reason." James thanked Mr. Breedlove and watched him until he entered his cabin.

James, Rhonda, and the Breedloves received an invitation to dine with the captain on the return voyage and accepted. Everyone at the table was open regarding their jobs and such but Curtis Breedlove and James Boutwell were evasive when queried. Mr. Breedlove just said he was on a diplomatic mission and James said he was his traveling secretary. The evening ended with brandy and cigars and Breedlove having very little to say. After an hour or so of listening to meaningless chit chat, James and Mr. Breedlove were ready to return to their cabins. Rhonda and Mrs. Breedlove seemed relieved to have been rescued by the men. The four of them walked out to the railing and watched the waves for several minutes. None of them said anything and they just enjoyed the cool night breeze and the gentle roll of the waves. After some time, they walked to their cabins, bid each other goodnight, and retired for the night.

James kept a close eye on all the passengers he encountered, but nothing further happened, and everyone seemed to be whom they appeared to be. On the night of the seventh day at sea, James and Mr. Breedlove were standing at the railing after dinner enjoying a cigar. Mrs. Breedlove hated the smell of cigar smoke and Rhonda wasn't crazy about the odor either, so they restricted their smoking to the saloon, or along the railing.

As they were smoking and enjoying the evening breeze, a woman walking along the railing approached them. She was approaching from Mr. Breedlove's side. James looked around and seeing no other individuals, changed places with Curtis. When the woman walked past James, she turned, and aimed a small pistol at Mr. Breedlove. Marshal Boutwell lunged, grabbed her wrist which held the weapon in that hand, lifted her arm so vigorously that he jerked her off her feet, and the pistol discharged harmlessly into the air. The woman swung at James with her other arm but missed as he leaned back. At this point James figured he wasn't being confronted with a lady, so he hit the woman square on the nose with his fist. She was out like a light with a very unattractive and bleeding nose and fell to the deck. Like the man, she somehow rolled under the restraining rope and fell into the ocean.

Mr. Breedlove just looked at James and said, "Beautiful night isn't it. I guess we should go in for the evening. I've been thinking, would you be so kind as to make the arrangements to have Mrs. Breedlove's and my meals brought to our cabin tomorrow. I think we will be more comfortable if we stay inside until we leave the ship." James thought that was an excellent idea and said he would take care of it.

The last day of the voyage went without incident. They arrived at the dock at New York harbor right after dark. After arranging for all the luggage to be taken off the ship, James, Rhonda, and the Breedloves disembarked. When they arrived at the end of the gangplank two obviously heavily armed men met them and showed their U. S. marshal badges. The older of the two men thanked Marshal Boutwell for keeping the Breedloves safe and asked if he had any problems. All James said was "No, not really. It was actually a pleasant trip." Curtis Breedlove looked at James but made no comment.

Chapter 23

James and Rhonda said their goodbyes to Mr. and Mrs. Breedlove. Curtis Breedlove shook hands with James and thanked him for keeping him safe. Marisa hugged Rhonda and said that she would miss her company. They stood on the platform and watched the Breedloves and two U. S. marshals board a train headed for Washington, D.C. After getting a taxi, going to the hotel, exchanging the steamer trunk for Rhonda's valises, and returning to the train depot, they caught a train bound for Texas. The only ones who weren't happy to be going to Texas were the red caps that were loading all of Rhonda's bags. It was the morning of September 22, 1874.

After several delays, layovers, stops for wood, coal, or water, and changes of trains, James and Rhonda arrived in Dallas on September 27, 1874. James had sent a wire the day prior and had Maggie notified of their arrival time, or more accurately, the train they would be on. They arrived late, which was normal. Maggie and Rhonda embraced tearfully. They were elated to see each other again. James just stood off to the side. You would have thought they hadn't seen each other for years. Women!

After getting all of Rhonda's bags loaded in Maggie's wagon, James said that he had to send a telegram to the attorney general. The ladies said they would see him the next day for breakfast. After they rode off in the wagon, James headed for the telegraph office. He dictated a wire to the attorney general. *"Sir. Package delivered safely to NYC 9/22."* He told the telegraph operator he would be in the courthouse for an hour or so checking warrants and attending to other paperwork. In about an hour, the telegraph operator delivered a wire. James unfolded and read *"Thanks. GWC AG."* James just smiled. The response was curt but much better than if he had failed at his mission. He gathered up a handful of warrants, folded them, and slid them in his vest pocket. Tomorrow after breakfast he needed to get to work.

James got up early, took care of his bodily functions, and walked to the livery. He saddled his horse and rode to Maggie's. He stabled his horse behind the building and walked in the back door and down the hallway and into the foyer. Maggie and Rhonda were sitting at the kitchen table drinking coffee. Rhonda got up, poured James a cup of coffee, and placed it on the table. James sat down and placed his hat, crown down, on the table. Maggie said, "James Boutwell. I appreciate you taking care of my little girl. I know you are a capable and decent man but I still worried while the two of you were gone." James responded that he thought it would be unnatural if a mother didn't worry about her children. Maggie smiled slightly and made no comment.

Ling brought three plates. He had laden two plates with bacon and eggs, biscuits, and molasses. The third contained something that looked like bird food and a piece of dry toasted bread. Rhonda felt

James' eyes on her and said, "All that food on the ship caused me to gain some weight, I'm going to take it back off." James considered saying that it wasn't the food, but rather the amount of it that Rhonda ate but decided silence was the best plan.

While they were eating breakfast and chatting, approximately 1,300 miles away, Curtis Breedlove was leaving the Willard Hotel.

****

The Willard Hotel, affectionately known as "The Willard," began as a series of small houses on Pennsylvania Avenue, which were built in 1818. The houses were purchased by Henry Willard in 1847. Mr. Willard combined the buildings to make one four-story hotel. Some history had been made in the Willard place before Willard purchased the buildings. Henry Clay introduced the Mint Julep for the first time outside of Kentucky at the hotel's famous Round Robin Bar in 1830. The bar is still in working order today. Abraham Lincoln stayed in the Willard for ten days prior to his 1861 inauguration. Dr. Martin Luther King, Jr. polished his "I have a dream" speech while sitting in the Willard lobby.

****

Mr. Breedlove left the Willard and walked towards his horse-drawn carriage with a bodyguard on either side of him. As he was about to step into the carriage, a shot rang out. The bullet from a Sharps .52-70 carbine entered Curtis Breedlove's side, exited, and hit the marshal on his left side. The shooter escaped in the confusion. They took Mr. Breedlove and the marshal to a room on the ground floor of the hotel.

After some confusion, they brought a doctor to the hotel who attended to both men. At 9:30 AM on September 24, 1874, the attending physician pronounced Curtis Breedlove and Marshal Samuel Biglow dead. What exactly Mr. Breedlove was to testify about was a closely guarded secret. Even in the Washington, D.C., environment where no one could keep a secret, no one seemed to know what Breedlove had known that was so important. There was a lot of speculation, but no facts came forth. Between Curtis Breedlove's death in 1874 until mid-1876 thirteen notable Americans died under mysterious circumstances. Four committed suicide with a pistol, two drowned in the Potomac River, five had heart attacks, and two fell out of windows and broke their necks. Some of the dead were in Washington, D.C., at the time of death. Some were in New York City, and some were visiting foreign countries when they met their death.

James learned of Curtis Breedlove's murder when he was skimming through the third page of the Dallas Weekly Herald. It saddened him to learn that they had assassinated Mr. Breedlove. Curtis Breedlove seemed like a decent man. James started serving the Dallas warrants. Most were notifications

211

to appear in court as a witness, or to answer some minor charge. Most involved little if any danger. The important thing was James got paid $2.00 for each warrant he served. By the end of the day on September 25, James had served twelve warrants and three summonses. In two-and-a-half days he had made $30.00.

Now that he had a little cash in his pocket and wouldn't have to go into his bank savings from the horse sales and other money he had accumulated, he decided it was time to get back to the investigation of Thelma Goodrich. The girl's uncle had led James to believe that he knew who had killed his niece, but apparently wanted to make a game of finding her killer. Once the second prostitute was found dead in Fort Worth, James pretty much figured it had to be Mayor Scruthers or Reverend Smith who had killed both prostitutes.

James was sitting in the Dallas Café having lunch when Doctor Pickwell walked in, nodded to the marshal, and sat at an adjacent table. In a couple minutes the owner of the café walked over, sat a cup of coffee in front of the doctor, and said, "Doctor Pickwell, I'm sure sorry to learn that your sister died. It's a shame you had to go to Fort Worth for her funeral and missed the 4th of July celebration." After overhearing the comment, it added a new twist. James decided his best source of information was Maggie Branceer, so he got his horse and headed out for Maggie's place to find out how the good doctor might fit into the investigation.

James didn't plan on staying long so he just hitched his horse to the post in front of the building and walked in the front door. Rhonda was sitting in the foyer reading a book and stood when James came through the door. She said, "Well, I wondered when you would miss me and ride out."

James smiled and said, "I always miss you when I'm not with you, but this trip is to talk to your mother."

Rhonda smiled and said, "Is it customary to talk to the parent first?"

James turned red and started down the hallway. When he got to Maggie's office door, he met her coming out and said, "Maggie, I've got a couple questions for you if you have time."

Maggie smiled and replied, "I always have time for you, James Boutwell. Come on in, take a load off, and ask away."

James didn't know how to beat around the bush, so he just dove in. "Maggie, how well do you know Doctor Pickwell? Who came to Dallas first, you or him? And how long has he been examining your employees and treating them?"

Maggie said, "Whew, that's a lot of questions. Let's see, I've known Doctor Pickwell since he came here in 68 or 69, I'm not sure which. How well do I know him? I guess about as well as most people who I see from time to time. Most of our interaction has centered on the girls. He started examining and treating the girls when necessary, in 1870 as best I recall."

James was thoughtful and asked, "Did Doctor Pickwell get overly attached to any of the girls? Did he ever use the services of one of the girls?"

Maggie said, "I probably shouldn't say this because all I have is my female intuition, but I think Doctor Pickwell was taken with Thelma Goodrich. He seemed nervous in her presence, and I kinda suspected there was more than a doctor patient relationship between the two of them. I never observed him doing anything inappropriate. It was just a feeling I had."

James thanked Maggie and walked out of the office. He stopped and talked with Rhonda for a few minutes, kissed her on the cheek, and walked out to his horse. He mounted and took off for Dallas. He had a doctor to talk to.

When James got to town, he went straight to Doctor Pickwell's office, dismounted, tied his horse to the rail, and walked inside. Doctor Pickwell was sitting in his office chair writing on a pad. He looked up when James walked in the door and said, "Marshal Boutwell, what can I do for you today?"

James looked at Doctor Pickwell and said, "I understand you were in Fort Worth on the 3rd and 4th of July of this year."

Doctor Pickwell replied, "Yes, yes I was. I went to attend my older sister's funeral. I hope you aren't here to tell me that's a crime."

James ignored the sarcasm and said, "Are you aware that a Fort Worth prostitute was killed sometime on the night of the 3rd or early morning of the 4th?"

Doctor Pickwell said, "I think I heard something about the murder while I was at the depot in Fort Worth waiting to board the train to come back to Dallas. Is there a point to these questions, Marshal?"

James asked, "Did you have more than a doctor patient relationship with Miss Goodrich?"

Doctor Pickwell was taken off-guard and said nothing for a few seconds, and then said, "I grew quite fond of Thelma; and yes, we went beyond a normal doctor patient relationship. I'm not proud of getting involved with the girl, but I fell in love with her. I know it was stupid, but I did, nonetheless. But I certainly didn't kill Thelma Goodrich. She never rejected me, nor was she ever unkind. She just had no interest in a relationship beyond what we were doing. As far as the prostitute in Fort Worth, I know nothing about it beyond what people told me."

Marshal Boutwell thanked Doctor Pickwell for his time and got up and left the office. If James was any judge of humans, Doctor Pickwell was telling the truth and seemed sad over the death of the girl. Marshal Boutwell rarely misjudged people, and he hoped that he had the doctor pegged right.

****

Unbeknownst to Margaret Dever or Marshal Boutwell, a cowhand who had been sweet on Marie

LaPierre when she worked in the same vocation in Abilene, Texas, found out she was in Fort Worth and went there to find her. He had tried to see her at Dever's place. She had asked him to leave and promised to meet him in an alley down the street from the brothel. Miss LaPierre had told the man she had no interest in him, they argued, and she turned to walk back to the brothel. The man choked her to death with her own scarf. The cowboy later was overcome with grief concerning murdering Miss LaPierre and took his own life. So much for the connection between the deaths of the two prostitutes, but Marshal Boutwell had no way of knowing the facts surrounding Miss LaPierre's murder.

****

When James left the doctor's office, Marshal Framington's deputy came running up and said, "There has been a killing on the Bar T and Sheriff Baggett is gone out of the county for a few days. Marshal Framington said you needed to go out to the ranch and arrest the killer."

James looked at the deputy and asked, "And who exactly is the killer?"

The deputy said, "A cowboy on the ranch named Lamar Frederickson. He got into an argument with Mark Johnson, the foreman, over some work that hadn't been done. Johnson fired him and as the foreman walked away, Frederickson shot him in the back and killed him. Frederickson got his gear together and lit out before anyone could stop him."

James walked to the jail where Marshal Framington was sitting at his desk. James said, "Let Fred Benton out of the cell. I need him to help me track down this Frederickson fellow."

Marshal Framington said, "Apache Fred is being held for the murder of the Goodrich girl. I can't let him out of jail." James walked over to a peg on the wall with the jail cells key hanging on it, took the key, and opened Benton's cell. James told Fred to go the livery and get his horse. They would get on the trail of the killer as soon as James could get his saddle horse and the packhorse ready.

Marshal Framington said nothing at all.

Chapter 24

Fred Benton came into the livery as James was finishing putting provisions in the panniers. He walked up to James and said, "I'm sorry to hold you up, I had to make a stop at the privy. I don't mind helping you track this man, but I'll have no part in killing him if it comes to that."

Marshal Boutwell said, "Fred, I may need your help in tracking the man and I may not. I just thought you might like to get out of that cell and stretch your legs for a day or two. Just help me make sure I don't lose him if we end up in rough country. I'm sure you're more than a fair tracker."

Fred said, "I'm not the best, but the best taught me, Indians."

James decided he would go by Maggie's and let Rhonda know he would be gone a few days. He stopped in front of the building and dismounted. Fred said he would stay with the horses. James walked into the foyer and found Rhonda reading. Maggie came out of the kitchen and said, "Marshal Boutwell, I need to talk to you. I'd forgotten something you might need to know. I guess I'm getting old or have too much on my mind." James walked into the kitchen and sat down. Maggie said, "This may be nothing, but a man named Himey Swinton came over here two or three times from Fort Worth and asked for Thelma each time. I could kick myself. He is tied up somehow with Reverend Smith and the church.

Church folks probably wouldn't approve of his using a brothel, so he rides over here in his buggy. Unless he just bumped into a church client from here that uses my establishment, and knew him, people wouldn't know what he's up to. I'm sorry I didn't think of this sooner."

James didn't say anything as the information had him lost in thought. He suspected that Maggie's priority was protecting the identity of her clients. The men who frequented her establishment were men of substance from Dallas, Fort Worth, and the surrounding area. They weren't individuals who would want their name associated with a brothel. He could understand Maggie's reluctance to share information with him regarding her clients. He wondered how much more she might have failed to share with him.

He thanked Maggie, walked into the foyer, and sat down beside Rhonda. He explained that a man had murdered Mark Johnson, the ramrod at the Bar T ranch. He said he would be gone for a few days until he tracked down the man who had committed the murder. Rhonda kissed James, stood, and said, "Be careful. I don't want to lose my handsome marshal." James blushed slightly and walked out to the waiting horses and headed for the Bar T ranch.

When James and Fred arrived at the ranch house, Ike Turnbull met them. He greeted them coarsely and said, "I want Frederickson hanged. He shot Mark in the back because he was mad about being fired. He shot him like a dog. Mark was a good man, and Frederickson was a piss poor cowhand at best. The irony of this is that I would have fired him a couple times, but Mark asked me to give him another chance. If I'd followed my instincts, Mark would still be alive."

James said he understood and wanted to know the direction Frederickson had taken when he fled the ranch and that a description of the man would be helpful.

Turnbull said, "Frederickson is a tall drink of water, probably 6' 2" or so, sandy colored hair, has a pock-marked face, and walks with a slight limp from where a steer stepped on his foot. He headed east. He talked about his family being in Shreveport, Louisiana, so I expect he headed there figuring a lawman wouldn't follow him that far or out of Texas. I guess he figured Sheriff Baggett would run out of steam once he saw he was leaving Dallas County. Baggett's a good man but he stays within his jurisdiction." James thanked Turnbull and he and Fred turned their horses towards the east.

There wasn't much in the way of horse or cattle traffic to the east of the ranch house and Fred picked up the tracks of a lone rider after about thirty minutes of crisscrossing back and forth as he slowly rode along. Fred would slowly ride and then dismount when he saw something in the grass that caught his attention. Once Fred found the trail left by Frederickson, they started following the distinctive tracks left by his horse. They held their horses to a slow trot. There was no reason to hurry as it was about 185 miles to Shreveport, Louisiana. James was prepared to follow Frederickson all the way there if necessary, but he sure hoped it wouldn't be.

James figured Frederickson would feel more comfortable after he got to Willis Point. That would put him in Van Zandt County, and in his mind, out of the jurisdiction of Sheriff Baggett. Willis Point wasn't much, just a small post office for the ranchers and homesteaders in the area, a trading post and rustic saloon. Fred knew the place well and said that Frederickson might just stop there to drink and buy some supplies. Normally, cowpunchers didn't have much money. Frederickson had left without getting his pay, so he was likely to look for a little work in exchange for some grub and supplies. Anyway, Willis Point would be a good place to stop if you were on the run.

Frederickson had a full day's head start on James and Fred. It was around fifty miles from the Bar T to Willis Point, so the killer would already be there or perhaps had already passed through. Fifty miles was more than James wanted to travel in one day, so they stopped in the late evening and made camp. James asked Fred to take care of the horses and he would get some bacon and beans and a pot of coffee going. Thirty minutes later Fred had the horses picketed and eating grass, and he and James were eating beans and drinking coffee. After their second cup of coffee they turned in for the night.

The next morning, slightly after daybreak, they were on the trail again. They only took time for a cup of coffee which James brewed while Fred took care of getting the horses ready to travel. During the early afternoon, they arrived at Willis Point. As Fred had said, it wasn't much. There were two horses outside the trading post and saloon. James dismounted and started for the door and Fred led the horses to a hitching rail.

Once inside, James gave his eyes a few moments to adjust to the dimly lit room and then walked to the rustic bar. A large fat man walked up and said, "What'll it be, Mister?"

James looked at the man and said, "Only a little information. I'm looking for a tall man, sandy hair, pock-marked face, and who walks with a limp. Has he come through here yesterday or earlier today?"

There were two men sitting at a table drinking. One of them said, "You a lawman? We don't much cotton to lawmen."

James turned his body slightly to keep the men in his line of sight, ignored the man's comment and said, "Barkeep, I think I asked you a question."

Before the bartender could respond the man at the table who had made the comment stood and started to say, "I said." And that was as far as he got.

James pulled his pistol and walked to the table and stuck the revolver right against the man's nose and said, "I doubt you would be badly injured if I shot off a round into your brain pan, but it may come to that." James reached down and pulled the man's pistol out of its holster, looked at the other man and said, "Take your pistol out real slow."

As the second man was taking his pistol out James heard a gun cock. He turned just in time to see the bartender with a shotgun and then a blur as a large knife flew across the room and embedded in the man's right arm and protruded out the other side. The impact of the knife caused the bartender to drop the shotgun and it went off when it hit the floor. The 00 buckshot pellets tore a hole in the bar. James struck the talker along the side of his head with the man's pistol. He then picked up the second man's pistol from the table and stuck it in his waistband.

James walked back to the bar and saw the bartender was as white as a ghost. The big bowie knife had made a mess of his arm. As he was looking at the bartender, Fred walked up, grabbed the man's wrist, and jerked the knife free. The bartender passed out and fell to the floor bleeding like a stuck hog.

James walked over to the last man still standing and said, "Guess it's kinda up to you to answer my question. Has the man I described been through here?" The man couldn't get the answer out fast enough and confirmed that the man James had described had been in the saloon the night before, slept in the stable, and rode out east earlier this morning.

James smiled, thanked the man, and said, "See, that wasn't all that difficult. If the bartender had just answered my question, he wouldn't have a sore arm and your friend wouldn't wake up with a sore head." James unloaded both pistols and threw them behind the bar. He then walked around the bar, opened the breech on the shotgun, and took out the spent and live shell. He walked out of the building, mounted his horse, and said, "Fred, thanks a lot. You saved my bacon back there. I got a little careless. I know to never turn my back on anyone. That was dumb on my part." Benton neither agreed nor disagreed, and said nothing at all, just nodded his head, and they began riding east.

Fred said there was another trading post and makeshift saloon about thirty miles farther east. If they hurried on, they could probably get there around 7 PM. Fred was confident that Frederickson was headed for the trading post. There was nothing between Willis Point and Maxom's trading post. James and Fred took off holding their horses to a brisk canter. Slightly after sunset, they arrived at the trading post, which was to become the modern-day Mineola, Texas.

Fred stayed with the horses and James entered the saloon. As he walked through the doors, James saw a pock-faced man sitting at a table by himself. James looked at the bartender and said, "You have food here?"

The bartender said he could rustle up some chili and cornbread. James replied, "Bring three plates if you please and a bowl of chopped onions." The bartender looked confused but walked away through a door.

James pulled his pistol and walked to the table the pock-marked man was sitting at and said, "Keep your hands where I can see them, stand up, and take off your hat." The man complied. James saw the man had a full head of unruly sandy hair. James said, "It would be the biggest coincidence in history if you were anyone other than Lamar Frederickson." James tossed a set of manacles on the table and said, "See how these fit." While Frederickson was putting the cuffs on his wrists, James relieved him of his pistol and stuck it in his waistband. James hollered. "Fred, come on in. I've got us some hot chili on the way."

James, Fred, and Frederickson ate their chili. James and Fred enjoyed the chili. Frederickson seemed to have little appetite but got a few bites down. After they finished eating, James took Frederickson to the makeshift stable that was attached to the main building. He threw the man's saddle and a ground cover down and cuffed him to a post. Fred got the saddles and panniers off their animals, put down their ground covers, and the three men turned in for the night.

The next morning Fred got the horses ready to travel, and James kept an eye on Frederickson as he saddled his horse. As Frederickson was saddling his horse, James said, "Just so you know, if you try to get away, I'll have my friend here hamstring you. Then you will have to drag yourself to the gallows instead of just limping."

Frederickson was sniffling and said, "I let my pride and temper get away from me. Johnson was a decent sort, I just thought I deserved another chance and lost my temper."

James replied, "You'll need to tell all that to the judge, but I suspect you're gonna be hanged no matter your excuse. Killing can't be condoned."

James, Fred, and the prisoner set out for Dallas, spent one night on the trail and got to the Dallas jail mid-day the following day. James got Frederickson locked up while Fred took the horses to the livery and got them situated.

Marshal Framington was sitting at his desk and asked, "Boutwell, where's your other prisoner. You didn't let him escape, did you?" James just ignored the marshal and told the jailer that Fred Benton would be along as soon as he got the horses taken care of.

James decided he needed to take a ride to Fort Worth. But right now, what he wanted was a nice T-Bone steak at Maggie's, and then to get a decent night's rest.

Chapter 25

It was September 30, 1874, and James had been investigating the death of Thelma Goodrich off and on for about three months. Trips to Austin, going after criminals, and the France trip had interfered with his investigation. Still James was persistent despite the delays. The killer of Thelma Goodrich was out there walking around, free as a bird, and James was committed to finding him. Himey Swinton was to be his next interview.

James rode to Maggie's, had a steak dinner, a couple of drinks, and spent the evening with Rhonda. As they sat in the foyer and talked, it suddenly occurred to James that Rhonda would soon return to Denver. He said, "Rhonda, when are you leaving to go back to Denver?"

Rhonda replied, "Actually I'm not going back, or at least, I'm not going back anytime soon. I have a fellow I'm quite interested in, and I want to see how that works out before I make any commitment to return to Denver."

James said, "I've got a few years on you, I travel all over Texas chasing wanted men, and occasionally I have to take extensive trips to pick up or escort a prisoner. On any given day, I'm just one bullet away from being injured or dead. Is that the type of man you want to hang your future on?"

Rhonda replied, "James Boutwell, I think I have been in love with you all my life. Certainly not by name, but I've loved everything you represent since I was a little girl. I realize that being married to you would have its days and nights of worry. But the truth is I would worry about you all the time anyway and wouldn't have you coming home to look forward too. Yes, I'm younger than you, but I'm not a little girl, and I know my own mind. It wouldn't be fair to another man if I didn't marry you, because I would always be thinking of you."

James was thoughtful for a few moments and then said, "I've never met a woman I had any real interest in before I met you. I'm concerned about our age difference, not so much now, but in a few years. Be that as it may, how would you like to marry me?"

Rhonda's response was "Yes, yes of course I'll marry you. When would you like to tie the knot?"

James replied, "I'll leave that to you and your mother. If you're happy with the arrangements you make, it'll be fine with me. I've got to make a trip to Fort Worth tomorrow to talk to another man about the Goodrich killing. If all goes well, I should be back tomorrow evening before dark, or at least I hope so. We can discuss this wedding more then, but I will really be happy with whatever you and Maggie decide."

Rhonda said, "I'll tell Momma. I think our marriage will please her and will relieve her mind to know that you and I are going to be together. She has a lot of respect for you. Be careful James, someone doesn't want you to solve this mystery of who killed Miss Goodrich."

228

James was thoughtful for a couple moments, and then said, "No, Rhonda, I'll tell Maggie. I owe her that respect." With that James turned and walked down the hallway to Maggie's office and knocked on the doorjamb.

Maggie looked up from her paperwork, saw James, smiled, and said, "Come in. What's on your mind?"

James was just a little nervous but got right to the point. "Maggie, Mrs. Branceer, I've asked Rhonda to marry me and she has accepted. I've come seeking your blessings."

Maggie got up, walked around her desk, embraced James, and said, "James Boutwell, I couldn't be happier. I know you will be a wonderful husband to Rhonda and a great father to my grandchildren." She took James arm and walked to the foyer. When they arrived, she looked at Rhonda and said, "Rhonda, I couldn't be more pleased. You both have my blessings to marry."

James and Rhonda embraced, kissed, and James got on his horse and rode back to Dallas.

The next morning James ate breakfast, walked to the livery, saddled his horse, and headed out to Fort Worth. He was riding through a shrub-filled arroyo with large boulders scattered randomly around, seemingly without rhyme or reason. As he was daydreaming about his upcoming marriage to Rhonda, he felt a sting in his right upper arm, followed immediately by the sound of a rifle shot.

James grabbed his rifle from its scabbard, rolled out of the saddle, and came off onto the ground on his left side of the horse. He looked at his arm and saw the bullet had taken a divot out of the flesh. Other than producing a good bit of bleeding, it had done no real damage. James figured the drygulcher was ahead of him, but he couldn't be sure. He wriggled across the ground and got behind a boulder. He hoped he had guessed right about the direction the shot had come from. After a few minutes James heard a horse whinny ahead of him and to the right, perhaps thirty yards off. He had guessed right, the drygulcher was ahead of him, and had been waiting for him to ride into the trap.

Whoever had shot at James wasn't a very good shot, or he was just trying to scare him off. Thirty to forty yards should have been an easy rifle shot, and James should be on the ground bleeding from a sizeable hole in his body. Instead, he was just nicked. James started easing from rock to rock being careful not to allow himself to be visible for more than a second or two. As he got nearer to where the sound of the horse had come from, he heard someone scolding the horse as he was having difficulty trying to mount the animal.

James ran towards the sounds and when he cleared the boulder, he saw a man just starting to ride away. James shot into the air, levered another round into the chamber of the rifle, and hollered, "If you put spurs to that horse, I'll shoot you out of the saddle." The man stayed still in the saddle and put up both hands. The man's back was towards James so he couldn't tell who the man was for sure, but he had a suspicion.

James said, "Keep your right hand raised where I can see it and get off the horse to your left. If you do anything fast, you will be toting a hunk of lead." The man dismounted and turned towards James.

****

Meanwhile, at Maggie's, Rhonda and her mother were sitting in Maggie's office discussing wedding plans. Rhonda remembered a newspaper she had saved that had pictures of wedding dresses in it. She excused herself and went upstairs to get the paper. She found the paper in a few minutes and as she started down the stairs, heard a loud voice say, "You bitch, you'll either give me all the money in that safe or I'll put a few cuts on your face until you cooperate. Then I'll slit your throat with this here Bowie knife."

Obviously, Rhonda's mother was in terrible trouble. Suddenly, she realized that she still had the pistol James had given her. He hadn't asked for it back, so she put it in the top drawer of her dresser when she unpacked from the trip to Paris. She retreated to her room, took the Webley pistol out of the drawer, checked the cylinder just as James had taught her, and saw that it contained five cartridges.

Rhonda started down the stairs as quietly as she could. Thankfully, all the girls were in their rooms, either reading or perhaps napping, so the building was eerily quiet. She heard her mother loudly say, "You son of a bitch, you may get the money, but you won't get far with it. There is a U.S. marshal here in Dallas and he'll nail your hide to the wall."

Rhonda heard the man say, "How is he going to know who robbed you? Do you think I'm stupid enough to leave here with you alive? If you cooperate, I'll take the money and leave with just you dead. If you put up a fuss, I'll kill every person in this brothel, starting with your daughter."

Rhonda was running everything James had taught her through her mind: don't think about shooting, don't talk to whoever you think you need to shoot, and don't hesitate. Rhonda tip toed down the hall to her mother's office. When she got to the office door, she rehearsed in her mind what she would do. "Cock the hammer, step through the door, point the pistol with both arms extended towards the target, and squeeze (don't jerk) the trigger. If the target keeps moving, keep cocking the hammer and keep shooting!" When Rhonda came around the door opening, her mother was leaned over trying to get the safe open. The man was about five feet from Rhonda and slightly to her left. The man saw her movement out of the corner of his eye and started turning. Rhonda started shooting! The man fell with the first shot but still held the pistol in one hand and a large knife in the other. Rhonda took a step forward, cocked the hammer, and fired again. The second shot hit the man in the face and tore off a large hunk of his jaw and exited the side of his neck. He still held the gun and knife. Rhonda cocked the pistol again and fired. The third bullet struck the man in the chest area and he started gasping for breath. The man's body relaxed and both weapons fell from his hands. Unbeknownst to Rhonda, the first bullet was fatal. The man's reflexes just hadn't told him to drop his weapons before she fired the second and third shot.

Rhonda and Maggie ran to each other, and both broke down in tears. After sobbing for a few minutes, both women regained their composure. When they looked past the body, Ling was standing in the doorway with a shotgun in his hands.

Maggie said, "Ling, please saddle a horse, or take the buggy and go to Dallas and find Sheriff Baggett. If he isn't around, I suppose you can find that worthless Marshal Framington, but I doubt he will come because we aren't within the city limits. Sheriff Baggett's deputy will be fine. I'm sorry I'm so scatter-brained and babbling. I know I'm not making sense. I'm just a little upset."

Ling said he would take the buggy, go to Dallas, and find either the sheriff or his deputy and bring one of them back.

Everyone in the building had either been awakened or startled by the gunshots. All the girls were in the foyer huddled together and wondering what had happened. Maggie and Rhonda came down the hall with Rhonda still holding the pistol in her hand. She had completely forgotten she was even holding the weapon. When Maggie walked into the foyer all the girls were talking at once, but they all asked essentially the same question, "What was all the shooting about?"

Maggie asked all the girls to sit down and then explained that a man had tried to rob her and planned to kill her. She went on to say that Rhonda had heard the commotion and came to her aid. Fortunately, Marshal Boutwell had trained Rhonda well in how to use a firearm while they were preparing for their trip to France. Maggie laughed a very nervous laugh and said, "If I didn't know better, I would have thought she was an accomplished gunfighter."

Rhonda walked out of the foyer and up the stairs to her room. No matter the necessity, killing a human being was a dreadful thing to do, just dreadful. She knew she would see the dying man with a large portion of his face missing for a long time. She lay on the bed and sobbed until she finally fell asleep.

After explaining what had happened, Maggie asked them to go back to their rooms and went to check on Rhonda. She quietly opened the door to Rhonda's room and saw that she was crying. She decided to leave her alone and let her deal with killing the man in her own time.

In about an hour, Ling returned with the deputy. Sheriff Baggett was still out of the county and wouldn't be back for a couple days. The deputy had the forethought to bring a wagon with which to haul the body back to Dallas. Just as a perfunctory act, the deputy checked to make sure the man was dead. He was. With Ling's help, he dragged the man out of Maggie's office, out the rear door, and got him loaded on the wagon.

Once they loaded the body into the wagon, the deputy walked back into the building and told Maggie that he had seen the man hanging around Dallas for the past few days. He went on to say that there would have to be a coroner's inquest, but it would only be a formality. It was obvious that the man had attempted to rob her and that her daughter had come to her defense. The man's knife and pistol were still lying on the floor next to the body when the deputy arrived. That substantiated the fact that the man had attempted to rob Maggie.

The deputy left with the body. Maggie went into the kitchen to have a cup of coffee and try to steady her nerves. She could only imagine how upset her daughter was. The ordeal had shaken Maggie to her core. She knew she kept too much cash on hand, but she didn't want people in Dallas to know her business. The reality was, whether she had a great deal of money in the safe or a little, a thief would assume it was a gold mine.

Maggie and Ling got some soap and cold water and headed to her office. They had a bloody mess to clean up. She certainly didn't want Rhonda

to see all the blood and gore and relive the shooting.
Once was enough to have to deal with the incident!

Chapter 26

James walked towards the man, relieved him of his pistol, slid it under his own gun belt, and slapped him across the face with the back of his hand. The man lost his balance due to the impact of the blow and fell. James reached down, grabbed his arm, and jerked him erect. The man's saddle had a large opening in front of the crotch area, which was the style of some saddles. James placed a cuff on the man's right wrist, pushed and prodded the other cuff through the hole and across the horse's withers, and cuffed the man's left wrist. Having immobilized the man, presuming he couldn't walk off carrying a horse and saddle, James walked back and got his horse and led it to the man's mount.

James took the reins of both horses and led them well off the trail. The man was stumbling and whining but didn't fall. When James came to a large rock laying on the ground he stopped, laid the reins of the man's horse on the ground, and rolled the large rock on top of the leads. He then pulled on the straps a couple times to make sure they wouldn't come loose. James was satisfied that the horse's reins were secure.

James walked around the man's horse, pulled the rifle out of its scabbard, and ejected all the shells onto the ground. He looked at the man and said, "As I'm sure you knew or have guessed I'm on my way to Fort Worth. I'll be there a few hours, maybe more, and will ride back with or without a prisoner. Unless I forget where I left you, I'll pick you up on my way back to Dallas. If I were you, I'd stand real still. If you scare your horse and he managed to pull loose from the rock that is holding the reins and runs off, you'll either have to run very fast or get dragged to death."

The man pleaded, "Please, Marshal Boutwell, don't leave me like this. Some people in Dallas hate me. If one of them came along they might abuse me, or even kill me."

James smiled and said, "If I had my druthers, I'd leave you out here for the buzzards. But, if anyone harms you, I'll be sure and track him to the ends of the earth or until I have something better to do. Whichever comes first? You're going to have a few hours to meditate, use the time wisely." James mounted his horse and rode off towards Fort Worth.

When James got to Fort Worth, he stopped at the city marshal's office, and asked where he could find a man named Himey Swinton.

The marshal said, "Reverend Swinton is the territorial elder for the church. I guess you would find him at the church unless he's out taking care of some church business, visiting the sick, or escorting his wife to the mercantile store. She seems to like to go there at least once each day to keep current on the gossip around town."

James got directions to the church, walked out of the marshal's office, mounted his horse, and headed in the direction of the house of worship.

When he arrived, he saw a middle-aged man sitting on a bench under a large tree, enjoying the shade, and reading a book. James dismounted, walked towards the tree, and when he got to within a few feet of the man, said, "Are you Reverend Swinton?" The man stood, offered his hand and replied that he was.

James said, "I'm Deputy U. S. Marshal James Boutwell and I have a few questions to ask you." Marshal Boutwell waited a few moments and assessed Swinton's reaction to his statement. He observed a noticeable twitch at the corner of the man's mouth. James didn't know what the reverend was upset about, but the minister didn't like the way the conversation was starting out one bit. James said, "Reverend Swinton, I'm not very good at beating around the bush, so I'll get right to the point. I'm in Dallas investigating the murder of a prostitute named Thelma Goodrich. Do you know the woman?"

Reverend Swinton looked around in all directions and said, "Marshal, this could ruin me and my ministry if any of this conversation got out. I'm married and I'm quite sure my wife wouldn't understand. And I'm equally sure that my congregation and superiors wouldn't be forgiving of my lapse of fidelity. I'll answer your questions, but I would hope you keep the content of our conversation confidential."

James replied, "I'm here for answers. If you've done nothing wrong, or at least nothing wrong regarding man's law, you've got nothing to worry about. I'll either arrest you today or thank you

239

for your candor. Either way, I'll ride back to Dallas this afternoon. I'll warn you ahead of time. You don't know what I know about your exploits, so I suggest you not lie to me. Not even a little!" Marshal Boutwell waited a few moments for his words to sink in and said, "Now, back to my question, Reverend Swinton, did you know Thelma Goodrich?"

Reverend Swinton looked at the ground for a few moments and replied, "Yes, I knew her, but not in a biblical sense. On one of my visits to Dallas, Reverend Smith introduced me to her. Miss Goodrich was only a go-between and made the arrangements for me to visit with another of the young ladies named Jenny Lee who worked in the establishment. That was my only contact with the poor unfortunate soul."

James said, "Thank you. And you're sure you never used the services of Miss Goodrich?" Reverend Swinton reaffirmed that he hadn't. James continued, "Where were you on June 20 and 21 of this year? And where were you on July 2 of this year?"

Reverend Swinton breathed a sigh of relief and said, "I was in Denver, Colorado, for a church meeting from June 18 through the 22. As far as I know, I was in Fort Worth during the entire 4th of July holiday period. I can check my calendar to be certain, but I have no memory of going outside of town that entire week. That's the time when the unfortunate young woman was killed here in Fort Worth if I'm not mistaken."

James said, "I'm presuming that if I send a wire to your church association in Denver that they will confirm your presence at the meeting and the dates."

Reverend Swinton replied, "Absolutely. I'm sure you're judging my conduct, but as a matter of explanation, my wife and I have grown apart over the years. Our children are grown and gone, and she has no interest in the sexual aspect of marriage. That doesn't make what I did acceptable but at least I had a reason for my transgression."

James said, "I didn't ride to Fort Worth to judge you, just to ask you some questions. I expect we all have a way of justifying things we probably shouldn't do. But you needn't justify your decisions to me. Thank you for your honesty. I'll be heading back to Dallas now." James shook hands with Reverend Swinton, mounted his horse, and headed back east. He had a prisoner to pick up about halfway to Dallas.

About halfway through Fort Worth, James suddenly realized he was hungry. The ride and the excitement of being shot, while ever so slightly, had given him an appetite. As James rode down the street, he saw the Cattlemen's Café, stopped, hitched his horse, and went inside. He ordered chile rellenos and coffee. As he was eating, the thought of leaving the man attached to his horse's saddle crossed his mind. But someone would discover the body with his manacles on the man and put two and two together. Besides, the government had commissioned him to uphold the law, not administer its justice. Unless the drygulcher resisted arrest, James was honor bound to take him in for trial.

James rode out of Fort Worth headed towards Dallas. About halfway on his ride he came to the spot where he had left the drygulcher. He rode back into the rocks and found the man standing by his horse. He had wet his pants and immediately started whining about having to piss his pants when James rode up. Otherwise he seemed to be alright. James undid the left cuff and pulled it through the opening in the saddle. He reattached the manacle to the man's wrist and told him to get on his horse. The ride to Dallas was uneventful.

When James and the man rode into Dallas, the gawkers came out in droves, pointing, and whispering. When they arrived at the jail, James helped the man off his horse and guided him into the office. The jailer was sitting at a desk reading an old newspaper. When he looked up his mouth fell open.

James looked at the jailer and said, "Lock up this piece of trash. If he isn't here in the morning when I stop by to check on my way to breakfast, you will need to pack your clothes because you will share the cell with this piss-ant and be headed for prison. Do you understand?"

The jailer said, "Yes, Marshal Boutwell, you can bet your bottom dollar he will be in that cell anytime you need him."

James thanked the jailer, walked over to Fred Benton's cell, and asked him how he was doing.

They talked for a few minutes and James said, "The circuit judge will be here in a few days. Your luxurious accommodations here at town expense will end when I get an opportunity to speak with him. Lamar Frederickson and your new cell mate will stand trial when he sets a court date."

James walked out and crossed the street to the Dallas Hotel, washed up, put on a clean shirt, and headed for Maggie's. When he came back down the stairs into the lobby, the entire room was abuzz. Everyone was talking about the Branceer girl killing the man who tried to rob her mother. James walked over to a man and asked, "Did he say the Branceer girl. Do you mean Rhonda, Maggie's daughter?"

The man said, "I don't know if her name is Rhonda, but according to Sheriff Baggett's deputy, Maggie Branceer's daughter shot a man who was attempting to rob and planning to kill her mother. The deputy sheriff said she walked into her mother's office as cool as a cucumber and shot the man three times. According to the rumor mill, you taught the girl how to shoot and gave her the pistol she used to kill the bandit."

James didn't say anything. He walked out, mounted his horse, and started for Maggie's. When he arrived, it was slightly after sundown and there were no horses tied to the rail. He rode around back, stabled his horse and walked in the back door. He walked down the hall and into the foyer. When he peered into the kitchen, Maggie and Rhonda were sitting at the table drinking coffee. Rhonda jumped up, ran to James, and put her arms around him. She was softly crying, and said, "It was horrible, James. Killing that man was horrible. I never, in my wildest dreams, considered how killing a man would make me feel."

Maggie looked at James and said, "It's a funny world. I didn't want Rhonda to go to Paris. If she hadn't gone with you to France, she wouldn't have needed to know how to handle a pistol. If you hadn't trained her in how to shoot, she wouldn't have known how to use the pistol. And, if she hadn't kept the pistol, she wouldn't have been able to protect me. So, you see a confluence of events saved my life. I'm glad I'm gonna be around to attend your wedding, and hopefully, get to play with grandchildren."

James smiled and replied, "I'm glad you're gonna be around too, Maggie." James paused, looked at Rhonda, and said, "Killing a human being is a horrible experience and there certainly isn't anything about it to enjoy. Even the worst of men have someone who cares for them. There are times when we must respond to evil in a harsh and lasting fashion. If you hadn't acted swiftly and calmly, your mother would no doubt be dead and perhaps you as well. You're quite a woman. I'll try to remember not to make you mad." As he was finishing, Peaches came strolling in and rubbed against his boot. He didn't know what it was about that darn cat; he didn't even like cats.

Rhonda asked Ling to put a steak on the fire for James and poured him a cup of coffee. She turned to James and said, "Well tell me about your day!"

James laughed and went over the high points of his day's activities and finished by saying, "I thought my day was exciting, but it dims in comparison to yours." They talked for a bit, kissed, and James rode back to Dallas, stabled his horse, and hit the sack.

Chapter 27

Marshal Boutwell finished his breakfast and walked to the jail. When he walked in the door, he went to the cell where Fred Benton was sitting on a cot, and asked, "Fred is there anything you need to do around Dallas? Maybe go the barbershop for a hair trim or get a bath."

Fred thought for a couple seconds and replied, "I guess a bath wouldn't hurt and I'd like to check on my horse at the livery. Can I have a couple hours?"

James said, "Sure Fred, go ahead, and take as long as you need. I'll probably still be here when you get back. Just be careful and stay out of the saloon. There are some folks that may still think you killed the woman." Fred got up, put on his hat, and walked out of the jail. James had told the jailer he didn't need to worry with locking Benton's cell door, that way he wouldn't have to bother the jailer when he needed to go to the privy.

James turned to his two prisoners and asked, "Have you both had breakfast?" Both men nodded in the affirmative. James asked the jailer to let him into the cell which contained the drygulcher. After the cell was unlocked, Marshal Boutwell walked inside and took a seat in a chair he had taken from the office. James looked at the man for a few moments and began, "You are in a heap of trouble. Judge Hiram Blackstone will be here on Monday, October 5. He will hold the trial for you and the other back-shooter. The judge will no doubt order Lamar Frederickson to be hanged. As it stands, you're looking at probably ten years in the territorial prison for attempted murder. I think I can make a pretty good case that you murdered Thelma Goodrich. If Judge Blackstone is convinced by my circumstantial evidence, Fredrickson will have company on the gallows."

The drygulcher just sulled up with tears running down his cheeks and said nothing.

James got up and walked out of the cell, turned to the drygulcher, and said, "I'm going back to the Dallas Café for another cup of coffee. I'll be gone for ten or fifteen minutes. Why don't you decide if you have anything you would like to tell me when I get back?" James enjoyed his coffee and chatted with a couple men who were eating breakfast. After a few minutes he returned to the jail.

Marshal Boutwell walked back into the cell, sat down in the chair, and said, "Well, are you ready to talk?"

John Earl Framington, city marshal of Dallas, was more than willing to talk. In fact, when he started, it was like the floodgates had opened.

****

James rode to Maggie's, hitched his horse, and walked in the front door. Rhonda greeted him with a kiss and said, "Marshal, let's have some lunch. Ling fixed some chili just the way you like it."

As they were eating, James smiled at Rhonda and said, "You do understand that we won't have Ling once we get settled in Austin. I don't know what I'm getting myself into. I've never seen you cook anything. I hope you can cook well enough that I can still keep my gun belt on without it falling to my knees."

Rhonda threw her napkin at James and said, "I can cook. I'm not as good at it as Ling, but I have other qualities you might enjoy that Ling can't provide. I think you will be all right. I guess I'll have lots of time on my hands to practice while you are off chasing outlaws." James thought it best to just be quiet, so he continued working on his bowl of chili. Rhonda continued. "Momma and I figured that Saturday, October 17, would be a great day for our wedding. Momma suggested that the wedding should be soon so you wouldn't get cold feet and ride off into the sunset."

James replied, "Not much chance of my changing my mind. It's taken me a long time to find someone I wanted to spend my life with. I doubt anything will change my mind now." James stooped, kissed Rhonda, and said he had to get back to Dallas. When James rode up to the jail, there was a crowd of onlookers. James thought, "Oh, shite, what's happened now?"

When Marshal Boutwell walked through the crowd and into the jail, Doctor Pickwell was attending to a gunshot wound the jailer had received. Doctor Pickwell turned to James and said, "He'll live. Marshal Framington won't." When James walked to the cell, he saw a bullet hole right between the marshal's eyes and a pool of blood on the cell floor. Framington had confessed to attempting to kill Marshal Boutwell on two occasions and had implicated the man who had paid him to kill the marshal. But, without the now dead marshal's testimony, it would only be James' word against the man who had hired the marshal to kill him.

Marshal Boutwell turned to Doctor Pickwell and asked, "When will I be able to question the jailer?"

The doctor said, "I'll finish in a few minutes and you can have at it. The jailer was lucky. The bullet just grazed his head. I suppose he moved his head at just the right instant. The killer no doubt thought he was dead. Framington apparently didn't move his head as well as the jailer." As the doctor finished his statement, Fred Benton walked into the jail. James cursed his decision to let him out of jail. It would be helpful if he could identify the killer. But, on the other hand, the assassin might have killed Fred had he been in his cell.

James walked to Frederickson's cell and asked, "Did you see the man who shot Framington?" Fredrickson said he had seen the shooting but had never seen the shooter before. He gave James a loose description of the killer. James turned to the jailer and asked, "Can you identify the man who killed Framington? By the way, what's your name?" The jailer replied that his name was Melvin Merkel, and he had never seen the man before either. Merkel provided a reasonably good description: dark hair, scar above his right eye, and a dark mustache and chin whiskers. James knew he couldn't be so lucky but asked anyway, "Did you hear Marshal Framington tell me the name of the man who hired him to kill me?" Merkel said he was sorry, but he hadn't. When James turned to Frederickson, the back-shooter said that he hadn't heard the confession either. The fact that neither man had heard the confession wasn't surprising as Framington had talked in hushed conspiratorial tones when he was telling James his story. At times it had been difficult for James to hear every word.

James realized it really didn't make any difference whether the jailer had heard the confession or not. The man who hired the killer didn't know Merkel hadn't heard or that he couldn't testify against him. Once the man who had hired the killer realized that the jailer was alive, the killer would try again. Fred Benton had been in the bathhouse when the shooting of Framington had occurred. If Frederickson had heard anything, no one would believe him anyway. People would think he was just trying to save his own skin. Melvin Merkel was the key to flushing out the killer.

James looked at Fred Benton and said, "This may seem a little strange since technically you are a prisoner, but I need your help. I need to deputize you as a deputy marshal and leave you here to protect Mr.

Merkel until I can make arrangements for a place to hide him until the trial next Monday."

Fred didn't seem very excited about being a lawman, especially after the way the marshal had treated him, but he consented. Fred Benton made it very clear he was only doing this as a favor to James. Marshal Boutwell swore Fred Benton in as a deputy U.S. marshal, walked over to the weapons rack, and removed a coach gun. Merkel told him the shells were in the top desk drawer. James took out two, opened the breech, inserted the shells, and handed the scattergun to Fred. James told Benton that he would be back in an hour or so and to not let Merkel out of his sight. Whoever had tried to kill him would try again.

James went to the sheriff's office and discovered from the deputy that Sheriff Baggett still hadn't returned from his trip. He asked the deputy if he knew of an empty house that he could use for a couple days. The deputy thought for a minute or so and said, "There is an empty house on the edge of Dallas as you head north. The owner left Dallas a few weeks ago to go back east and left it unlocked so people could see it if they were interested in buying. I see no reason you couldn't use it. It's about a quarter-mile from here."

James went to the livery, got a small wagon and horse, and went to the jail. James talked to Fred for a couple minutes and then walked Merkel out to the wagon and had him lay in the back. He started north to find the house the deputy had described.

When he arrived at the house, he took the jailer inside. James and Merkel pulled down the window curtains and sat back in a couple chairs in the living room. James cautioned Merkel to keep the lanterns trimmed very low so that a shooter wouldn't be able to see his silhouette as he walked past a lamp and get a clear shot.

James looked directly at Melvin Merkel and explained that he was using him for bait. After it got dark, Fred Benton would take to side streets, making sure he wasn't seen, and enter the house from the back. After Benton got settled in, James was going to leave and return the horse and wagon. James assured Merkel that Benton was more than capable of protecting him. The idea was to make the killer think the jailer was alone in the house, and hopefully he would enter to finish the job. The problem was James and Fred would have to guard Merkel until the killer tried again, or until Monday, October 5, whichever came first.

About an hour after dark, Fred knocked on the back door of the house. James made sure it was Benton and opened the door. After Fred entered, James locked the door and propped a chair against the doorknob. James cautioned Fred and Merkel they weren't to use the outhouse. There was a chamber pot in each bedroom. They were to use them and never leave the house. James would go to the café, get one large meal, and deliver it in a basket. Two meals would let the cat out of the bag and reveal that the jailer was being guarded. James told Fred that he was sorry he couldn't spell him from time to time, but the killer had to be convinced that the jailer was alone. James promised he would come and stay long enough that Fred could get a nap for a couple hours.

Merkel was in place. The plan was in place. And Fred had secured the back entrance. They were as ready as they could be.

James had cautioned Fred that killing the assassin wasn't an option. Unless Fred had to kill the man to save his own life, the killer had to be taken alive. Without the killer's cooperation and testimony, the man behind all the killings would go Scot free.

****

Scot free, also sometimes written as scotfree, scot-free, and incorrectly as Scott free has been around since the 11th century. The term has nothing to do with the Scottish people or the Dred Scott case. Scot is from the Old Norse word "skot" which means something to the effect of payment or contribution. In English, scot translated to tax.

The term Scot free was first used regarding municipal taxes levied by Edward the Confessor in England. Each person in a village would be obligated to pay a share of the scot (tax), which was called their lot. Those who didn't pay, such as the poor or the wealthy, that could get out of paying were in effect "scot free."

****

On Saturday morning October 3, James delivered a half dozen biscuits, a large bowl of molasses, and a mug of coffee to the house. There were cups, saucers, and knives and forks in the kitchen, so they were all fixed up. James walked out of the house, mounted his horse, and said loud enough to be heard up and down the street "Keep the door locked. I'll bring you more food this evening."

James rode out to Maggie's to let Rhonda know that he wouldn't be able to come and see her until the first of the week. He was trying to catch a killer. Actually, it was two killers. Rhonda said that she understood. And that she might ride into Dallas late Sunday morning and eat lunch with James if she could find him. James said he would rather she stay at Maggie's. The man who ordered the killing of Framington suspected James knew he was the man who had been ordering the killings. He might abduct, or more likely, have his assassin abduct Rhonda to get James in a position where he could be killed. If Rhonda stayed out of Dallas, James would have one less worry. Rhonda said she understood and would stay at Maggie's until the ordeal was over.

Confident he had done everything possible to set the trap, James kissed Rhonda, walked out, mounted his horse and headed back to Dallas. The waiting was the hard part. James had to stay close in case he was needed, but well away from the house.

About all he could do was sit around the jail or nap in his hotel room. He hoped this would be over soon!

Chapter 28

James went into the Dallas Café and ordered a large meal, had the food placed in a wicker basket, and took the grub to the house in which they were hiding Melvin Merkel. James sat and visited while Fred and Melvin ate. When they finished eating, James told Fred to take a nap and he would hang around for a couple hours. After allowing Fred to get a little rest, James took the breakfast and dinner utensils, placed them in the basket, and rode off to return the pots to the café.

James went to his room and tried to rest. Taking a nap was impossible because he was restless and worried. This entire investigation in Dallas had been a fiasco from the very beginning. He wasn't used to so much inactivity, so many questions, so many possibilities, and so little in tangible evidence with which to form an opinion. Other than meeting Maggie Branceer and Rhonda, he felt like his entire effort had been a waste of time. Finally, he knew who had tried to kill him on the two occasions and who had hired the two assassins. But he still didn't know with certainty who had killed Thelma Goodrich. He had a pretty good idea, but opinions weren't evidence or admissible in court.

James was in his own element in taking on robbers, killers, and other outlaws. Apprehending outlaws had its inherent danger, but the reality was that most men in the west weren't very proficient with firearms. When it came to returning fire at someone who was shooting back, most men would become so nervous that they would be lucky to hit a barn door. Some probably couldn't hit the barn! In fact, the typical cowboy only carried a pistol to dispense with a longhorn cow if he couldn't handle the animal in any other way or to keep his horse from getting gored by the ornery critter. Once a cowboy got a few drinks under his belt, he would be lucky not to shoot himself in a gunfight.

Investigating something as complex as the killing of Thelma Goodrich, with so many potential killers was more in line with the investigative skills of the Pinkerton Agency. A deputy U. S. marshal had no training in investigative work. Frontier marshals just did the grunt work of capturing killers and transporting prisoners. After the investigation of the killing of Miss Goodrich, it would thrill James to death to get back to his regular duties. James reminded himself that he was the idiot who wired the attorney general and insisted on being placed in charge of the investigation. Sometimes your ego and a big mouth can get you into trouble. Since accepting the commission as a deputy U.S. marshal, James hadn't failed in an assignment. He wondered if this would be the first.

After lamenting his assignment and its results James fell into a fitful asleep. Early Sunday morning, well before daylight, James woke up. He hadn't slept soundly all night and now he was awake. He decided to go to the house he was using to hide the jailer.

Since he wasn't resting anyway, he might as well make sure everything was all right. He decided, since it was less than a mile to the house, to walk and take the back streets to be inconspicuous while getting to the house. He came out beside a house that was catty-corner across the street from where they were hiding the jailer. James pressed himself against the building, looked around the porch, and up and down the street. He saw nothing and started to go back to the hotel. Suddenly, he saw a match light across the street and down a couple of houses.

When James saw the flash of light, he thought it was mighty careless of a killer to give his position away. On the other hand, if the assassin thought he was all alone on the street, he might think it made no difference. And there was also the possibility that the occupant of the house just decided to go out on the porch and have a smoke. Occasionally, James could see the glow of the man's cigarette. Then there was nothing. No movement. No glow of the cigarette.

James was in a good position to watch the house they were using to hide the jailer, so he didn't move. It was the early morning hours of the 4th of October. The moon was changing from the last quarter to a Waning Crescent. There was enough light to see movement, but there was less than half the moon's reflection of the sun's rays. James didn't see anyone open the door to go back into the house. He waited for around a half hour and saw the silhouette of something moving between houses. There wasn't enough light to tell anything about the object other than it was large and no doubt a man. James backed up and went around the back of the house he was using to hide beside. He crossed a little clearing between houses as quickly as he could and took up a position almost directly across the street from the house the jailer was hiding in.

James had no way of knowing if Melvin or Fred were awake. He could intercept the man but catching him walking around early in the morning hours wouldn't prove he was up to no good. And, if by some chance this man wasn't the killer, James would be giving up the ruse he had worked to establish. James saw the outline of the man slowly step up on the porch of the house Fred and Merkel were in. The man stood still for a few moments. There was no light coming from within the house so the man would have nothing to see. In a few seconds James saw another match strike and thought "Why would he be lighting another cigarette?" Then he saw the faint glow of a lantern and said, "Oh, shite."

Before James could move the man kicked open the door and threw the lantern inside. The lantern broke and the wall the lantern hit burst into flames. No sooner had the man thrown the lantern, than he came staggering out the door and fell on the porch. James took off running. When he got to the porch, the killer was lying on his side with a large knife handle sticking out of his chest. Fred's aim had been about perfect. The blade missed the man's lung and heart but sure took all the fight out of the assassin and produced a lot of bleeding.

James stepped on the man's exposed arm, relieved the assassin of his pistol, and put manacles on his wrist. He then rolled the man onto his back, grasped his other wrist, and placed a manacle on it. James ran inside and saw Fred and the jailer beating the wall with blankets trying to get the fire put out. After a couple minutes, the fire died down and then went out. James asked Fred to go and roust out Doctor Pickwell. After telling the doctor there was a wounded man who needed medical attention, Fred went to the livery, got the wagon, and came back to the house.

In ten minutes or so Fred drove up with the wagon. They got the killer loaded in the wagon and James and Melvin sat on the back as Fred drove to the doctor's office. They got the man out of the wagon and into Doctor Pickwell's office and placed him on his back on an examination table. When James looked at the man in the office's light, he saw the man had dark hair, a scar above his right eye, and chin whiskers. He had his man!

Doctor Pickwell said they all could leave. He would take care of the wounded man. James said, "Reckon not." He asked Fred to escort Melvin to the jail and to lock themselves inside. He would stay with the killer.

Doctor Pickwell was able to pull the Bowie knife out of the man and get most of the bleeding stopped. He bandaged the wound and said, "He's all yours, marshal. I didn't give him any laudanum, so he knows what's going on. I'll just take a walk while you question him."

James looked at the man and said, "Do you have a name?" The man said nothing. James pulled his pistol, flipped it, and caught it by the barrel and said, "Are you sure you don't want to talk to me?" The man said nothing. James brought the butt end of the pistol briskly down on the man's nose. Blood and snot flew in all directions.

The man's eyes started tearing, and he said, "You broke my nose. But you'll have to do better than that to get anything out of me."

James said, "Oh, I can do a lot better if you force the issue. Court goes into session tomorrow. So, I've got all day and night for us to visit. I may not influence you to talk but I guarantee you, you'll never be able to walk to the gallows when I get through with you."

The man said, "They're gonna hang me whether or not I talk, so why would I want to tell you anything?"

James said, "I've always heard that confession was good for the soul. And I guarantee you that confession will be good for your physical body. You can walk to the gallows while you're whistling Dixie or you can go to your death with every part of your body aching and bleeding, and your teeth in a sack. It's your choice."

The man said, "I'm called Dell Hardaway. A man named Jonathan Scruthers contacted me and hired me to kill you. When I got here from Fort

Worth, he had changed his mind, and told me to go to the jail and kill the jailer and Marshal Framington. I guess the jailer moved his head at the instant I fired. Framington was dead when I walked out of the jail."

James said, "Killers aren't smart, but I didn't think you were dumb enough to suffer needlessly. You made a good choice for you and me both." James wondered to himself if he would have been able to torture the man. The past few years of arresting the worst of the human species had hardened him. Still, James was by nature a compassionate man and hated needless violence. Anyway, Hardaway talked so what James might have done was a moot point.

James walked to the door and hollered for Doctor Pickwell. When the doctor answered, James asked him to go to the jail and get Melvin Merkel and Fred Benton and bring them to the doctor's office. When everyone was in the room, James asked Hardaway to repeat his confession. When Hardaway finished telling his story, James asked Fred to take the assassin to the jail and lock him up. He told Melvin he could go to his small sleeping quarters behind the jail.

It was about 6 AM and James saw no reason to wait until later in the day to arrest Mayor Scruthers, so he headed to the mayor's house. When he got to the house, he banged on the door. In a couple minutes Mayor Scruthers said, "Who is it?"

James responded, "It's Marshal Boutwell. I'm here to arrest you for conspiracy to commit murder and the murder of John Framington." The mayor said to give him time to get dressed and he would be out. James figured that Scruthers would either get dressed and surrender or commit suicide, so he waited on the porch to see which it would be. In a few minutes the mayor came out the door dressed in his suit and said, "You're wasting your time, Marshal. You won't be able to prove anything." James didn't say anything. He checked to make sure Scruthers wasn't carrying a weapon, pulled a set of manacles out of his vest pocket, and placed them on the mayor's wrists.

They walked down the street to the jail. When James opened the door and steered the mayor inside, Scruthers saw the assassin locked in a cell, and partially collapsed on the floor. When he composed himself a little the mayor stood and said, "I didn't tell him to kill anyone. It will just be my word against his. People in Dallas will believe me, you'll see. I'll walk free on Monday."

Chapter 29

The Honorable Judge Hiram Blackstone arrived on the noon stage from Fort Worth on Sunday, October 4, 1874. Sheriff Baggett and Marshal Boutwell met the stage and greeted the judge. James knew the judge by name but had never met him. J. L. had met him several times through the years. Judge Blackstone was known as a no-nonsense arbiter of the law. He would show leniency if there were some type of mitigating circumstances, but if it was a killer who killed without just cause, Blackstone's solution was always the same. He would order the man hanged.

Sheriff Baggett and Marshal Boutwell escorted Judge Blackstone to the Dallas Café where they had lunch and discussed the four cases that the judge was to hear. They shared no details or evidence. That would have to wait for the trials. They merely summarized the charges that would be levied against each man. Judge Blackstone's ears perked up when he was told that one of the accused was the town's mayor. The judge said nothing, but he had absolutely no sympathy for a government official who committed a crime.

Once J. L. and James finished their meal, they sat and watched Judge Blackstone eat and eat. The judge was a large man, perhaps 300 pounds and stood a full six feet tall. When he sat down to eat, he was as serious as he was on the bench. Finally, about the time J. L. and James finished their third cup of coffee, the judge slid his chair back. J. L. and James slid their chairs back and started to get up. The judge said, "If my memory serves me correctly, they serve a fair-sized piece of apple pie in this place?" J. L. and James watched as Judge Blackstone polished off two large slices of apple pie. Now that the judge was fortified until supper, he went to the Dallas Hotel, and got a room. He didn't forget supper. At 7 PM, Judge Blackstone walked back to the Dallas Café, had three bowls of beef stew, and finished off all the apple pie in the café.

The next morning, Judge Blackstone got dressed and went back to the Dallas Café. Six eggs, several slices of bacon, a half dozen biscuits, about a pint of molasses, and four cups of coffee later, the judge was ready to preside over the trials. The trials were to be held in the Cattlemen Saloon. When James, J. L., and Judge Blackstone walked into the saloon, a table had been positioned for the judge and chairs arranged for the jury. Two more tables were provided, one each for the prosecution and defense. The crowd that was gathered to watch the proceeding had to stand as there was no other seating available other than the witness chair.

Judge Blackstone settled into his chair, unpacked his valise, and placed a well-worn law book and Bible on the table. He struck the tabletop with his gavel and said, "Court's in session. The gallery will keep their mouths shut during the proceedings." There were two lawyers in the courtroom. One represented the prosecution and one for the defense. Judge Blackstone looked at Sheriff Baggett and said, "J. L., let's get on with it. Bring the first accused."

Sheriff Baggett left for a few minutes and returned with Fred Benton, aka, Apache Fred. The young prosecutor stood and said, "Your honor, if it pleases the court, I would like to drop all charges against Mr. Benton. He has been in an unlocked cell and could have walked off at any point. He's helped Marshal Boutwell on at least two occasions. In fact, Marshal Boutwell deputized him on at least one occasion, and there is absolutely no evidence to support the charges."

Judge Blackstone said, "If there was no evidence against Mr. Benson, why was he in jail? Who was the idiot that kept him locked up?"

The young prosecutor replied, "That would be the late Marshal Framington Your Honor."

Judge Blackstone said, "Well, Mr. Benton, you're free to go or you can stay and watch the proceeding. If you're going to be a witness, I must ask you to wait outside the saloon. Please accept the court's apologies for the way you have been treated. And, thanks for your service in helping Marshal Boutwell." The judge looked at the prosecutor and said, "OK, what's next on the docket?"

The defense attorney stood and said, "Your honor, all the defendants have elected to waive a jury trial and throw themselves upon the mercy of the court."

Judge Blackstone replied, "So be it. The jury is excused." The men elected to stay and watch.

J. L. left and returned after a few minutes with Lamar Frederickson. The sheriff led Frederickson to the defense table where he sat down. The prosecutor called Isaac Turnbull as the first witness. Turnbull turned out to be quite colorful and was cautioned twice by Judge Blackstone for his language. Three cowhands who had seen the murder were called, and all three told the same story. Mark Johnson, the Bar T foreman had fired Frederickson, and when he turned and was walking away, Lamar shot him in the back. The defense lawyer asked each man a cursory question or two but there simply wasn't much in the way of defense for the cold-blooded murder. Judge Blackstone told Frederickson to stand up and asked him if he had anything to say in his behalf.

Lamar Frederickson had tears in his eyes and said, "What I done was wrong, horribly wrong. I got mad cause Johnson fired me and shot him without thinking. I wish I could take it back."

Judge Blackstone looked at the young man and replied, "It's a sad thing when a man lets his temper cause him to do a horrible thing. Lamar Fredrickson you will be hanged by the neck until you are dead on Thursday, October 8, at 9 AM, and may God have mercy on your soul." With that, Judge Blackstone said, "What's next?" Sheriff Baggett left with Frederickson and a few minutes later returned with Dell Hardaway.

Judge Blackstone looked at Hardaway and said, "You look like you've been through the mill. You're upright, so I guess you're able to stand trial." The jailer, Doctor Pickwell, Fred Benton, and Marshal Boutwell were all called as witnesses. They had all heard Hardaway's confession concerning killing Marshal Framington and trying to kill the jailer. Each recalled Hardaway's confession almost word for word. Again, the lawyer who was serving as the defense had little to say.

Judge Blackstone told Hardaway to stand. The judge said, "Killing for hire is despicable and loathsome. As far as I'm concerned, this type activity places you at the bottom of the human species. Dell Hardaway, I find you guilty of murder. I will suspend sentencing as I understand you are to be a witness for the prosecution at the next trial." The judge looked at Sheriff Baggett and said, "Bring the last accused please."

J. L. led Hardaway to a seat at the prosecution table and left to get Mayor Scruthers. In a few minutes, Sheriff Baggett returned with Jonathan T. Scruthers, technically still the Mayor of Dallas and a practicing attorney. Judge Blackstone looked at the lawyer acting as prosecutor and said, "Call your first witness." Dell Hardaway was called to the stand and told the court of being hired by Scruthers to kill Marshal Boutwell and then Scruthers had changed his mind and told him to kill the jailer and Marshal Framington. Marshal Boutwell was called and told of Marshal Framington telling him of Scruthers hiring him. The thrust of it was Scruthers had hired Framington to kill Marshal Boutwell by any means necessary. The only caveat was that he wasn't to get caught or implicate Scruthers. Framington hadn't gotten the job done so Scruthers hired Hardaway.

Scruthers acted in his own defense. He objected, saying that Marshal Boutwell's testimony was hearsay. The judge pondered a few moments and said, "Marshal Boutwell is an officer of the court. I'm going to give his testimony due consideration."

Mayor Scruthers took the stand in his own defense. The assembled crowd was murmuring, and Judge Blackstone struck the tabletop with his gavel, and said, "If you folks want to hear Mr. Scruthers testimony, shut up, or I'll have Sheriff Baggett remove you all from this courtroom."

Mayor Scruthers said that Hardaway was lying and Framington had lied to Marshal Boutwell about being hired to kill him on two occasions. Another possibility was that Marshal Boutwell was lying and Framington hadn't told him anything. Framington was dead anyway so what he might have said to Marshal Boutwell couldn't be corroborated and was therefore of no consequence, anyway.

When Mayor Scruthers finished his testimony, Judge Blackstone asked if there were any other witnesses. The prosecution had nothing further. Judge Blackstone said, "Sheriff Baggett and Marshal Boutwell filled me in on what's been going on in Dallas these past weeks. Obviously, all this involves the death of a young woman in some manner. Mr.

Scruthers, before I pass sentence on you, I want to ask you a question. This community has been subjected to the senseless murder of a young woman and needs closure. Did you kill one Thelma Goodrich? The penalty for killing or having two people killed will be no more severe than one."

Mayor Scruthers said, "Your Honor these men are lying. I've asked no one to kill anyone on my behalf. If Hardaway killed Framington, it was his idea. I had nothing to do with it." Scruthers never responded one way or the other concerning the death of Thelma Goodrich.

Judge Blackstone told Scruthers to stand and said, "Jonathan Scruthers, I find you guilty of murder, and conspiracy to commit murder in that you hired agents to kill on your behalf." The judge told Hardaway to stand. When Hardaway was standing next to Scruthers, the judge continued, "Mr. Scruthers you're obviously an intelligent man, but also lacking in personal courage. Hiring someone to kill on your behalf is the mark of a man of weak character and lack of mettle. I don't want either of you reprehensible creatures to soil the gallows before that young cowboy is hanged. He doesn't deserve to die accompanied by the likes of the two of you. Dell Hardaway and Jonathan Scruthers, you both will be hanged on Thursday, October 8, at 9:30 AM, and may God have mercy on your souls."

With that Judge Blackstone said, "Is there any other business to be heard by this court?" No one said anything, so the judge struck the tabletop with his gavel and said, "This court is no longer in session, and you can reopen the bar."

The judge stayed overnight at the Dallas Hotel. Marshall Boutwell said he would like for him to join them at Maggie's Pleasure Palace for a T-Bone steak. The judge smiled and said he would be more than happy to accompany him. J. L. and James looked at each other and wondered at the smile. They knew the judge loved food, but they suspected there was something else at work here.

James got a buggy from the livery and picked up Judge Blackstone from the hotel at 6 PM. They made the short trip to Maggie's and entered the foyer. Maggie and Rhonda were standing in the foyer when they arrived. James started to introduce Judge Blackwell to Maggie, but she said, "Hiram and I have known each other for a few years. How are you, dear?" The judge blushed slightly but smiled and replied he was fine. Rhonda kissed James, and he introduced her to Judge Blackstone. The group headed for the kitchen for a private dinner.

While they were eating James told the judge that he and Rhonda were to be married at 2 PM on October 17, and that he knew the judge had a busy schedule, but if he could perform the wedding ceremony they would be pleased and honored. James hadn't said anything to Rhonda or Maggie, but he didn't want Reverend Smith to do the ceremony. The judge allowed that it would be his pleasure to perform the wedding ceremony for Maggie's daughter, and he would adjust his calendar to be there.

After dinner, James and the judge prepared to return to Dallas. Maggie said, "James, you go on to Dallas. Hiram and I'll visit for a while and I'll take him back to Dallas in my buggy." James and Rhonda just looked at each other. James kissed Rhonda and said he would be by the following morning for coffee and to discuss their plans for the move to Austin.

The following morning, James and J. L. had breakfast with the judge and watched him deplete the egg stock in the café. They all shook hands, the judge got on the morning stage, J. L. went to his office, and James headed for Maggie's. When he arrived, Rhonda met him in the foyer, and they walked into the kitchen. Rhonda poured him a cup of coffee and sat down across from him. Peaches made her appearance and started weaving in and out around his boots. Rhonda said, "James, I'm so pleased you like Peaches. Momma gave her to me, and I want to take her to Austin with us." James lied, and said that would be wonderful, he'd always kinda wanted a cat.

The thrust of James' ride to Maggie's this morning was to find out if Rhonda had any criteria for a house for them to live in when she came to be with him in Austin. James reminded her he didn't make much money as a deputy U. S. marshal, and whatever he found would have to be modest. Rhonda replied that she wasn't marrying him for his money and knew that they wouldn't be living in luxury. She told James to just find whatever suited them and their budget and she was sure it would be fine.

James said he would be back from Austin by the 15th at the latest and would try to find a new suit to wear at the wedding. With everything settled, or as settled as could be, James got up, kissed Rhonda, and headed back to Dallas.

He got his gear from the hotel and caught the train to Austin. It was October 6, 1874, when he left Dallas. On October 8 at 9 AM Lamar Fredrickson was hanged in the town square of Dallas. After Frederickson's body was removed and taken to the undertaker, Scruthers and Hardaway were brought from the jail. At 9:30 AM, Jonathan Scruthers and Dell Hardaway were hanged together on the same gallows. Jonathan Scruthers had the last laugh and never confessed to murdering Thelma Goodrich. Notwithstanding the lack of a confession, the long ordeal of the investigation concerning the murder of Thelma Goodrich was over and Marshal Boutwell could close the case and get on to other things.

As James boarded the train, he noticed Thelma Goodrich's uncle standing on the depot platform looking at him. The man didn't say anything, wave, or greet him, he just looked. James thought to himself "What's his presence here all about? I would have thought he would have thanked me for bringing his niece's murderer to justice."

Chapter 30

James arrived in Austin and went directly to the courthouse. After checking all the new warrants and prioritizing them, he went and looked in on the judge. They exchanged pleasantries and James told him about his upcoming wedding. The judge congratulated him and wished him happiness with his bride to be.

James selected some warrants for the local area around Austin. Most were mundane stuff, but they paid him $2.00 each for serving them. Next on his list of things to do was to find a suitable place for him and Rhonda to set up housekeeping. He asked around and found a vacant house on 9th Street within easy walking distance of the courthouse. The house wasn't much, just a small wood frame dwelling with two small bedrooms, a living room, kitchen, and an outhouse. Unfortunately, it would have to suffice until he could do better. James made the financial arrangements to buy the house, gave the owner a small down payment, and moved his gear into his new home.

On Saturday, October 10, James rode to the Lazy M ranch to arrest a cowhand for shooting a man in a saloon brawl. The ranch was around fifteen miles west of Austin and an easy ride. James had left Austin at 8 AM and arrived at the ranch house shortly after 9:30 AM. He stopped his horse in front of the ranch house and tied the horse's reins to the hitching post. As James walked towards the front door, it opened, and a large man sporting a long beard appeared. James said, "I'm Deputy U.S. Marshal James Boutwell."

The man looked James over and replied, "I know who you are. I've seen you in Austin. I'm Micah Madison, the owner of the Lazy M, who is it you want?"

James said, "I have a warrant for a man named Delbert Freeman. Folks have told me he works on the Lazy M spread. Does he work for you, and if so, where can I find him?"

Madison replied, "Yeah, he works for me. You'll find him around a mile from here branding calves. I'll ride out there with you." Madison went to the corral, roped a horse, saddled him, rode up to where James was waiting, and said, "Let's go, Marshal."

When Marshal Boutwell and Mr. Madison arrived at the branding site, Freeman and two other men were working at branding calves. Marshal Boutwell dismounted and walked over towards the men. Madison stayed on his horse but moved the animal around, so he was on the far side of the men from Marshal Boutwell. James said, "Delbert Freeman, I have a warrant for your arrest for attempted murder." None of the three men moved. James looked at Madison and asked, "Which man is Freeman. I don't want to have to take all three men to Austin." Madison pointed out Freeman and James told the man to take off his gun belt and let it drop.

The man hesitated and James said, "You need to understand, I hunt and arrest men for a living. Many of them were no doubt a lot better with a gun than you. If you don't follow my instructions, it will force me to put a bullet in you and probably take you to Austin draped over your horse. Now, I'll only tell you this one last time, remove your gun belt and let it drop."

Madison spoke up and said, "Son, I'd do as the marshal asked. You're no match for him with a gun, and if by some miracle you somehow got lucky, they would hang you for killing a U. S. marshal." Freeman hesitated for a few moments, undid his gun belt, let it drop on the ground, and walked towards Marshal Boutwell.

When Freeman got to within a few feet, James said, "That's far enough. See if these manacles fit your wrists." Freeman put the manacles on and walked over and mounted his horse. James removed Freeman's rifle, looked at Madison and said, "Thanks for helping defuse that situation. I have no desire to kill anyone. If you would, take care of his rifle, gun belt and pistol." Madison just nodded.

James got Freeman locked up in the Austin jail and got on with serving other warrants and making arrests. On the morning of the 15th, James visited the judge and told him he would be back in a few days, and with a wife. The judge wished him well. On October 16, James caught the train to Dallas with a suit bag over his shoulder.

Everything was going like clockwork. Maggie, Rhonda, and the girls had the backyard of Maggie's decorated with flowers and several chairs for those who would attend the wedding. Not many folks in Dallas knew Rhonda, but just about everyone knew, or knew of Maggie and her place of business. Some were ambivalent regarding her business, and some thought it unseemly, but they all knew she was a woman of substance who made charitable contributions in the community. James rode to Maggie's and walked in the foyer where he was met by mother and bride to be. The three of them had a private dinner and Maggie asked Rhonda to excuse them please. Rhonda looked puzzled but didn't say anything, excused herself, and went upstairs to her room.

Maggie looked at James and said, "I'm going to tell you some things that Rhonda doesn't know. I've always told her that her father was killed during the Civil War, and that is technically true. But the whole truth is that he and two other men stole a Confederate gold shipment being carried by a courier. Robert Branceer made it to our house and left a sack with me for safekeeping. Rhonda was in school when he stopped at our cabin, so she didn't see him. Later that day, a Union patrol killed him. I used part of the gold to start this business."

James was thoughtful and said, "I'm going to forget what you told me. I don't think Rhonda needs to have her image of her father tarnished. And, it's not my place to tell her anyway."

Maggie smiled, thanked James, slid an envelope across the table, and said, "I want you to have this. You and Rhonda deserve to have a comfortable life, and this will help you somewhat to get established."

James opened the envelope and saw Maggie had stuffed it with $100.00 bills. He started to say that he couldn't accept such a gift when Maggie said, "You take good care of my little girl, James Boutwell. I know you are a good man and couldn't be more pleased that you are marrying Rhonda. Now let me get her so you two can see each other for the last time until the wedding ceremony."

Rhonda came down the stairs carrying Peaches and sat down in the foyer. When James sat beside her, she wanted to know what her mother wanted. James told her she just wanted to give him some money to help them get established in Austin. Rhonda looked a little skeptical but didn't say anything. After visiting for a few minutes, they kissed and said they would see each other the following afternoon.

James got up early on October 17 and went to the Dallas Café to have breakfast. He was as nervous as a cat in a room full of rocking chairs. It wasn't just every day that a man got married. He decided to go to the sheriff's office and kill some time with J. L. They sat and talked for a half-hour or so. James had asked J. L. if he would stand with him at the wedding and the sheriff had allowed it would be his honor. James said he would see J. L. at the wedding, left, and went to the barbershop. He got a shave and soaked in a tub of warm water. After scrubbing his hide with a brush, James got out of the tub and put on his brand-new suit.

The noon stage was on time and Judge Blackstone got off the stage and wanted something to eat. James took him to the Dallas Café. James cautioned him not to eat too much as there would be enough food at the wedding reception to feed a small army. After Judge Blackstone had three bowls of chili and three cups of coffee, he was ready for the trip to Maggie's. James drove the judge to Maggie's in a two-seat surrey that Maggie had provided. J. L. had said he would come to Maggie's with a buggy and drive himself and the judge back to town.

The wedding went off without a hitch. Rhonda was beautiful in a long white dress. After the ceremony, the crowd assembled at a group of tables in the yard and started eating and drinking some rather potent punch to the sounds of a Mariachi band. As James and Rhonda were sitting and enjoying the music, the telegraph operator from Dallas came rushing up, handed James a telegram, and said, "I was reluctant to bother you at your wedding, but thought you would want this as soon as possible so I brought it straight away. Congratulations, Marshal Boutwell, Mrs. Boutwell."

James looked at the telegram for a few moments, wondering what could be so important that it had to disrupt his wedding. He unfolded the paper and read, "*James and Rhonda. Stop. Marisa and I wish you both the best. Curtis.*" James shook his head and mumbled, "Well I'll be hornswoggled." James wondered how Curtis Breedlove could have possibly known that he and Rhonda were getting married, and especially the time and date. Then he smiled and realized that Curtis Breedlove probably knew pretty much whatever he wanted to know; about anything he was interested in knowing about.

****

As it turned out Curtis Breedlove wasn't killed by the assassin, but he had been wounded and the U.S. marshal was killed as claimed. Mr. Breedlove was treated by a doctor who was sworn to secrecy. Mr. Breedlove was then hidden away until he recovered sufficiently to testify to a small group of men. Curtis Breedlove told a bearded man who everyone called Mr. President and the other select few men about a planned coup d'état that a small group of men were planning. They had a great deal of money at their disposal and filled positions of great influence in government and commerce. Mr. Breedlove cautioned that this wasn't some group of harmless windbags flying by the seat of their pants. This group was well funded and serious in their intent to restore the South to prominence.

After Curtis Breedlove left the meeting, he went into seclusion until he and Marisa could be placed on a ship back out of the country. They were covertly placed on a steamer headed for London,

England, and used the names of Mark and Nancy Fisher. Having performed a great service for their country, they lived out their lives in relative obscurity in a beautiful village outside London. Their true identies was never discovered by locals and they were never bothered.

The President and the group took Breedlove's testimony seriously, very seriously. In fact, his testimony was taken so seriously that the men that Curtis Breedlove had identified started meeting unexpected tragic ends.

****

James and Rhonda took the surrey to Fort Worth and spent two days and nights in the best hotel in town. Fort Worth was just beginning to recover from the cattle related recession but had some good restaurants and musical theaters that had survived. They caught a couple musicals, ate some fine food, and enjoyed getting to know each other in a biblical sense. When they returned to Dallas, they stayed overnight at Maggie's and left the following day for Austin.

When they arrived in Austin, they went to their new home straightaway. Rhonda was pleased with the house, or at least acted like she was. James left Rhonda in the house and went to the Texas State Bank. He had his account changed to James and Rhonda Boutwell and made a sizable deposit. With the proceeds from his horse sales, his savings, and the money from Maggie, they were in good financial shape for the 1870s.

On October 29, 1874, the telegraph operator delivered a telegraph to Marshal Boutwell's office in the courthouse. James unfolded the wire and read, *"James. Stop. Reverend Smith killed himself last night. Thought you might like to know. Stop. J. L."* James was thoughtful for a few moments and wondered to himself what was to become of Emma Smith, the reverend's wife. He supposed the church would place her in a church provided facility where she could be cared for.

James supposed the reverend's sins had weighed on him until he couldn't stand the guilt of becoming entangled with a prostitute any longer and ended his own life. James had no way of knowing, but Smith's longtime friend Jon Scruthers was dead in large part due to him trying to protect the reverend from a murder charge. Sometimes life can get complicated and overwhelming. Anyway, James thought no more about the reverend's death and never revisited the killing of Thelma Goodrich, the investigation, or how he had brought her supposed killer to justice. The fact that Jonathan Scruthers never confessed to murdering Thelma Goodrich was troubling. Normally, a man would want to cleanse his soul before dying. He lay the telegram aside and thought no more about the matter.

James and Rhonda got down to life as a married couple. They had three children: Maggie Mae born June 4, 1875, James Mark born March 7,

1876, and Elizabeth Joan born December 8, 1877. James continued to serve as a deputy U. S. marshal until his retirement on June 1, 1904, right after his sixtieth birthday. He served his last few years with the U. S. Marshal Service as the director of the Austin marshal service region. From time to time after his retirement he would consult with law enforcement on cases they were working on, but for the most part, just enjoyed his seclusion and his grandchildren.

Maggie lost the sporting house to a terrible fire in 1883 and moved to Houston, Texas. Houston was close enough she could see James, Rhonda, and her wonderful grandchildren occasionally. But Maggie was far enough away she wouldn't be underfoot. She made several train trips over the years to visit in Austin, Texas. When Maggie Mae was born, James and Rhonda realized they would need more room. They used the money Maggie had given James to purchase a large house and sold the small one they had lived in. The new house had a room set aside for Maggie's visits. Hiram Blackstone stopped in Houston and visited Maggie from time to time, but she never remarried.

On the morning of August 7, 1912, James was sitting in his favorite rocker drinking a cup of coffee and reading the newspaper when he suddenly had a massive heart attack and died. James and Rhonda had been married just shy of thirty-eight wonderful years. After James' death, Maggie sold her home in Houston and moved to Austin to be with

Rhonda. Maggie's grandchildren were grown but two lived in Austin and it delighted her to see her great-grandchildren grow up. Maggie Branceer died in 1916 of some unknown illness that claimed her within two weeks of the onset of the disease.

Rhonda Boutwell never remarried. Like she had told James years before, it would be unfair to marry anyone but him. She died in a nursing home in Austin on November 3, 1940, surrounded by her three children and five grandchildren. They buried Rhonda next to her beloved James who had been waiting for her in a small cemetery just outside Austin, Texas.

Epilogue

On a chilly Sunday morning on November 1, 1874, a woman parked her buggy, had a red cap load her bags, and boarded the 9 AM train at the Fort Worth train station headed for California. She entered a Pullman car and took a seat beside a middle-aged man who was wearing a clean and well-tailored suit. The man smiled and introduced himself as Jeffrey T. Blunkett. Mr. Blunkett was traveling to Tucson, Arizona, to start a new job with a bank. The woman smiled in return and said, "My name is Emma, Emma Franklin. I've been in Dallas visiting my sister, and now I'm on my way to visit relatives in San Francisco. I'm recently widowed."

Emma and Mr. Blunkett chatted as the train rumbled along. Mr. Blunkett seemed to be a very nice man, unlike her former husband who snuck out of their house in the middle of the night and visited whores.

Emma sat deep in thought. The note to the whore claiming to be Reverend Smith and asking the Jezebel to pack up and meet him so he could give her money to start a new life worked like a charm. The chloroform she had taken from Doc Pickwell's cabinet had put the whore to sleep and choking her was easy enough. No one would suspect a crippled woman of a murder!

Unbeknownst to Emma, she hadn't quite got away Scot free. Elmer Goodrich had seen Emma hitch the buggy up and rode ahead to Fort Worth. When he saw Emma board the train at the Fort Worth station, and the red caps load her luggage on the train, he boarded, and sat in the next Pullman car. Elmer sat and read a newspaper he had brought along and bided his time.

****

On the morning of November 2, 1874, three cow hands were driving a few head of cattle across the railroad tracks which ran alongside the Double SS ranch close to the Arizona state border. The cattle had drifted off the ranch and crossed the tracks. When they crossed back across the tracks, they saw a woman's body lying in a splayed position alongside the tracks. Someone had cut her throat!

Thelma Goodrich could now rest in peace.

Ironically, Jonathan Scruthers spent a lot of money and gave his life trying to protect his lifelong friend Simon Smith from a murder he hadn't committed. Reverend Smith had only been guilty of succumbing to one of life's oldest temptations.

The Lawman

The Ike Branson Story

Chapter 1

The man was freezing to death. What northern New Mexico lacked in summer rain it more than made up for in winter snow, ice, and freezing rain. The temperature had continued to drop all afternoon as he tracked the man who had robbed the Taos National Bank, killed the teller, and wounded a woman who was in the bank to make a small withdrawal. An errant bullet had struck the woman. The bullet probably wasn't even fired by the bandit. Nonetheless, it looked as if she would lose her arm because the bullet shattered the bone in her forearm. The practice of medicine had come a long way since the Civil War. Surgical techniques which were used to repair a shattered bone were in their infancy in 1872 and practiced basically in large eastern hospitals. Removing the injured arm was the archaic treatment of the day in small towns in the west.

Ike Branson was a Deputy U.S. Marshal who lived and worked out of Albuquerque, New Mexico. He was in Taos to serve a warrant on Frederick Anderson, who had made the mistake of taking a mail pouch while robbing a train. The sheriff of Taos County had sent a telegram to Albuquerque requesting Branson's help in tracking down

Anderson. Branson wasn't crazy about the idea of riding the 130 miles to Taos, but he liked the idea of riding the train even less. Ike had taken Blaze, his midnight black gelding with a white flame shaped splotch on his forehead, on one train ride. The experience had scared the animal to death and made him skittish for days. Nope, Mother Branson didn't raise no idiot. He wasn't going to make that mistake again.

Branson rode out of Albuquerque on January 3, 1872 and arrived in Taos during the afternoon three days later. Ike got Blaze settled into the livery and gave him a good rubdown and a scoop of oats. After tending to Blaze, Ike went to the Taos Café to get a bite of food and some hot coffee. Just as he finished his beefsteak and beans, Sheriff James T. Bidwell walked into the café, pulled up a chair, and sat down at Ike's table.

After saying hello, Bidwell said, "Branson, you're a day late. Anderson came into town this morning, robbed the Taos National Bank, killed a teller, and headed north towards Pueblo Peak. There's a bad storm coming in tonight or tomorrow, might be best to wait a day or two before going out after the bandit."

Branson leaned back in his chair, lit a cheroot, expelled a lungful of smoke, smiled, and replied, "I'll leave in the morning. No reason to leave now and fight the storm and darkness. Do you have a recent likeness or wanted poster on Anderson?"

Bidwell responded, "Nope, I haven't had time to get a handbill made up. Anderson is about 5' 10" tall, sandy colored hair, and has a nasty scar on his right cheek from when he worked as a cowpuncher some years ago and got too close to a longhorn steer. You won't have any trouble identifying him. The scar is horrible looking."

Branson sarcastically said, "I'll have him come out of the rocks and let me look at him before I shoot. It always pays to be sure who you're shooting at before you kill a man."

Bidwell smiled and simply said, "Guess so. Do what you think is best marshal." Bidwell got up and walked out of the café.

Ike got up, paid for his meal, walked across the street to the Taos Hotel, got a room, and settled in for the night. It felt good to get his boots off and stretch out his 6' 2" frame. The clerk had started a fire in the wood stove, and it was warming the room. Within minutes, Branson was fast asleep.

As was his custom, Branson was up before daylight. He washed his face in the Minton wash bowl, ran his fingers through his dark brown hair, and then slicked up his long droopy moustache. After pulling on his boots, he picked up his rifle, left the room, walked down the stairs, and turned in the room key. He then walked through the lobby and into the hotel dining room. The smell of coffee and bacon frying awakened his senses and reminded him he was hungry. He ordered three eggs sunny side up. In just a few minutes the eggs, a side of bacon, two biscuits, and coffee refill were in front of him. People began drifting into the dining room to eat. Everyone was complaining about the cold weather and allowed that a snowstorm was on its way. Ike listened to the talk about snow and went under the assumption that as miserable as it might be, it would be equally wretched for the man whom he would be following.

As Ike walked to the livery, light sleet pelted the exposed parts of his face. His mackinaw jacket repelled much of the wind and the slouch hat repelled the bulk of the sleet. Nonetheless, it was a cold and miserable day. And judging by the sky, the weather would get worse, maybe much worse…

The Lawman – *The Ike Branson Story*

Will be available during the spring of 2020

Bill Shuey is the author of several books and the weekly ObverseView column. He travels extensively in his Recreational Vehicle with his wife Gloria and his fly rods.

He can be contacted at: billshueybooks@gmail.com or WWW.billshueybooks.com